CODE OF SILENCE

Copyright 2015 Larry LaVoie

ACKNOWLEDGEMENTS

Although this is my 14th novel, I couldn't have completed it without help from my wife, Anna, who gave many hours of draft review, suggestions and inspiration. No novel would be as enjoyable to read without thorough editing. I thank my editor, Sharon Shafa, for her eye for detail and generous support.

FACTS

Code of Silence is a novel set in the Pacific Northwest during the early days of World War II. Many of the events are factual accounts of what happened at the time. Among them are the following:

1. Franklin Delano Roosevelt did use his son, James, on a secret mission to inform our allies we would soon be joining the European war. The trip was eight months prior to the bombing of Pearl Harbor and the United States entering the war.

2. Japanese submarines were active during the early days of the war and attacked the West Coast of Canada and the United States on several occasions, most notably the shelling of Fort Stevens, near Astoria, Oregon. Of the Japanese attacks, perhaps the strangest, (and most unbelievable), were the dropping of incendiary bombs on Oregon forests from an airplane launched from a Japanese submarine.

3. There was heated debate over the internment of persons of Japanese ancestry, many of whom were American citizens. In spite of the debate, President Roosevelt issued Executive Order 9066. More than 120,000 Japanese Americans along the coastal areas of the United States were uprooted and moved to inland internment camps, where they were held for the duration of the war.

4. The sinking of merchant ships by Japanese submarines off the western coast of the United States was discounted by the Navy. Most were

declared to be accidents with rational explanations. Newspaper accounts of the events were discredited. When the Japanese government could not confirm the effectiveness of their attacks through newspaper accounts, and the American public did not panic, they ruled the attacks ineffective, and ordered their submarines from the coastline of Oregon, Washington, and California, and sent them into battle in the Pacific.

5. CAP, or Civil Air Patrol, was formed in December 1941, to aid the military in patrolling the boarders and the coastlines of the United States.

6. In June 1942, Japan seized Attu and Kiska, two islands in the Aleutian Chain off Alaska. It was the only U.S. soil Japan occupied during the war in the Pacific.

CODE OF SILENCE

A World War II Novel

5

Chapter 1

Philadelphia, Pennsylvania, November 9, 1941

"...Gaston Carson, the 175-pound halfback from New York City has scored the final touchdown of the season, and what a season it's been for Navy. Head Coach Swede Larson has led his team to the third victory in a row over Army with wins of 10-0 in '39 and 14-0 last year. It looked like it might be another shutout victory until a late second quarter touchdown by Army made the game an even match, but in the final minute of the game, Gaston Carson proved his mettle, pulled a rabbit out of the hat with a 45-yard run for a touchdown and sealed the deal. It's Navy over Army for three years in a row! I'll bet Army fans are asking themselves, 'How long can this go on?'" The announcer put his hand over the microphone and said to one of his engineers, "Okay, fellas, I'm going to wrap it up now." He took his hand away. *"This is John Wilkinson broadcasting as part of the National Broadcast System. Good night to football fans, everywhere."*

Gaston Carson sat in the locker room holding his helmet in one hand and a cup of water in the other. The room hung heavy with the smell of dirty socks, sweaty bodies, and musty uniforms. He watched as Sam Booth dumped a keg of water over their coach. Arthur Knox was in the corner with a few others, on one knee, offering up a prayer of thanksgiving. Ray Swartz was ready to get some beer and celebrate. It had been an unusually good year, and there was much to celebrate. Their nine- game season had ended with five shutout victories, and only one loss, to Notre Dame. The Fighting Irish were having a great year themselves with an 8-0 record. Gaston took a slap on the back and congratulations from Gene Flathman, a guard that weighed a good hundred pounds more than he.

Gaston was in his own world reflecting on how his life would be changing. This was his last season of football, and his last year at the academy. This time next year he and his classmates would be serving their country at home or abroad as crew members on ships, aides in the Department of the Navy, engineers, statisticians, and accountants. These men he served with were the finest the nation had to offer. There was a lot to celebrate, but he was saddened by the fact this would all end and they would be scattered about. He hoped to be on an aircraft carrier; James Donaldson hoped to serve on a battleship; and John Harrell would be heading to submarine school. Football had brought them all together to win battles on the gridiron; soon they would be defending their Country. Gaston was struggling to get his mind around it.

*****

In April 1941, eight months *before* the Japanese attack on Pearl Harbor, President Roosevelt needed a person he could trust for a secret mission. He called on his eldest son, James, because he was the man the President trusted most. The mission was to assure our allies around the world that the United States would soon be joining the war. If news of the trip reached the press, it would have dealt the Roosevelt Administration a crippling, if not fatal, blow. The country at the time was strongly against the United States getting involved in the conflict in Europe.

In the past James had served his father as Administrative Assistant to the President, and was later appointed Secretary to the President. There were rumors that James had the greatest influence of anyone in Franklin Delano Roosevelt's administration. But, after allegations he used his influence with his father for personal gain, James resigned from his White House position, and the

President was left without anyone he truly trusted.

On December 9, 1941, two days after the attack on Pearl Harbor, the morning after President Roosevelt had delivered his "Day of Infamy" speech to Congress, he had need of another person for a secret mission, but this time his son, James, was on active duty and was not available. He chose another man, a much younger man, but one he knew he could trust.

It was 5:00 a.m. The President's Chief of Staff found Midshipman Gaston Carson in his bunk at the Naval Academy in Annapolis, Maryland. The United States had been at war with Japan less than 24 hours.

Unlike the President's son, Gaston Carson wasn't chosen for this secret mission because he was blood. Gaston wasn't related to Roosevelt at all, and had never served the President in any official capacity. The young man wasn't in politics and didn't run with the Washington crowd. Gaston Carson was chosen because no one would suspect he was on a mission for the President. Gaston was as far from politics as anyone the President knew. There was no one better suited for the job, and he knew Gaston could be trusted.

At 22 years old, Midshipman Carson had a vision of graduating from the Academy and serving his Country as an officer in the US Navy. He wanted to serve on one of the new aircraft carriers, like the USS Enterprise. It was a dream about to be realized, but a dream the war was about to cut short.

Gaston was sitting uncomfortably on a straight-back wooden chair in the ante-room outside the President's bedroom, waiting for Franklin Delano Roosevelt's aides to finish dressing him. *It's a miracle,* Gaston thought, *I was a vagrant roaming the streets of New York City, and here I am in the White House only ten years later.* It was a miracle, of sorts, or maybe fate. Gaston was born into poverty ten years before the stock market crash of 1929. The son of a prostitute and a father he had never met. By way of his circumstances, he should have been running with the many gangs that roamed the back streets and alleys of New York City during the Great Depression. But he was here in the White

House waiting for the President to finish dressing.

The day before, with a handful of midshipmen, Gaston had listened closely to a large Philco radio in the recreation annex at the Naval Academy. President Roosevelt was addressing the nation following the vicious attack on Pearl Harbor. Gaston knew, at that moment, his life would change forever, but he never imagined he'd be sitting in the White House, waiting for the President to join him. In a few days the naval academy would be nearly vacant. It was nearing the Christmas Holiday and many would be going home to their families, maybe for the last time, before going to war. With no family, Gaston had planned on spending the holidays visiting friends. Christmas dinner was scheduled to be with his girlfriend, Cheryl, her sister, and mother. With the reality of war setting in, for many this would not be a Christmas to remember, but one to forget. His girlfriend's father had been in Pearl Harbor and they had not heard from him.

Gaston shifted his thoughts to the last time he had been in the White House. It had been with a group of classmates his freshman year in high school. He didn't even see the President that time. That was nearly eight years ago. Now, dressed in his midshipmen's winter dress uniform, he toyed with his cap and stared at the ornate carpet at his feet. His mind was spinning. *This must be serious,* Gaston thought, *it's still dark outside and the President is barely awake. Hell, I'm barely awake. Am I in trouble? Why would the President summon me to the White House in the middle of the night?*

"Gaston," the President said. "Once you've finished counting the threads in the carpet or whatever you're so interested in, I want you to join me for breakfast." Roosevelt was sitting in a wheelchair. He was wearing a red silk smoking jacket over a white shirt. He had a white scarf draped around his neck.

"Yes sir." Gaston grinned and flushed a little. "I missed mine this morning."

Breakfast was served in the President's chamber. Aides brought in a small table and covered it with a white linen cloth. Eggs, bacon, toast, orange juice, coffee and tea, in silver containers, were served.

As they finished breakfast sitting across from one another at the small table, Roosevelt took a sip of steaming tea. "Gaston, I'm not going to keep you in suspense any longer. The Japs are a formidable enemy and they caught us sleeping in Pearl Harbor, literally with our pants down. The sons-a-bitches didn't have the decency to warn us they were coming. They led us to believe we could settle our differences peacefully. Instead, they blindsided us with a cowardly Sunday morning attack. I'm sure you know our Pacific Fleet has been devastated. Thank God we sailed our aircraft carriers prior to the attack."

He took another sip of tea and removed his cigarette holder from his mouth. "There's talk the Japanese are planning an attack on our mainland next. It's a highly heated debate among my staff. Frankly, I don't know who is right. That's where you come in."

"Me, sir?" Gaston swallowed hard. He wanted to speak. *Better wait for the President to get around to it himself.* He couldn't help himself. "Sir, it's my last year at the Academy. I'm thinking of dropping out and joining the war. There's some talk they may be commissioning officers early to get them into battle."

Roosevelt shook his head. The cigarette holder in the corner of his mouth moved up like a flag at half-mast. "I understand your youthful enthusiasm to serve, and I'm going to give you that opportunity, but I need you in another capacity."

"But, sir, I can fight as good as any man, and with the war and all, I will probably get field promotions, even if I don't go in as a commissioned officer. I'll be an officer before you know it. Heck, I'm older than many of the volunteers. I could be an officer in no time."

The President laughed. "Son, I wish I had your energy, and frankly your naiveté. Seriously though, I need someone I can trust to tell me the truth and to keep a secret. The people on the West Coast are starting to panic. They have convinced themselves that there is going to be an invasion by the Japanese on their shores. There are submarine sightings and, sadly, hostilities against the Japanese population in Seattle, San Francisco, and Los Angeles. I need someone to be my eyes and ears on the West Coast. After careful consideration, I've decided you're that person. As of today you will be on special assignment answering only to the Commander in Chief; that's me."

"What about my commission? With all due respect, sir, you have the entire Army and Navy at your disposal. They're far more experienced than I. I was going to serve on an aircraft carrier."

Roosevelt laughed. "That's what I'm talking about. I've been following your progress at the Academy. Number one in your class in every endeavor; that touchdown against Army was a stroke of genius; this is a natural for you. As for why I need you, I haven't time to go into all the details, but suffice it to say we're in a political climate that makes it impossible for me to know who I can trust. It's created by powerful people that surround me. Hell, half the people around here tell me what they think I want to hear. The other half has political ambitions of their own. Many would like to see me fall on my ass, literally!" He removed the cigarette from the holder and put in another. He lit it and drew in a deep breath.

"Gaston, I'm going to be honest with you. From the day we met you've been honest with me. Painfully honest at times. Do you think you can still do that from the West Coast?"

"Sir, it's true I have always been honest with you, and I don't want you to think I wouldn't be under any circumstance, but I'm still a kid. Let me finish school, serve my time in the Navy and then I'll do anything you ask, I promise."

"Gaston, if it was last week, you would have swayed me with that argument, but this is today; the world is a different place than last week. You mentioned you wanted to quit the Academy and join the fight. I'm asking you to do that, right now, for me."

Gaston stood up. "Yes, sir."

"At ease, son, I'm not finished."

Gaston sat back down. He felt his cheeks flush again. He had never felt so uncomfortable in his life.

"There is near panic out West," FDR continued. "The Navy is calling for a good portion of its arsenal to be sent to patrol the coastline. The Army wants to establish posts every twenty miles along the beaches from Seattle to San Diego. I need to know what's actually happening, in Oregon especially. The Japs want us to divert our limited naval fleet to protect the West Coast while they expand their empire into the Pacific. We need every last man we can enlist to fight the battle in the Pacific and in Europe. I need to know that I'm not sacrificing our war effort by limiting our resources off the Pacific Coast. You're going to make sure I have a clear picture."

Roosevelt reached in his breast pocket and pulled out an envelope. "This will help with your expenses and aid in your transition to civilian life." He slid it across the table. "You will be operating undercover, meaning you will dress like the civilians. You will answer to no one but me. That's very important. There will be those who will demand to know who you are answering to. Don't tell them you answer to me. If you must, you can tell people your orders come from Washington. That's it!"

He pulled out a small card. On one side was the President's seal, a picture of Gaston, the word 'Diplomat' and a telephone number on it. "If you get into serious trouble, this is your ticket out. I don't expect you'll use it, being the resourceful man you are, but just in case. And Gaston, I'm counting on you to be straight with me. The Nation is counting on you."

Gaston finally touched the brim of his cup to his lips. The coffee was cold. He wondered what the President was sending him into. He had never been west of the Mississippi. He needed time to think. He felt guilty that the first thing that came to his mind was *what about Cheryl? What would he tell her?* "How secret is the job, sir?" he asked. "I mean, my girl, Cheryl, she'll know something is going on if I just up and leave."

"Tell her you've quit the Academy and have taken a job with the Government. You'll be working as a civilian assigned to the Coast Guard Station in Yaquina Bay, Oregon. You will be able to collect your mail at that station and can take up housing there. As a diplomat you will be able to travel freely, ask questions, and pry into reports of ship sightings or, God forbid, a Jap invasion."

FDR gave a stifled laugh. "As far as the Commander at the station is concerned you are on special assignment. What they won't know is that you are reporting directly to me. Also the FBI will undoubtedly want to know who you are. Try and keep a low profile and tell them as little as possible, short of getting yourself thrown in jail."

"Why not just tell them I'm your eyes and ears?"

FDR leaned back, briefly studied the President's Seal on his gold cigarette case, before opening it and removing a cigarette. He placed it in his long ivory cigarette holder, slid it between his teeth, and lit it. A bellow of blue smoke streamed from his nostrils. "Trust me son, if they know you're working directly for me, the truth will escape you like a dog chasing its tail. You must keep it a secret."

*****

Cheryl Barton stood at the porch of her parents' colonial-style home on the outskirts of Annapolis. She wore a light button down sweater and pleated skirt and shivered in the crisp winter air. Her father, an ensign serving on the Arizona, was officially listed as missing in action, meaning they hadn't heard from him since the attack on Pearl Harbor. She had been crying off and on the past two days, but had run out of tears. She had comforted her mother and younger sister as bravely as she could, but fearing the worst, they had each burst into tears in the depth of the night when they were alone. Staring down the long drive, waiting for Gaston to arrive, she was thankful she had finally stopped crying. Fifteen minutes earlier Gaston had called and told her he would be by shortly. His call was a welcome flicker of light in two of the darkest days she had ever known, but there had been something in Gaston's voice that told her he was hiding something. It was unusual for him to come by in the middle of the week. She hoped nothing was wrong.

Her lips curled up as she saw a car pull into the driveway, but vanished when she realized it wasn't Gaston. A dull gray sedan crept slowly up the gravel drive and stopped an unusually long way from the front of the house. Two Navy men in their winter dress uniforms approached her. She panicked. "Mama!" She turned and opened the door to the house. "Mama, come quick!" Dread overtook her. There was no mistaking why they were there.

It took over an hour for Gaston to maneuver his 1936 Plymouth coupe through the Washington traffic. In the short time since the declaration of war, the Capitol was already a madhouse of activity. It seemed the city had doubled in size overnight, and, in fact, it had. The country was at war, and Washington DC was swelling with contractors, lobbyists, military personnel, and, of course, politicians. It was more traffic than he'd ever seen. As he maneuvered his dirty, brown, two-door sedan through a seemingly endless mass of vehicles, he considered what he would tell Cheryl. He had been given an assignment directly from the President. How could he keep from lying about it? If he told her the truth, she probably wouldn't believe him anyway. He hated to lie. It went against every fiber of his being. *It shouldn't be that hard*, he thought. When his mother was alive, he had to lie just to survive. Telling the truth often got him a beating from one of the many men in his mother's life. After she was gone, he had made a promise to himself never to lie again. Still this wasn't that simple; it was all right if the President told you to do it, wasn't it? He decided he couldn't lie to Cheryl. He wouldn't lie to her. She was his steady girl. They would probably marry one day. It wasn't right to keep secrets from someone you loved. He let out a long sigh as if the world had been lifted from his shoulders. He was content that she could keep his secret.

As traffic closed in around him, he felt the heavy burden of the President's actions come over him. Ever since that day, long ago, when he slept in James Roosevelt's bedroom, he had wanted to be an officer in the Navy. He remembered seeing the pictures of James' father in his naval uniform. He was a tall, handsome man standing by his son. Gaston imagined the man was his father and he was the boy in the picture. Now, that same man had taken away his dream. He would never serve his Country as Commander of a ship. He would be lucky if he ever set foot on a ship. He clamped his jaw to keep from crying. He was a civilian, and every other man his age was fighting the war.

When Gaston turned into the long drive, he found a dark house with Cheryl, her mother, and sister sitting in the living room. In spite of the chilly December day the front door was wide open. Immediately he knew something was wrong. "What happened?" he asked, as he entered the house, but by the look on Cheryl's face, he already knew.

Cheryl ran up to him and put her arms around him. "Daddy was killed when the Arizona went down," she whispered. "Mom and Lilly are pretty upset."

Gaston hugged her tight, "He was a brave man serving his Country," he said, trying to comfort her. "How are you holding up?"

"Gaston, the goddamned Japs killed my dad!" She broke into a hysterical fit and started pounding his chest. "They killed him! They killed him!"

Gaston wrapped his arms around her again and held her trembling body close to him. He felt the wetness of her tears on his shirt as they streamed down her face. He was without words. What do you say to someone who has lost their father?

He had never known his father, and his mother had died when he was twelve. As he held her tight and tried to comfort her, he wondered what his life would have been like if he hadn't been rescued from that alley in a New York City ghetto so many years ago. His eyes grew misty as he thought about that day.

"She's dead, you little shit. She ain't no use to me now. Get your things and get out!" a man called Slade was yelling at him.

He only knew him as Slade, a tall thin man in a shiny blue suit and slicked back hair. Even though it was hot weather, a white silk scarf was draped over his shoulders like he was some kind of royalty. An unlit cigar seemed to be permanently attached to the corner of his mouth. Slade was his mother's john. She'd given him strict orders not to be present when Slade was around, but his mother was dead, lying lifeless on the bed, and he had nowhere to hide.

"You hear me, boy? Get yer ass out of here and don't come back or you'll get what's commin' to ya!"

Gaston gathered his clothes from a dresser drawer. He found a battered suitcase in the closet and his mother's purse. He rummaged through her purse and took out a pack of cigarettes, one crumpled dollar bill, a Standing Liberty quarter and eleven pennies. He stuffed the money in his pocket and his clothes in the suitcase and walked out on the street. It was summer; the August air heavy with humidity from a passing storm. The concrete burned the soles of his bare feet. A worn pair of sneakers, the only shoes he owned, hung by the shoelaces around his neck. He lugged the suitcase as far as he could, and when he could no longer walk, he found a dark spot and collapsed. He found a thick newspaper by a garbage can. That night he slept on a bed of newsprint, behind a brownstone house. He was scared, hungry, and more alone than he had ever known. Little did he know that the place he had chosen to sleep his first night alone in a noisy city would change his life forever.

He felt the cane in his side. "Wake up, boy. Are you okay?"

Gaston looked up at a very tall man with wire-rimmed glasses and a long cigarette holder in his mouth. The man had steel braces on his legs and a cane in each hand, still he stood tall.

Gaston rose to his feet, speechless. He would surely go to jail. The man looked to be someone important. In the street beyond the man was the largest, most luxurious vehicle he had ever seen. He looked up at the man wearing a black silk hat and a wide grin.

"Come on lad, let's get some breakfast. I'll bet you have a hell of a tale for me."

Something about the man told Gaston he could trust him, or possibly it was his desperate circumstances, but Gaston decided he'd let the man give him a ride in that grand and luxurious automobile. The man held himself upright with two canes. He watched as the man labored his way back to the car, refusing to be helped by the driver. The driver reached for Gaston's suitcase, but he was having none of that. After a bout of tug of war, the man relinquished and let Gaston take care of it.

Gaston climbed up into the back seat of the open carriage. The black leather seats were hot from the morning sun, but Gaston had spent a cold night with little protection and it felt good. The man in the silk hat let the driver assist him to the seat beside Gaston. Gaston felt like they were the star attraction in a parade as they slowly drove down the street. "Gee, mister," Gaston said, "you must be rich."

He looked down at Gaston. "We are all rich. You have your whole life ahead of you. I have the White House."

At the time Gaston had no idea what the man was saying. They pulled up to a large brick house. Several servants came out to assist the man as he got out of the car.

After a bath and a change into his cleanest dirty shirt, they had breakfast served. "You don't know who I am, do you?" the man asked.

Gaston stared at him with wide eyes, shaking his head. "Someone famous, I suppose. You don't get a house like this or a car like that unless you're a gangster, or you're famous."

Roosevelt laughed again. The lad was getting to him. "It's okay, eat up. You look like you could use a good meal. When was the last time you ate?"

Gaston shook his head and took a mouthful of oatmeal. Suddenly, it came to him: the man on the front page of the *New York Times*. He had seen the paper before he laid it out for a mattress. "I know who you are," Gaston said, after swallowing hard. "You're the new Governor of New York."

"Bravo boy. How'd you know that?"

Gaston took a drink of orange juice. "I read it in the *New York Times*."

"Well, boy, you know who I am, now tell me your story."

"Gaston, darling, you said you had something important to tell me," Cheryl said, breaking the silence.

Gaston, shaken back to reality, grimaced. "Somehow in the

scheme of things, it doesn't seem so important anymore."

"What are you doing out of uniform? You didn't go off and enlist!"

"Worse, I'm afraid. You know I have less than a year left at the Academy."

"Of course; well, what is it?"

"I had to drop out, but I've been asked to serve our Country in another way."

"What way? Why are you being so elusive?"

Gaston picked his words carefully. "I'm going to the West Coast on a special assignment."

Cheryl started to laugh. "A special assignment! You a spy? Are you sure they're that hard up for G-men? No, it's something else. Come clean with me, Buster. You're breaking up with me, aren't you?"

Cheryl's demeanor went from inquisitive to anger. "That's it; you're breaking up with me and going to war! I hate you Gaston Carson!" She turned to go away.

Gaston grabbed her arm. "I'm going to serve out the war in Oregon at the request of the President. If I can, I'll send for you." He pulled her to him and kissed her on the lips.

She pushed away from him. "You're not telling me the truth. You think you can kiss me and I'll let you get away with that? Oregon! That's half way around the world."

"It's not that bad. It's only 3,000 miles." His attempt at making light of the situation failed.

"You *are* breaking up with me. You can't run away and expect me to wait for you."

Gaston was becoming frustrated with the conversation. "What do you want me to do? We are at war!" He looked at Cheryl's mother still sobbing in the arms of her younger daughter. "Sorry, Mrs. Barton. I'm so sorry for your loss. I didn't know Ensign Barton that well, but he was a good man. I can't imagine what you're going through."

"Thank you, Gaston. I'm sorry the two of you didn't have the opportunity to get to know each other better. He would have liked you."

"Gaston is breaking up with me, Mother!" Cheryl turned and ran out of the room.

Mrs. Barton shook her head and stood up. "Gaston, go ahead and do what you have to do. I'll talk some sense into her. If it's meant to be, you'll come back after the war and she'll be waiting." She gave him a knowing smile.

Gaston hugged her. "I have to catch an airplane tomorrow morning. Imagine me flying across the country!"

"Stay safe. We'll miss you."

Cheryl's sister got up from the couch. "Kill some Japs for me, Gaston. And hurry back. If Cheryl won't have you, I'll be a lot older by then and *we* could get married."

Cheryl stormed out from her bedroom. "Lilly, you little brat!" She ran up to Gaston. "I'm sorry. I love you. Please don't do anything dangerous. Gaston, I'm going to miss you. I'll wait...I promise, I'll wait 'til you come back."

Chapter 2

The four Wright R-1820 Cyclone 9 engines of the Boeing B-17 roared to life and the plane shook like an earthquake had struck. Gaston, dressed in combat flight gear, adjusted his earmuffs to dull the steady drone of the engines. In front of him were a parachute and a duffle bag stuffed with gear. He would be picking up additional items when he reached his destination, a remote Coast Guard station on Yaquina Bay, on the Central Oregon Coast. By way of instructions, he was briefed by two men in dark suits. Civilians! *I, too, am now a civilian*, he reminded himself. The last remaining evidence of his prior life was the pair of shiny black dress shoes on his feet. He didn't have a clue how this was going to work out; a young, able-bodied man, serving as a civilian, when most young men were going to war. He went over the instructions that had been given to him. Communication with the White House would always be at midnight West Coast time, by way of the ham radio installed in the Yaquina Station Headquarters building. He had been given a special call sign. To Gaston, the assignment seemed more like he was spying on his own countrymen. It didn't seem like he'd be doing anything significant to fight the war.

As the turbochargers revved up, a high-pitched whine was added to the overwhelming beat of the giant bomber's propellers as they sliced through the morning air. Soon they started to taxi down the runway at the newly commissioned Washington National Airport.

In his head, Gaston went over his instructions in detail. He wasn't allowed to write them down. Everything had to be memorized. *I'm a G-man*, he thought, *I might as well be working for the FBI!*

*****

When news spread of the attack on Pearl Harbor, widespread anger spread across the country. On the West Coast, anti-Japanese paranoia spread rapidly. Many feared the attack on Pearl Harbor was orchestrated from within; that Japanese spies had aided their homeland in planning and carrying out the attack. Though the war had barely started, there was widespread fear that the Japanese would attack the West Coast of the United States. Already there was talk of incarcerating those of Asian descent to prevent Japanese spies from mingling with Japanese Americans, who were scattered throughout the Pacific Northwest. San Francisco had a large concentration of Japanese, both first and second generation. All up and down the coastal areas of Washington, Oregon, and California, there were pockets of Japanese, mostly on farms raising fruit and vegetables in the fertile river valleys.

*****

Gaston looked around the bay of the aircraft. This B-17, soon to be dubbed the Flying Fortress, was a model E. It had been in service only a few months and was being ferried back to Seattle for service and upgrades. For this trip, the bombs had been removed to make room for an auxiliary fuel tank, a few other passengers, and cargo, but the thirteen machine guns remained. It was an experience he would long remember. Not only was it his first flight in an airplane, it was the most advanced airplane in the Army's arsenal at the time. But the B-17 wasn't welcomed by all branches of the service. As a midshipman, there had been arguments as to whether the airplane was cutting into the Navy's territory as the guardians of the American coastline. The argument was, with the heavy armament and long-range, the B-17 bomber would only be good for patrolling the many miles of coastline, watching for an enemy invasion. That was the job of the Navy, not the Army! Regardless of the political turf fighting, Gaston had to admit, the B-17 was an impressive piece of hardware. He was seated in a waist gunner's position. A 50 cal. machine gun was mounted in front of him, but the ammo belt had been removed.

This must be terrifying in battle, Gaston thought. *Imagine a Zero attacking from the side and having to shoot it down or die trying.* He would be glad to take his chances on one of the naval aircraft carriers, a destroyer, or a minesweeper any day. He looked at the parachute stuffed in a space next to him. *A lot of good that will do if the plane goes down. Like I'm going to jump from an airplane. No Way!*

"Hey, you going to Seattle?"

Gaston looked up at a tall man in a brown leather pilot's jacket. His attire told Gaston this was a man who might fly one of these things. "Actually, I'm heading to Oregon. How about you?"

"The name's Jason Whitman. I'm heading to Boeing. They're going to teach me how to fly one of these tubs."

"Oh, I thought you *were* the pilot."

Jason laughed. "The biggest thing I've ever flown is a kite. I dropped out of Yale and joined the Army Air Corps. Somebody's got to drop bombs on those Nazi bastards."

"I'm a midshipman at Annapolis, or was, until yesterday. Just Gaston Carson now. Don't have a clue what I'm going to do in Oregon."

"Climb out of that seat and I'll show you around this tub."

"They let you walk around when this thing is flying?" Gaston wasn't at all sure he wanted to wander around an airplane. He wasn't certain anything made out of metal should be this high off the ground.

"Come on, stretch your legs, it'll do you good."

Gaston unlatched his harness and wrestled himself out of the tight quarters. They held onto the bare metal ribs of the fuselage as they made their way forward along a narrow walkway.

"Gaston, meet our pilot, Joe Reams, and copilot, Denny Frye," Jason said. "These guys not only fly these birds, they tell Boeing how to make them better. We're lucky to be flying with them."

Joe let go of the controls and looked up at Gaston. "You're the civilian we're dropping off in Portland. Is your dad a congressman or something?"

"Pardon?"

"We were told you were a *VIP*. I figured your old man was a member of Congress or ran the Navy or something."

Gaston didn't know what to think. "I never knew my dad, and the closest I ever got to Congress was a White House tour when I was in high school. You got me pegged all wrong."

"Welcome aboard, anyway. I'd have the stewardess serve drinks, but..." he waved his hand, "what you see is what you get."

"Lots of gauges and things," Gaston said, looking at the instrument filled cockpit.

"This here is the altimeter," Jason said reaching over the pilot's shoulder.

"Get your cotton pickin' hands off my controls!" Joe yelled.

"Sorry," Jason said, backing up. "Just trying to teach this guy something."

"See that cloud bank up ahead? Those are thunderheads. You better take your seats unless you want your brains scattered on the bulkhead. And fasten your harnesses. The ride's about to get interesting."

"That guy's a dick," Jason said, walking Gaston back to the waist gunner's seat.

"He's the pilot," Gaston said. "Better do as he says."

Gaston squeezed back into his seat and started to strap himself in just as the plane dropped suddenly. It felt like they had hit a giant hole in the sky. As he was lifted from his seat he grabbed the harness and held on. Jason was not so lucky. He went flying and crashed into the sheet aluminum paneling of the fuselage. As quickly as the plane lost altitude, it leveled off and then started climbing again. Gaston managed to finish buckling in. He turned to see Jason picking himself up. "Are you okay?"

"Just a bump. I'd better take my seat."

"Good idea," Gaston said, smiling.

They had been in the air nine hours when the copilotshined a flashlight in Gaston's eyes and tapped him on the shoulder. "We've got some rough weather coming up. It's snowing hard in the Rockies and we're starting to ice up. We're going to try and take the plane lower, but there aren't any guarantees."

"I don't understand," Gaston said.

"See that," Denny said, wiping the frost off the side of the sheet metal above Gaston's head. In the glow of the flashlight he could see the inside of the plane had turned white with frozen condensation. "We've got to get lower or we'll ice up solid."

"What happens then?"

"We go down like a rock in a pond. I'd better get up front."

I must have been asleep, Gaston thought. He could see it had turned dark outside. He checked his watch and did the math. "Nineteen-hundred in Oregon. We're another three hours out," he said, to the darkness. He felt the plane change altitude, a gradual descent. After a few minutes he felt a drop of water hit his face. He looked up and saw more drops. It felt like it was raining inside the airplane. *It must have worked*, Gaston thought.

A few minutes later he heard Jason call out. "Hey, Navy! You awake?"

"Yeah."

"We got problems."

"Yeah, what?"

"At this altitude we'll be lucky to make it to Portland."

"Great, what's wrong?"

"We've been in the air nine hours. Portland is 2400 miles from DC. By my calculation we'll run out of gas over Idaho."

"They must have already done the math on that," Gaston said.

"Yeah, but we've been bucking a headwind the whole trip and we're practically hugging the ground. The air down here is thicker and our fuel is burning up fast."

"Why don't you go up and tell the test pilots they're doing it wrong?" Gaston smiled. *The smart ass knows just enough to get us in trouble.* Before the thought was out of his mind, he heard the first engine shut down.

Chapter 3

Portland Air Base

"Captain, we've got a B-17 overdue out of Washington DC. The last communication was an hour ago. They were spotted on radar over Pocatello." The young woman delivering the message was a member of the Civil Air Patrol.

"Thanks, I'll take it from here." The captain put down his cup of coffee and headed for the communication shack. "What have you got on the missing B-17?" he asked, entering the communication room. The airman manning the radio took off his headset. "We lost them on radar. It was either a controlled descent or loss of engine. We tracked them until they were too low to be picked up by ground radar."

"Was there a distress signal?"

"Nothing yet, sir."

"Contact the station where they were last spotted and see if they have a bearing where we can start a search.

"Yes, sir."

*****

"It's a good thing we made it over the mountains," the pilot said, as the second engine stalled. He tapped the fuel gauge. "Damn Wright engines burn fuel like a hungry tiger. We should have been able to make 2400 miles with fuel to spare."

"Joe, I told you we should have scheduled a fuel stop in Denver."

"Yeah, yeah, a lot of good that does us now. Find a soft spot and we'll try and put her down easy."

"I saw the lights of Pocatello a while back. There should be a major highway going west from there."

"I don't like it, landing this ton of bricks on a highway. Probably telephone wires or power poles alongside. I don't want them taking this tub out of my pay."

"Well, I haven't got anything better. Is there an airfield around?"

"Are you nuts? We're out in the middle of no-man's-land."

"Check the charts; we're not that far from civilization."

Denny grabbed the charts and studied them. "This is what you get when you give the navigator the day off." He folded the map and twisted it sideways. "Wait a minute!"

"Speak to me, Denny."

"I'll be damned! Joe, you've got to be the luckiest son-of-a-bitch on the planet. Ten miles due west and we have American Falls, Idaho. There's a landing strip that parallels the highway."

"Well quit flappin' your jaw and see if you can raise them on the radio."

"I think we're going down!" Jason yelled.

"I hope you're wrong," Gaston yelled back.

"Brace yourself."

Gaston felt the same thing Jason did. The plane went into a downward pitch and was dropping rapidly. He saw landing lights go on and outside the window was nothing but white. Snow covered every surface he could see.

Without fanfare the plane settled and the props caused the plane to be caught in a white-out blizzard. The B-17 slowed abruptly and came to a halt. Before Gaston could unbuckle his harness, Denny was standing over him with his flashlight. "Ladies and gentlemen, I think you will want to thank Captain Joe Reams for another perfect landing. Welcome to American Falls, Idaho. We will be here long enough for you to clean the shit out of your britches, and see if we can garner enough fuel on the Army's credit to get us the rest of the way to Portland." He started clapping. Gaston and Jason joined in.

Inside the tin Quonset hut that served as a terminal, they warmed themselves beside a pot belly stove. Gaston used the toilet and helped himself to a cup of coffee from a large metal pot setting on the stove. "I knew we were in trouble," Jason said to Gaston. They huddled around the stove while the pilot arranged to have aviation fuel pumped into the tanks of the aircraft.

Gaston took a cautious sip of coffee. "This stuff will grow hair on your chest."

"You think this is a scheduled landing!" Jason was near hysterical. "We were that close to meeting our maker."

"Still it beats the alternative," Gaston said. "We're here on the ground. Cool down. No-harm-no-foul."

"Incompetence is what I call it! These guys should be in jail. What they did was criminal."

"You got a problem, Army, maybe you'd like to hoof it to Seattle." Joe Reams stood three inches taller than Jason and was a good thirty pounds heavier.

"Just sayin'," Jason said. "I didn't mean it."

"Then take it back." Joe put his face three inches from Jason's face.

"All right, you two. Go to your rooms and face the wall." Denny slipped between Joe and Jason like he had refereed in a past life.

Gaston stood back with his coffee and took in the scene. He wondered why people would get upset so easily. "How long before we get in the air again?"

"Man, you're too anxious. Believe me; the war will be waiting for you when we get there." Joe grabbed a tin cup from a hanger beside the stove and poured himself a cup of coffee. "I'll call ahead and let them know where we are. No sense taking off in this storm at night."

"All right, if we crash here for the night?" Gaston asked the man in coveralls.

"I got a couple of extra blankets in the store room. All right by me if you bed down next to the stove. I ain't seen nobody else since sundown. This snow keeps falling you ain't goin' nowhere, no way, no how."

Gaston breathed a sigh of relief. As uneasy as he was with flying, the only thing worse in his mind was flying with pilots who were tired.

The storm broke and the B-17 lifted off the frozen runway at daybreak. Gaston watched from the waist gunner's seat as the Flying Fortress rose into a crystal-blue sky. In two hours they were circling around snow covered Mt. Hood and searching for the runway at Portland-Columbia Airport. As the plane taxied to the hangar a stream of vehicles trailed it until it stopped.

"Looks like we've got a welcoming committee," Joe said, opening the main cabin door.

At the bottom of the stairs, a man dressed in a black suit and heavy black overcoat stood with an umbrella. "I'm here to escort Mr. Carson to the Coast Guard Station at Yaquina Bay," the man said.

Joe turned to Jason who was standing at the door behind Joe. "I told you he was a dignitary."

Gaston came up behind them dragging his heavy duffle bag. "You fellas afraid to put your feet on the ground?"

"I was just admiring your welcoming committee. You're the son of a congressman, aren't you?" Joe asked.

"Sorry to disappoint you. I'm serving my Country just like the rest of you."

"Somehow I find that hard to believe," Joe said. "I was told by my Commander, you were special cargo. If you don't know these people, how do I know it's safe to leave you with them?"

Gaston laughed. "Get out of the way. I'm nearly a day late for my appointment." He pushed past the others and lugged the bag down the stairs. On the tarmac another man, also wearing a suit, grabbed the duffle bag. "I'll help you with that." He hefted the bag into the trunk of a 4-door Chrysler New Yorker.

"Gosh, I've never seen one of these before," Gaston said, admiring the shiny black vehicle. The man in the overcoat opened the rear door for Gaston. "We can ride in back and I'll brief you on the way."

"Gaston Carson," Gaston said, holding out his hand.

"Introductions can wait. We've had our team waiting since last night."

"Team? I don't understand."

"You'll be briefed shortly. We're only a few minutes from the hotel."

Gaston got the message. *No questions until he got to the hotel.* He sat back on the plush velvet seat. The man got in the car next to him.

"I understand you had to make an emergency landing," the man said.

Oh, small talk is okay, Gaston thought. "One of our engines shut down. We were able to touch down on a snow-covered runway in Idaho. American Falls, ever hear of it?"

"Only last night. The Director was all over our asses asking where you were."

"Sorry. As far as I could tell it couldn't be helped." *Why the hell was J. Edgar Hoover looking for him?*

"Understood. I guess the pilot didn't know who he was transporting."

"Am I missing something?" Gaston asked.

"You are aware of your meeting with the Portland field agent?"

"I guess I missed that part of the briefing," Gaston said.

The man nodded. "Hoover will love this," he said under his breath.

"Pardon?"

"I get that you are important, but nobody comes into our jurisdiction without reporting to the Deputy Director in the field. Hoover found out you were headed here and has been on our asses about it since yesterday. Don't your people follow protocol anymore?"

"Whoa, hold on a minute. I haven't the slightest idea what you're talking about. I was assigned to the Coast Guard Station at Yaquina Bay. I'm sure they can answer any questions you have."

"That will have to wait."

They pulled into the front of the Benson Hotel and the doorman opened the door to the car. Inside, they walked across the marble floor and past the carved wooden and polished brass reception desk, to the elevators. A bellboy pushed a cart behind them. The only thing on the cart was Gaston's duffle bag.

"Eighth floor," the man in the overcoat said to the elevator operator.

Once inside room 808 the man handed the bellhop a dime. "Thanks. That will be all." The door closed. Inside the plush hotel room the man motioned for Gaston to take a seat. Gaston pulled a chair from an ornate desk and sat as he was instructed. The man removed his overcoat and placed it on the bed. He knocked on a door connecting 808 to the room next door.

Two men dressed in dark suits and matching neckties entered and stared at Gaston for a minute. "Gaston Carson, I'm glad to meet you. I'm Wilson Manfred, FBI Director of the Portland Field Office."

Gaston stood. "Glad to meet you, too. You mind telling me what all the secrecy is about? My mind is spinning with questions."

"Your file said you were direct. Go ahead; ask away, but first I have a question for you. Who do you work for?"

"Who I work for is none of your business."

"I got a call yesterday from the Director himself asking me to find out who you report to. Would you mind telling me who that is?"

Gaston pulled out a piece of paper. He had written Coast Guard Commander, Thurston Goodman. He looked at the paper. "It says here, Coast Guard Commander, Thurston Goodman. I've never met the man, but I hear he runs the Yaquina Bay Station."

"We know you attended a secret meeting at the White House the morning of December 9. Who were you meeting with?"

Gaston didn't like where this was going. Maybe this was what the President was talking about. *Were there really those who were spying on the Oval Office? How did he figure into all of this?* His instructions were clear, he didn't answer to anyone, but *The Man* himself. The best he could do was to make the meeting short and keep his mouth shut. "I don't know of a meeting at the White House. I've been assigned to the Coast Guard Station at Yaquina Bay. That's all I know. You clearly have me confused with someone else."

The other man spoke. "Mr. Carson, I'm Frank Billings, Assistant to the Director here in Portland. We're not trying to pry into your private affairs, but as an American citizen there is certain protocol you must follow. We are charged with protecting the citizens in our district and we need a minimal amount of information to carry out our charge. There is only one way you could have been given passage on that aircraft, a direct order from the Commander in Chief himself. Why would Roosevelt give you passage on that airplane?"

Gaston knew they were grasping at straws. Jason was an Army Air Force recruit and he surely didn't have orders from FDR "Look, I'm civilian and you're civilians. The only protocol I *have* to follow is outlined in the Constitution of the United States. Attached are the Bill of Rights and certain Constitutional Amendments. If you want any information, talk to Commander Goodman. I need to be on my way. Commander Goodman is sure to be wondering why I haven't reported in." Gaston got up to leave.

"You clearly don't understand the rules," the Director said. "This isn't the end of the discussion."

Gaston picked up his bag. "It is for now. Are you going to arrange transportation to my destination or am I to figure it out on my own."

"There's a car waiting downstairs," Director Manfred said.

On leaving the hotel, the car was blocked by a crowd of demonstrators. "What's going on?" Gaston asked.

"A bunch of anti-war demonstrators. The police will have them cleared out in a few minutes."

Gaston saw the police were already on scene and appeared to have several people in custody. The signs held up were not necessarily pro-Japan, but were rather anti-war no matter what. One sign said, *Negotiate Peace,* another said, *Japan is not our enemy*!

As the car eased through the crowd, down the street was a larger demonstration. One sign read *Death to all Japs.* In spite of the close proximity of the two demonstrations, there didn't appear to be any clashes between the two. *Maybe that was what the police were trying to avoid,* Gaston thought. "Is there a lot of Japanese sympathy out here?" he asked.

"Just the opposite, if you ask me," the driver said. "Most of the arrests have been for people attacking the Japanese. We even had an incident where a Chinese restaurant owner was attacked."

Chapter 4

The three-hour drive to the Coast Guard Station took Gaston through the little town of Tillamook and down the coastline through a number of tiny fishing and lumbering communities. He saw people going about their lives, apparently unaware that the country was at war. There was not a uniform or military vehicle to be seen. Occasionally, a logging truck would round a curve and force the driver to pull dangerously close to the edge of the narrow road. "Bastards think they own the road," the driver shouted once, pulling the car to a stop with the front tire nearly in the ditch.

Gaston sat in the back seat with plenty of time to contemplate the meeting he'd had in Portland. The FBI was certainly on edge, but he didn't know if they were just doing their job or asserting more authority than they were charged with legally. The country was at war and that may call for extraordinary measures: it wasn't considered in any discussions or training at the Academy. He had to consider he was working directly for the President, and didn't know if there were any others to watch his back. He felt alone, very alone.

Eventually they reached the fishing town of Newport and the Coast Guard Station located on the north side of the bay, just east of the new Yaquina Bay Bridge. The driver stopped the car. "Mr. Carson, you're on your own from here. Do you need help with your bag?"

"No, I'll be fine. Thanks for the ride." Gaston got out and grabbed his bag. Again he felt alone. He stood outside the guardhouse with his duffle bag at his side. *Now what*, he thought. He was in civilian dress. A young seaman with an MP armband came out of the tiny house and inquired to his business.

"Gaston Carson, here to see Commander Goodman."

"May I see your identification, sir?"

Gaston wasn't carrying any papers. Whatever orders he was traveling under had been forwarded verbally; at least he hoped they had been. He pulled out a Virginia driver's license and the I.D. card that had his picture. *US Diplomatic Service.* He handed them to the seaman. "I believe the Commander is expecting me."

Within a few minutes, a car with a young woman at the wheel arrived at the gate. She had beautiful dark shoulder-length hair, green eyes, and an infectious smile. "Mr. Carson," the woman said, getting out of the car. "You can stow your bag in the back seat and ride in front with me."

They drove along a gravel road to a line of barracks painted white with red trim. "You know my name, do you mind if I ask yours?" Gaston asked.

"Alice," she replied. She stopped in front of a house also painted white with red trim, to match the barracks. "This is Officer's Quarters. You can take a few minutes to freshen up and the Commander will pick you up at 1400 hrs. You can wait inside. I'll park the car and be right in to get you settled."

Gaston checked his watch. He had twenty minutes for a hot shower, and a shave if he hurried. Inside the house was a reception desk with a typewriter and a phone. To the right of the desk was a flight of stairs, behind it an archway that appeared to be a kitchen area.

"Mr. Carson, your room is up the stairs on the left. Your name is on the door."

Gaston looked at the young woman again. Her hair was curled under in the popular page-boy style. It went well with her girlish freckled face. She smiled, showing dimples in both cheeks, and perfectly white teeth with a slight lipstick stain.

"Is there something else, Mr. Carson?"

"You have a lipstick stain on your teeth," he said, touching his front tooth.

Her face turned red. She pulled out a hanky and scrubbed her front teeth.

"I think you've got it," he said, grinning.

"Will there be anything else?" she asked, sarcastically.

"I'd like to take a shower and shave. Are the facilities in my room?"

"You'll find a community shower and bathroom at the end of the hall. You will be sharing it at times with up to four officers, so I'd advise you to clean up after yourself."

"Yes, ma'am."

"My name is Alice. Miss Alice Fitzpatrick. You may address me as Alice, or Miss Fitzpatrick. Never, under any circumstances, are you to refer to me as Fitz, as you may hear from some of the less gentlemanly officers." She gave him a broad smile. "You'd better hurry, if you want to make a good first impression on Commander Goodman."

Gaston lugged his bag up the stairs, found the room with his name neatly stenciled on a cardboard insert on the door. "Home sweet home," he said, eyeing the tiny room. He noticed a musty smell, like the room had been closed up for awhile. Taking up most of the floor space was a white metal rail bed with sagging springs. On one wall were a four-drawer dresser with a mirror above it, and a white bowl with a matching pitcher sitting on it. A small desk sat beside it with a radio that took up most of the surface. On the back wall was a single small window with four panes overlooking the bay. He pulled back the black-out curtains. On that wall there was also a portable closet for his suits, and a shoeshine kit in a square metal can sat neatly on the floor. A fold-out ironing board was attached to one side of the closet. The iron was sitting on a shelf at the top of the closet. *All the comforts of home*, he thought, as he searched through his duffle bag for something to wear.

After shaving and taking a quick shower, he dressed in a new pair of freshly ironed navy blue slacks, a white dress shirt and a pullover maroon long sleeved sweater. He had heard it was chilly the year around on the Oregon Coast and had packed as appropriately as he could, considering his entire wardrobe was bought new and stuffed into the duffle bag only hours before his trip. He had sold his car to a buddy at the Academy for fifty dollars. He couldn't help but feel like he was being punished. He wanted so much to be serving like the sailors running around on the base. He had real doubts that his presence here would lend anything to the war effort.

He smiled in the mirror and ruffled his fingers through his short-cropped dark hair. *This should be acceptable.* He was sitting on the side of the bed, dusting off his dress shoes when there was a knock on the door. "Mr. Carson, are you decent?"

He recognized the voice of Miss Fitzpatrick. "Be right there," he said, tying his shoes. He opened the door. She was standing there with her dimples showing. She was pleasant to look at.

"The Commander is waiting downstairs."

"Just a second," he said, grabbing a suit jacket from his duffle bag. He shook out the wrinkles as best he could and carried it in his left hand. "Thank you, Miss Fitzpatrick. Would you like to lead the way?"

At the bottom of the stairs he saw Commander Goodman for the first time. He was as tall as Gaston, about six-feet and ruggedly built. He had a no-nonsense face, a strong jaw and ruddy complexion, common for someone who has spent a lot of time in the weather, or one who drank heavily. Already a five-o'clock shadow was showing on the Commander's face. He was casually dressed in winter khakis and a navy-blue windbreaker with US Coast Guard embroidered in small letters on the left side. His shirt collar had the triple silver bars of his rank. He looked younger than Gaston had imagined.

"Mr. Carson," Goodman said, stretching out his hand.

"Commander Goodman, you are younger than I expected."

"You really want to get along with me, don't you?"

"Pardon me, sir. I spent three years in Annapolis and most of the Commanders I've met have gray hair."

"I'll take that as a compliment. Speaking of age, Mr. Carson, you don't look old enough to be a diplomat. Aren't there age limits for that?"

Gaston knew he was going to like this man. He had a friendly smile and looked like someone he could trust. He was also getting tired of the questions about his age. "I'm old enough to fight for my Country, sir. I've barely got my sea legs and this assignment came completely out of the blue. I hope you can fill me in on a few details."

"First, I need to see some I.D.," the Commander said.

"Of course." Gaston presented the picture I.D. he'd shown at the gate. He remembered the President telling him never to call the number on the card unless it was a life and death situation.

After checking the card, Goodman said, "Come with me, I have a private lunch arranged."

The Commander drove a dusty-gray Ford sedan. The headlights had been blacked out with the exception of a small slit designed to light up a minimal amount of road surface at night. Gaston got in the passenger seat.

"You ever been to the Oregon Coast before?" the Commander asked as they exited the base.

"First time, sir. I'm expecting to see a lot of it over the coming months."

They turned east and headed up the bay to the Newport Bay Front; a mix of tackle shops, fish processing plants, a few restaurants, and shops fronted by a boardwalk.

"Open the glove box and pull out the manila envelope; it arrived by courier this morning."

The large envelope was bent over double and stuffed into the small space. The front had his name and was stamped "FOR YOUR EYES ONLY". He opened it and read the letter.

Part one of Gaston's orders was to observe what the community was doing, investigate any suspicious activity or enemy sightings, and report the results of his findings to the White House.

Part two gave Gaston pause. He was to draft recommendations on how to deal with the situation. In other words, he was to give the President his opinion of how to handle things out West. *That makes me a Presidential Advisor*, he thought, off the record, of course. It all seemed simple enough to him. He folded up the letter and stuck it in his shirt pocket.

Gaston learned the Commander lived off-site in a large house overlooking the ocean in a remote area called Otter Crest, and rarely joined the officers for dinner.

Gaston was told he could join the officers for dinner in the Officer's Mess, if he desired. That evening he met the other two officers who shared Officer's Quarters, over the dinner table. The officers at the table had known each other for a number of years and seemed comfortable telling stories on each other. Mostly they told stories on themselves.

Lieutenant JG Oberman was nearing the end of his second four-year tour and the other, Ensign Danny Pastor, was an old salt who hadn't been able to collect the rank that should follow ten years of service. In fact, Danny Pastor had managed to piss off every senior officer he'd served under and had been passed over repeatedly for promotion; thus midway through his third tour of duty he'd managed to stay a rank equal to what Gaston would have received had he graduated the Academy.

Ensign Pastor bragged he had not taken command of anything larger than a rowboat in his time in the Coast Guard. He readily admitted he drank too much, smoked too much, and swore, well, like a sailor, but he had managed to stay in the service in spite of his shortcomings, and now, with the war, he was almost certain to keep his job for the duration. Neither Oberman nor Pastor was married and both made Officer's Quarters their home. All the other officers were married and lived off base.

"If you insist on eating with us, you need to tell us a little about you," Ensign Pastor said. "Isn't that right, Oberman?"

Oberman, who outranked Ensign Pastor didn't seem to mind the casual way he was addressed. He smiled and nodded.

"I'm originally from New York City," Gaston said. "When I was twelve, I went to live with an uncle who sent me off to prep school. After high school, I was accepted into the Naval Academy at Annapolis. I played football; you may remember I made the last touchdown of the year against Army. One month later the war broke out. I dropped out of the academy, was put on special assignment, and ended up here." Gaston had rehearsed this several times. He knew there would be questions. He didn't want to get into a situation where there were too many prying questions, but he knew he had to be careful not to leave too many questions unanswered.

"What did I tell you, Oberman," Pastor said. "I said he came from money."

"I'll admit my uncle has money," Gaston said. "Unfortunately, he thinks I have to earn mine on my own." It wasn't a lie, Gaston reasoned. He could have told them it was Uncle Sam.

"Don't you just hate it when that happens?" Pastor said. "Me, I came from money, but I spent it all." He laughed.

Oberman, who had remained quiet, decided he was expected to say something, so he set down his fork and dabbed his mouth with a linen napkin. "When my tour is up, I'm going to join my father's firm. He has a factory weaving ladies' stockings out of a new material called nylon. Right now he's been switching the factory over to make parachute cords for the Army Air Corps."

"Interesting," Gaston said. "I read someplace that the synthetic material is better than silk."

"It gets a lot of attention. Most women would prefer silk, but that isn't going to happen as long as we're at war with the Japs, is it?"

It was 0300 when Gaston woke up and checked his watch. He had been sleeping restlessly his first night in Officer's Quarters. He heard voices coming from the room next door. *What the hell is going on this time of the morning?* he wondered. He got up and listened. He knew the noise was coming from Danny Pastor's room. He could clearly hear a conversation between a man and a woman. Then the unmistakable sound of bed springs being methodically exercised went on for a good ten minutes before he heard Danny tell the woman to get dressed.

Gaston stepped into the hall, barefoot and in his skivvies and quickly made his way to the head. While he was standing at the urinal, Danny walked in, fully dressed, looking none the worse for ware.

"Jesus, son," Pastor said, seeing Gaston. "You shouldn't have to take a piss this time of night. Better have Doc check you out. The Coast Guard's no place for a weak bladder."

"That doesn't seem to have stopped you," Gaston said.

"Yeah, but I've got an excuse. I drank a gallon of beer and just screwed the prettiest girl in town. Top that."

"No contest," Gaston said. He made his way back to his room and a few minutes later heard Danny ushering the girl down the stairs. "*It'll be a miracle if we win the war,*" he thought. He rolled over in bed and fell into a sound sleep.

By midmorning Gaston had crossed Yaquina Bay, by way of a large arched bridge that had been constructed only five years earlier. He drove south along the picturesque coast on US 101. He remembered the locals referred to it as the Pacific Coast Highway. The car he had requisitioned from the motor pool was a 1936 Dodge Coupe similar to the Plymouth he had sold. He had a full tank of gas, something that was already being rationed in the general public. He had been cautioned to be sure he was not traveling farther than the sixteen-gallon tank would allow him because the gas stations were few and far between, and they may not have fuel, anyway. He had yet to apply for rations, something that he reminded himself to do.

That morning at breakfast, Commander Goodman had handed him a note. A fisherman out of Winchester Bay, a fishing village sixty-five miles south of Newport, had reported seeing a submarine two miles off the coast. There were no allied submarines operating in the area so it was presumed to be a Japanese sub, or more likely a grey whale. Gaston was to do the investigation and share his findings with the Commander. This seemed reasonable to Gaston, since it fell within the scope of his orders.

As he maneuvered along the curvy road, he thought about the Top Secret letter containing his assignment. As he had been instructed, he found a stove and burned it along with the envelope it came in. He was relieved that Commander Goodman understood he could not share it with him.

Goodman had told him that he had also received a letter from President Roosevelt's Chief of Staff. He was asked to support Gaston in the investigation of any enemy activity whatsoever. As a civilian Gaston hoped to gain the trust of the people and get an unbiased opinion whether the sighting was credible or not.

After three hours without stopping, Gaston saw a spot high on a bluff where he could pull off the road. He parked the car, set the emergency brake and stood among the weathered and mangled coastal pine that were trying to survive the perpetual wind that tormented all living things exposed to the elements. He had a clear view of the ocean and could see for miles. It was an incredible sight. He looked around, and not seeing another living creature, relieved himself, making sure he was standing with the wind to his back. When he was finished, he removed a pair of binoculars from the passenger seat of the car and scanned the ocean. He saw several fishing vessels close in and a few farther out. He got back into the car and proceeded another thirty minutes to his destination.

Winchester Bay was both, fishing and a lumber town. The bay was tranquil and peaceful. Several fishing boats, with their outriggers reeled in, were moored along the dock. Gaston found a small restaurant called *Fish Tales* right on the dock. A rusty Model A pickup was parked out front. The air was damp and the smell of the sea was everywhere. Seagulls circled overhead and a Bald eagle plucked a fish from the water right in front of him. Overhead, dark clouds were gathering. In places the clouds had dropped down to the surface of the water. He stood mesmerized by the beauty of nature.

"Ya ain't from around here, are ya?" A voice woke him from his trance.

Gaston turned to see a bent-over man in coveralls. His face was as weathered as a dried apple. "I'm from up North. I was hoping to find Mitchell Williams. They said he fishes out of this port. You wouldn't happen to know him?"

"Ain't sayin' I do and ain't sayin' I don't. You got a handle?"

"Gaston Carson." He stuck out his hand.

"What's yer business with Mitch?"

"I thought you didn't know him."

"Now don't go puttin' words in my mouth. Don't see many strangers down this way."

"May I buy you a cup of coffee?" Gaston offered.

"Might be up for it, or somethin' stronger, if ya know what I mean." The old man rubbed the white stubble on his face. "This ain't the best place in town though. Follow me."

"I need to talk to Mitchell," Gaston said again, watching the old man wander off.

"That's what ya said. Ya ain't going to find him standing there."

Gaston caught up with the old man. "I didn't catch your name."

The hunched over man stopped and turned. "Now, I don't reckon I gave it."

"Then I'm going to call you Old Timer."

"That'll do as good as any. See that there blinking sign. That's where we'll be goin.'"

They walked in silence toward the blinking neon sign. It was red and flashed Olympia off and on. "What's Olympia?" Gaston asked.

"That'd be the best beer in these parts. Yer gonna buy me a pitcher and I'll tell ya what ya want."

"Fair enough."

The weathered sign on the building simply said "Tavern". The old man opened a squeaking door and held it for Gaston. Inside the dimly lit room, a cloud of smoke hung as dense as the fog that was starting to roll in.

"Manny, bring me an Oly and... whatever my new friend wants."

"I'll have coffee," Gaston said.

"That ain't gonna do," the old man said, shaking his head. "Can't trust a body that don't drink."

"Bring me an Oly, too," Gaston said. "Is that good enough?"

"If'n you don't drink it, I will," the old man said, with a new glimmer in his eyes.

The bar was made from a three-foot diameter log that had been split down the middle and mounted to two stumps nearly as large. The surface of the bar was worn from years of elbows and spilled drinks. *I'll bet Prohibition never reached this town*, Gaston thought as he sat on a hand carved wooden stool. It was as rustic as any place he'd ever seen.

"Drink up," the old man said, lifting his mug of beer.

Gaston grabbed his mug and took a sip. "About Mitchell?" Gaston asked again.

The old man pointed to a dark corner of the room. "Over yonder. He'll be in, in an hour or so."

"Where's he right now?" Gaston asked.

The old man took a long pull from his mug and let out a long sigh. "Now, that, I don't rightly know. We're in here and he's out there somewhere. What I do know is he'll be here round about an hour or so. You can take that to the bank, ain't that right Manny?"

"If you say so, J.P."

"Your name is J.P.?"

"Nope."

"But he called you J.P."

"Yep."

"Manny, why'd you call the old man J.P.?"

"Jesus, Morgan, I'm going to cut you off if you don't stop giving our visitors such a hard time."

"Don't give me any shit, Manny. I can take my business to Clair's Place. That'd teach ya."

"Clair wouldn't let an old fart like you through the front door."

"Excuse me, Manny," Gaston said, "my name's Gaston Carson. I drove down the coast from Newport this morning, and I'm looking for Mitchell Williams. The old man tells me he frequents this place."

"He's right about that. Ever since he saw that Jap sub, he's been scared to go out in his dad's boat. Been here every day for a week."

"What do you know about the sighting," Gaston asked.

Manny leaned across the bar. "I know it scared the shit out of that kid."

"So you don't think it was a whale?"

Manny started to laugh, then J.P. joined in. "There ain't no mistaken a submarine for a whale. Shit man, whales don't have numbers painted on their sides, now do they?"

"You got me there," Gaston said, seeing the humor. He lifted his beer. "I guess I'll just have to wait and hear the story for myself."

Gaston was nursing his second beer and J.P. was finishing the pitcher when a young man dressed in rubber knee-high boots and a yellow rain slicker came through the door. Gaston noticed through the open door that it was already getting dark outside.

"Hey, J.P. What's happening?" Mitchell came over to the bar. "By the way you were staring at me; you'd think I'd robbed a bank."

"Mitch, this here's Gaston Carson." He patted Gaston on the back. "Mind you, I'm not sure that's his real name. No self respectin' ma would name their kid Gaston."

"It's my real name," Gaston said, getting up from his stool. "Can I buy you a beer?"

"Hot damn, my ship has come in. I ain't never had anyone buy me a drink before...'cept my old man the day I turned 21."

"I'll take it from here, Old Timer," Gaston said, shuffling Mitch to an empty table away from the bar.

"I'll have another pitcher. Put it on money bag's tab," J.P. said to the bar tender.

Mitch set his beer mug on the table, climbed out of his rain gear. and piled it up on an empty chair. He sat in the chair next to it. "You some kind of reporter, Gaston?"

Gaston sat down across the table from Mitch. He leaned across and spoke in a low voice. "I'm investigating your story, but we have to keep it quiet, okay?"

"Sure, but wouldn't you want everyone to know if the Japs are storming our beaches?"

"First tell me what happened, from the beginning, then we'll decide how much we want the public to know."

For the next hour Mitch told how he was crabbing less than a mile off the coast when a submarine surfaced not a hundred yards from them. Gaston opened his notebook to a clean page and slid it to the kid with a pencil. "Draw me what you saw as accurately as possible."

To his surprise the kid was a pretty good artist. "You're sure the gun on the stern was facing toward the rear of the sub?"

"I ain't only sure, I'm positive."

"How about the numbers you saw. Are you sure about them?"

"Yes, sir, I am. I got out the binoculars and could see right through the fog."

"Fog? How foggy was it?"

"You know how it is that time of the morning. Everything is still and the fog hangs low to the water, but it wasn't so heavy that I couldn't see."

"What makes you sure it was Japanese?"

"I didn't figure we'd be dumping our garbage that close to shore, and we don't drink sake, do we?"

"Sake? You're sure it was sake."

"Well, not 100%, but I got the bottle. You can look at it and see for yourself. It's got Jap writing on it."

Gaston nearly jumped up from the table. "Finish your beer. I want to see the bottle." He went over to the bar. "Manny, buy J.P. one more, and ring up my bill. I've got to go."

Outside the rain had started falling in a steady drizzle. He had a quarter-mile walk back to his car. "There anyplace to get a room for the night around here?" Gaston asked, standing under the overhang at the front door of the tavern.

Mitch stood out in the open, apparently not aware it was raining, as he was dressed for it. "Not sure. You can try Mable Perkins. She sometimes rents out a room," Mitch answered.

"Let me see the bottle and I'll worry about a room later."

They crossed Highway 101 and headed for the docks. Gaston was already soaked to the skin through his light jacket. He made a mental note to pick up a rain slicker the first chance he got. Mitch was walking ahead of him down the narrow ramp to a string of fishing boats.

"This here is my dad's boat, '*Guppy*'. The name fits, don't you think?"

The boat was a metal tub about 30 ft. long. It was painted black down to the water line. The cabin was white. Gaston guessed it would do about ten knots with the diesel engine straining.

"You want to come aboard?" Mitch asked.

Gaston grabbed the rope rail on the gangplank and pulled himself up the steep ramp. On board, there wasn't much room. Crab traps covered nearly all of the rear deck. Inside the cabin, Mitch turned on an overhead light. Gaston was so wet he could see steam coming off his body.

Mitch lifted the seat on a bench beside a table and pulled out his trophy. "Here it is. Ain't she a beauty?"

Gaston took the quart-sized aqua-colored glass bottle and studied it. It had a wire bail holding a cork stopper in place. Around the base were several Japanese symbols and a circle within a circle, the symbol of the sun. There was no mistake; it was a Japanese beverage bottle. Now the question was, why were they dumping garbage this close to shore, and what were they doing there in the first place? Surely they wouldn't be so brazen to surface where they could be so easily seen...unless that was their plan. "Can I have this?" Gaston asked.

Mitch took the bottle from him. "I'll bet there are people who'll pay good money for a Jap bottle."

"What do you figure its worth?"

Mitch thought awhile, cocked his head, "Two dollars?"

"I'll give you one dollar and that's too much," Gaston said.

Mitch thought some more. "I really need two bucks."

"I'll tell you what. I'll give you two dollars and you give me a ride on Guppy and show me where you were when you spotted that sub."

Mitch checked his watch. "Be here at 6:00 sharp, tomorrow morning."

"Deal," Gaston said, reaching for the bottle.

"Let me see the money," Mitch said, hanging on tightly to the bottle.

Gaston reached in his pocket and pulled out two silver dollars. "You sure you're just a fisherman and not a car salesman?"

"Don't know for sure, but I ain't got any cars."

Gaston left with the bottle. Back at his car, he walked into the restaurant in front of where he was parked. A woman with her hair wrapped in a large bandana was cleaning up. A clock behind the counter said 7:15. The place was empty. "Are you closing?' he asked.

"My, don't you look like a drowned rat. Might just as well be closing. No customers, unless you want something."

"I could use a good meal and a place to stay. I was told Mable Perkins might have a room."

The woman looked him over. "What brings you to our town?"

"It's a long story. A cup of hot coffee would be nice, if you still have some."

"You gonna eat, too?"

"Depends, what have you got?"

"Sit down; I'll rustle up some leftovers."

Gaston set the bottle on the table and removed his soaked jacket. He hung it over a chair.

"You might want to remove your sweater too. Hang it over by the stove," the woman said. She set a plate on the table, left, and returned with a steaming cup of coffee.

After hanging his jacket and sweater on a chair back close to the stove, he grabbed the coffee and warmed his hands around the thick ceramic mug. He sat down and examined the plate in front of him. Meatloaf, mashed potatoes and gravy, a slice of buttered bread resting on a pile of green beans. He dove into the food. "This is good. You do the cooking here?"

"Cooking, cleaning, mopping. Worst part of the job is, I own the place."

Gaston smiled. "Well, I'm glad I caught you before you closed. Any idea where I can find Mable Perkins?"

"You've been talking to her. Just wanted to make sure you were okay before giving you a room."

"My name's Gaston."

"I know," Mable said. "You been talking to Mitch about that Japanese submarine."

"News travels fast around here." Mable pulled out a chair and sat across from him. He could see she was just starting to turn gray. He guessed she was in her fifties.

"Small town. The speculation is you are FBI."

Gaston smiled. "No, not FBI. Actually I'm on a special assignment."

"I get it. You reporters will do anything to get a story."

"You're Mable," Gaston said, reaching his hand across the table.

"Mable Perkins, but you already knew that. It's spelled just like it sounds. Is that a real Jap sake bottle?"

"I'm going to do my best to find out," Gaston said. "Now, about that room?"

Chapter 5

Off the coast of Oregon a submarine surfaced in the dense fog. The hatch opened and a crew member climbed out and stood on the deck. He unbuttoned his trousers and relieved himself, watching the stream arc over the side of the deck. He opened another hatch on the deck and removed a long, black object. Another seaman came through the hatch on the conning tower and made his way to aft deck. The two lifted the long object and slipped it into the water. They spoke in Japanese.

"See, it is as I told you," the first man said.

"How many do we have to place?" the other asked.

"Hundreds. We need to take advantage of the fog cover."

They disappeared inside the submarine, closed the hatches, and the sub slipped quietly below the surface of the water.

*****

Gaston had another restless night's sleep. He was able to use Mable's telephone and contact Commander Goodman to let him know he was going to be a few days in the Winston Bay area. He tried to remain vague about the meeting he had with Mitchell Williams, or about the early morning boat trip he was going to be taking. He rolled over in bed turned on a lamp and checked the time. Still too early to get up. He turned the light off. As he lay in the darkness he thought about the submarine. There was no doubt in his mind it was Japanese.

Finally 0500 rolled around and Gaston put his feet on the cold linoleum floor of the second-story room. He had not anticipated staying the night when he had left the day before and did not have a change of underwear so he pulled his boxer shorts and government issue T-shirt from the line he had hung them on after washing them in the bathroom sink the night before. They were still damp, but not as wet as they had been the day before. He decided Mable's house was a step up from Officer's Quarters. He had his own private bathroom on the second floor. After dressing, he made his way downstairs. Mable was already up and preparing breakfast on a wood stove in the kitchen. He walked in and immediately felt the warmth from the large stove.

Seeing Gaston enter, Mable motioned for him to sit on a bench at the large wooden table. "I'll have breakfast in a minute. Biscuits and gravy, scrambled eggs, back strap, sorghum and home churned butter for the extra biscuits. I've got buttermilk if you want."

"I eat all that, I'll gain a ton of weight," Gaston said. "You cook like this everyday?"

"The leftover biscuits will go to the restaurant. The meal comes with the room."

Over breakfast Gaston found out Mable's husband had been a fisherman. He was lost in a storm ten years earlier. They found his boat twenty miles up the coast crashed on the rocks.

"Never found him though," Mable said. "Lucky I stuck some away or I would have been a burden on my family. As it is, I do all right with the restaurant and letting the room once in a while."

Gaston said little. He was too busy eating as much as he could.

"You'll want to put some of that sorghum on your biscuit. It'll stick with you better."

"What's sorghum?" Gaston asked.

"Poor man's honey. Tastes a lot like molasses, but a little stronger."

Mable grabbed a biscuit, broke it in two and took a spoon of the dark syrup, and drizzled it on the biscuit. "Try it, you'll thank me later."

Gaston was a meat and potatoes kind of guy. He didn't care to try new things, but it seemed he had no choice. He took a bite, chewed it and swallowed. "Good," he said. "I think I'll take this with me. I've got a boat to catch."

The dock was a two-block walk from Mable's house. Gaston made the trip in less than five minutes. He was thankful the rain had stopped. A heavy fog had rolled in overnight and in the predawn light it was difficult to make out the details of the moored boats. He heard voices and walked toward them. "That you, Mitch?"

"Gaston, I wasn't sure you'd make it."

Gaston stopped at the bottom of the gangway. "Permission to come aboard?"

"Get your ass up here," Mitch said. "Dad's already got the engine warmed up."

Mitch introduced Gaston to his father. "Name's Oliver. My friends call me Ollie, my enemies much worse. You can call me Ollie."

Gaston laughed. He felt the rough calloused hands of Ollie as they shook. Ollie was a built like a tree stump, all five-foot-six of him. He looked like he had lived on the sea more years than he really had. "Spent my life in the woods, 'til a snag fell on me and nearly ended my time right there," Ollie said. "Bought a boat and been on the water nigh on 4 years now. Mitch joined me when he got out of school. Mitch cast off the bow rope!" Ollie gunned the engine and the *Guppy* crept away from the dock.

"You're okay with going out in this fog?" Gaston asked.

"Gotta make a living. I hope you're up for a long day. Mitch, get your friend a pair of gloves and some rain gear. No one comes aboard my boat that isn't willin' to work."

"No problem," Gaston said. "Are we going out where you spotted the sub?"

"That's where the crabs are," Ollie said. "I figure that sub's got no business with me. I ain't no threat to it."

Gaston wasn't so sure. If the Japs didn't want to be spotted they could put a cannon shell through the *Guppy* and they'd all be lost forever.

By the time they started tossing the crab traps, the fog had lifted. Gaston learned quickly and was keeping up with Mitch, dropping the large metal baskets as fast as he could. Before long a string of yellow floats trailed for over a mile behind them, each float marking the spot where a trap was resting on the bottom. "What do we do now?" Gaston asked.

"We wait a bit and then pull them in one by one with the crane."

Ollie idled the boat down and turned out to sea. The fog had lifted enough that he could see the shore. "Right there. That's where we saw her. You don't reckon she's still down there?"

"Hard to say," Gaston said, walking out on the deck. He watched as the ocean swells lifted the boat then rolled it in a nauseating rhythm. The diesel fumes seemed to hang over the deck. He had always been a little sensitive to the motion of the sea, but the diesel smell, a full stomach, and this particular rise and fall of the *Guppy* caused him to run for the rail. He lost his breakfast. *A fine sailor you are*, he said to himself. *Better take advantage of this land-based assignment while you can. You could be in the South Pacific on permanent sea duty.* He walked back into the cabin, embarrassed. "It's been a while since I've been on a small boat."

"Don't let it bother you," Mitch said. "When I first started helping my dad, I puked my guts out every day. Eventually I ran out of things to puke up."

"Thanks for that, Mitch. I feel much better."

"Mitch get your ass out there and see if that's another submarine." Ollie pointed to what looked like a periscope not fifty yards from them.

Gaston perked up and went out on the deck with Mitch.

"Damned if it don't look like something," Mitch said.

"Ask your dad to steer a little closer," Gaston said. He leaned against the railing trying to get a better look. "It looks like a periscope." He studied it intently. "It's no periscope. Ease up to it and let's see if we can snag it."

Ollie eased the boat alongside the tall black object. It was standing upright about four feet out of the water. The top of the tube had been cut at an angle. "You sure a submarine isn't attached to that?" Ollie asked.

"Positive," Gaston said. He had heard about such a thing, but had never seen one.

"Try snagging it with this," Mitch said, handing Gaston a grappling hook attached to a ten-foot-long pole.

Gaston managed to insert the hook into the top of the tube and pull the tube next to the Guppy. "I'll lift it up and you grab it," Gaston said to Mitch.

Gaston was able to lift the tube out of the water and Mitch grabbed it with both hands.

"Got it!" Mitch said.

"Hold on, I'll help you." Gaston removed the grappling hook and tossed the pole on the deck. He grabbed the tube and together they eased it out of the water.

"Pretty clever," Gaston said. "From a distance, to an untrained eye, you would swear it was a periscope." They laid the five-inch diameter bamboo post on the deck. It was weighted on one end so it would float upright. This was further proof that the Japanese were operating off the coast, but it also told Gaston information he could use against Japan. "Let's secure this so we can bring it in with us."

The next six hours were spent retrieving crab traps, and dumping the live crabs into a large tank filled with seawater recessed into the rear deck. By the time they stowed the last trap, the hold was filled with Dungeness crab. Ollie revved up the engine and the *Guppy* inched its way back to the docks.

Chapter 6

It was well after dark when Gaston pulled up to the guard shack at the Coast Guard Station. He showed the guard his I.D.

"What's that on your roof?" the guard asked, stepping up to the car and eyeing the bamboo post.

"Beachcombing," Gaston said. He drove straight to Headquarters Building, hoping the Commander would still be there. He had a little over two hours before he would make his first midnight call to the White House.

Unfortunately, the Commander wasn't there. The OD was Danny Pastor. When Gaston knocked, he lifted his head from the desk. "I didn't think you slept," Gaston said.

Danny wiped the sleep from his eyes. "It's been a quiet night," he said, as if that was a good reason for sleeping on the job.

"I'm going to use the radio. Is there a man on duty?"

"Petty Officer 3rd Class Wilbur Jones. Watch out for him."

"Why's that?"

"His girl jilted him. He's in a foul mood."

"Thanks, I'll keep that in mind." Gaston walked down the hall to the radio room. The radio shack was a small room with several pieces of modern equipment. It had recently been equipped with the latest radar equipment. From a tower on Cape Foulweather the radar scanned the sky for aircraft, as well as the ocean for ships. It was the first level of defense against an approaching enemy. Gaston peered into the dark room, lit only by the green glow of several oscilloscope screens. Radar was a new addition to the station, and still a novelty. The recruits were asking to be moved into classes where they could learn the new technology. In the classroom Gaston had learned the term radar was an acronym for Radio Detection And Ranging. He wondered if it would have the impact the manufacturers were promising. Could an invisible beam detect an aircraft farther out than a human with a pair of binoculars? All the radar stations were also equipped with personnel and binoculars just in case.

Gaston introduced himself to the radio man. He handed him the White House call sign. It was nearly 0300 hrs in Washington DC. *There must be a reason why FDR chose this time of the morning for communication*, he thought.

In fact there was a reason. 3:00 a.m. was a perfect time for the President. He was a light sleeper and rarely went to bed early. Many of his appointments went well into the night and sometimes the next morning. If he was going to communicate without the whole world listening in he needed to do it at a quiet hour. Even at that the messages were coded. Once the White House was contacted and FDR was on the other end, Gaston took the headset from Petty Officer Jones. "Take a break; I'll call you when I'm done."

"We have a reliable sighting of a Japanese submarine. The conning tower number is *I-26*. I recovered a fake periscope tube floating in the same vicinity as the sighting. They don't appear to be aggressive, but may be planting fake periscope tubes up and down the coast to try and panic the population. I doubt there will be an invasion. The coast is so lightly populated that nothing short of a full-scale assault would be effective. Without ships, which we can detect from miles away, it doesn't seem likely. There are many capes where the visibility is twenty or more miles along the coast and out to sea. Of course, that's on a clear day, of which there don't seem to be many. My take on the submarine is, it's nothing more than the Japs trying to scare the population. I'll keep you informed if I hear of any more activity."

"Good work, Gaston. Pass on the submarine identification to the FBI in Portland and the Coast Guard Commander where you are stationed. Do you have any recommendations?"

"Yes, sir. I think we should keep the sighting out of the newspapers. If the Japs are relying on us to spread panic by reporting this to the media, I recommend we don't fall into that trap."

"Thank you. I'll take that under consideration. By the way Hoover was in my office yesterday inquiring about you. I had no idea who you were. I want to keep it that way, understand?"

"Yes, sir."

Gaston's first communication with the President ended abruptly. He hoped if he got into trouble the President would have his back. In the meantime, he would pass along the information as ordered. Secretly, he hated giving the FBI Director anything after the way he had been treated. *Wouldn't giving him this information raise more questions about who I am working for?*

"All done, Petty Officer Jones," Gaston said, opening the door to the hallway. Jones was not in sight. He walked down the hall where he found Jones engaged in a joke telling session with Ensign Pastor.

Jones jumped off the desk as soon as he saw Gaston. "All finished, sir?"

"It's all yours. You can go back to saving our Nation again." Gaston smiled. "Mr. Pastor, would you tell the Commander when he gets in I have some information he'll want to hear."

"As you wish," Pastor offered.

"Tell the Commander I'll be in my quarters getting some shut-eye. He can wake me regardless of the hour."

"Got it. I'll let him know."

Gaston looked at his watch, 0107 hrs. It had been a long day.

The next morning, not hearing from the Commander, Gaston walked from Officer's Quarters to HQ where he learned the Commander had been called out for the day to a quickly scheduled meeting at Ft. Stephens.

Ft. Stephens was a good three hours north of Yaquina Bay Station, so there was no point in trying to get in touch with the Commander. Instead, Gaston decided to catch up on his letter writing. He had yet to hear from Cheryl and was concerned the events of their parting might have left her with the impression he didn't care about her feelings. Nothing could be further from the truth. In spite of the sudden notice he'd received to depart to the West Coast, he had made certain he saw her before he left. It was tragic and unfortunate he had to leave the day she found out her father had been killed. He supposed there would be a funeral of sorts, although he had read in the news that many of the service members lost in the attack would never be recovered. He hated the thought that Cheryl would have to endure such an event without his presence to comfort her.

December 17, 1941

My dearest Cheryl, I know this letter is coming to you while you are still grieving over your father's death. I also know you are probably upset with me for leaving for Oregon at such a difficult time in your life. I can't express how sorry I am. I truly wish I could be with you in this time of sorrow. Please tell your mother and your sister my heart is filled with grief for their loss.

I thought you might be wondering what I've been doing way out here. My goodness, this place is about as far from civilization as one can get. You can imagine how surprised I was to learn many of the houses around here don't have indoor plumbing. Outhouses are normal for most homes. I even came across a rural school that had only one room for eight grades. It was completely without plumbing. Can you imagine? While we lived in the big city with all the luxuries that we thought normal, there are many out here that think a toilet inside a house is not only unnecessary, but completely over the top as a need in life. Thankfully there are inside toilets in my quarters at the base. I'm afraid I wouldn't make a good pioneer.

I can't talk much of my assignment, only to say that the people out here are a good lot and are expecting their government to protect them from any foreign attacks. Somehow the people have it in their heads that the Japs will attack the United States and do it out here. I have to say there is a lot of talk of that. Although I haven't seen any Japanese, there is talk that there are several living in the area. I fear for their safety, as worked up as the locals are. I thought I might send for you once I got settled out here, but that was a foolish notion. My hours are long and completely unscheduled. It would be torture for you and disappointment for me to see you suffer under the poor amenities. Still you must know how much

*I miss you and am looking forward to the day we can be
together again.*
My love always,
Gaston
*P.S. Please don't try to mail me a Christmas present.
I'm not certain how well packages travel across the country.
Likewise, please understand my love will have to suffice until
we can have our holidays together again.*

He folded the letter, licked a three-cent stamp and stuck it on the upper right hand corner. He decided to take the letter to the post office in Newport, hoping it might speed up the delivery. While in town he stopped by a cafe on the Bay Front. The wind was blowing fiercely and the door to the cafe was nearly ripped from his hand as he entered.

He took a stool at the counter and ordered coffee. He noticed another man sitting three stools down. He was dressed in a brown suit with a yellow tie. He was smoking a large, drooping pipe and removed it periodically to take a sip of his coffee. He removed the pipe and held it while he addressed Gaston. "You hear about the lynching up river?"

"Lynching? Can't say that I did. I was down south yesterday. What happened?"

The man got up and offered his hand to Gaston. "I'm Mike Downs. I teach at Toledo Grade School."

"Gaston Carson, on special assignment," Gaston said, taking the man's hand.

"Oh, a newspaper man. How is it you're not in the service?"

"I am," Gaston said. Mike's comment grated on his nerves. "Just not in uniform."

"Then you'll have an interest in what I'm going to tell you." Michael Downs took a seat next to Gaston. "If you're not familiar with the area, my school is up the river a few miles."

"The only Toledo I've heard of is in Ohio," Gaston said. "Went through a little town down south yesterday called Florence, and it wasn't in Italy."

"Seriously," Mike said. "A man was lynched yesterday just because he was of Japanese descent."

"He was an American?"

"As American as you and I. His name was Terry Nakamura. The sheriff is keeping it quiet, but he had a wife and kid, for God's sake. Are we going to let the war turn us into barbarians?"

Gaston didn't know what to think. "Did you know him?"

"I taught his son. I met him a few times. He spoke perfect English. His father was a cook at the lumber mill kitchen. He was born here. This has been driving me crazy. You don't have any idea what I can do, do you?"

"I'm not sure what you mean?"

"Well if the sheriff is keeping it quiet, who do I go to?"

"First off, how do you know it's true? Maybe it's just a rumor."

"It's no rumor. I was there. I saw the whole thing."

Gaston was completely caught off guard. He was afraid something like this would happen. If it got out of hand, the West Coast could become a blood bath from vigilante groups attacking. "Can you give me a phone where you can be reached? I'll talk to a few people and see if there is anything I can do."

"Thank you," Mike said. "I hope you can help. I was so upset, I couldn't go to school today."

Gaston pulled out a tablet. "Better yet, I'll buy you a cup of coffee and you tell me everything you saw. I'll make sure the Commander of the Coast Guard Station gets it. Are you comfortable with that?"

"I'll buy you the coffee...and pie if you like. You can eat and I'll talk."

"Coffee will be fine. I'll write, you talk. Let's move to a table."

For the next hour Mike told his story. Gaston made certain he got all the details written, place, time, what led up to the incident, any others he could remember who were involved, the policeman who covered up the incident. It was a horrific story.

Gaston felt it was something he might be able to help with. He felt like he was here to make a difference, now he had to figure out if he could do that.

When he left the cafe, the wind was blowing at gale force and the rain was coming down in torrents. He got into his car and sat a moment shaking his head. *What had he walked into? Were people so scared they would murder their neighbors, just because they looked like the enemy? What about Germans? Were they going to attack everyone who had a German ancestor in their background?* He had to do something, to stop this craziness. As he sat, the windows fogged up. He wiped the windshield with his handkerchief. He sat for another minute before starting the engine. This assignment was going to be much harder than he imagined.

Back in Officer's Quarters he spotted Ensign Pastor in the hall. "You won't believe the story I just heard," Gaston said.

"I got time if you do."

"I thought you'd be catching up on your sleep."

"Sleep is overrated. Meet you in the dining room for coffee. I've got some news for you, too."

Alice had on her usual smiley face. She brought coffee and filled two porcelain cups to the brim. "Either of you want sugar or cream?"

Both waved her off, Gaston with the shake of his head and Pastor with a lewd comment.

"The war going too slow for you boys today?" Alice asked, leaving the room.

"You know where Toledo is?" Gaston asked in a quiet voice.

"I'd stay away from that town," Pastor said. "I got tangled up with a drop-dead red head a year back and almost lost my scalp to an Indian. You know they have a tribe still on the warpath?"

"Really?" Gaston looked into Pastor's eyes.

Pastor started laughing. "No, I'm pulling your leg. The redhead was real though. Seriously, don't mess with the Indians, if you run into one in a bar. They can be real mean when they're drunk."

"How about Japanese?" Gaston asked.

"In Toledo? Don't recall ever seeing any Japs there."

"One was hanged the other day," Gaston said.

"No shit!"

"I was having coffee on the Bay and this guy told me a story that was hard to believe."

"He told you they hung a Jap?"

"He told me they hung an American citizen who was of Japanese ancestry and the sheriff is covering it up."

"You can't cover up something like that," Pastor said.

"That's what I thought, but there's no mention in the paper. I checked."

"The paper doesn't come out 'til Friday."

"I stopped by to see if anyone had heard anything. They were all, 'what are you talking about?'" Gaston stirred his coffee to cool it down. "I got a full report for the Commander. I figured he'd want to know if there was a problem with the general population."

"It doesn't sound like something he would stick his nose into. He's got enough problems, rescuing fishermen and keeping people from the beaches."

"I suppose you're right. I'm going to run it by him, anyway."

"You want a smoke?" Pastor shoved a pack of Lucky Strikes toward Gaston.

"No thanks, I don't smoke."

"You don't smoke. Are you sure you're old enough to be away from your mother?"

Alice came back into the room and saved Gaston from another insult, or Pastor from a beating, she wasn't sure which. "I'm going home. Anything you need from me before I go?"

Pastor was about to say something.

Alice cut him short. "You keep your filthy tongue in your mouth." She looked at Gaston. "I have four brothers; I've heard and seen it all. Don't let this man corrupt you."

"No, ma'am," Gaston said. "I mean, yes, ma'am."

After Alice left the room, Pastor tapped the end of a cigarette on the table and lit it with a flip-top lighter. "I think she likes you. I'll bet she could give that candy-ass of yours a real ride."

"I've got a girl back home," Gaston said.

Pastor put his hand to his ear. "What was that? I thought I heard you say you have a girl back home."

"That's what I said."

Pastor leaned across the table. "What the hell does that have to do with anything?"

"You expect me to be unfaithful to my girl?" Gaston shook his head and smiled. "No way man, haven't you got any morals at all?"

Pastor threw up his hands. "There you go again. If I wasn't your friend, I'd think you were insulting me."

They heard the outside door slam shut and turned toward the noise. A drenched seaman was standing in the dining room doorway. A puddle of water was forming where he stood. "Mr. Carson, sir?"

Gaston stood. "I'm Carson."

"The Commander is on the telephone in headquarters. He sounds like he's a long ways away. He wants to speak to you, sir. Right now!"

"Thank you, I'll be right there."

"Oh, you don't need to go there. You can take it at the desk here. I rang and there wasn't an answer."

"Okay. I'll take it at the desk." He followed the seaman out of the room and picked up the telephone. "Carson, here." He spoke to the Commander a few minutes and hung up the phone. He went back into the dining room and turned on the radio. The radio was the size of a dresser and dominated the corner of the room. Several padded chairs were placed around it. Gaston played with the dial until a station came in clear.

"...Aleutian Islands. Fishermen reported seeing several Japanese supply ships and

submarines off the coast of Attu and Kiska islands. While the islands are sparsely populated they are US territory and the residents are considered Americans. This report makes it clear the war has entered a new dimension and could reach the beaches of the West Coast. Residents along the entire western coastal beaches are encouraged to speak up and report any unusual activity along the coastline."

Pastor put his cigarette out in an ashtray. "They'd be nuts to try and attack our coastline."

Finally, Gaston found something he and Danny Pastor agreed on. "Commander Goodman isn't going to be back for another day. He asked if I would get hold of the Civil Air Patrol and have them step up their plans to have daylight patrols along the coast."

"I'll go with you," Pastor volunteered. "Major and I have been known to throw back a few. He's a good man."

"I'll call ahead and warn him we're coming," Gaston offered.

Pastor let out a whoop. "No need to call. He's at the office. Give me your keys, I'll drive."

Gaston grabbed an umbrella from the stand near the door and opened it before stepping out into the storm. He ran for the car about twenty yards across a patch of grass that was rapidly turning into a small lake. He hadn't taken three steps into the yard before a gust of wind nearly ripped the umbrella from his hands. By the time he got control of it, it had turned inside out. He wrestled with it for a minute and dragged it behind him as Pastor played taps with the horn.

"I'm coming!" Gaston yelled, splashing across the lawn. He stuffed the broken umbrella into the back seat and slid in.

Pastor was laughing.

"How long do you think it'll take me to figure this place out?" Gaston asked. He laughed along with Pastor. "I'll bet you knew this was going to happen."

"Don't feel bad. Umbrellas are one of the most overrated accessories offered by the Coast Guard. Any seaman worth his salt knows the weather out here is either very wet with a lot of wind or very damp with no wind. Neither works well for umbrellas."

"You should teach a class for new arrivals."

"Why, you're learning just fine." He pushed his foot on the starter and the engine fired up. Both men removed their handkerchiefs and started wiping the fog from the windshield.

"Hell of a night for Goodman to send us on a trip."

"He sent me," Gaston reminded him. "You could be snug in the sack and having sweet dreams by now."

"And miss out on all the fun?"

"Fun, what are you talking about?"

Pastor shook his head and slowed the car as they were waved through the gate.

The office, Gaston discovered, was a bar named the *Blue Whale*. It was 1900 hrs. The place was nearly empty. Three men on barstools were trading stories. All three turned to look at Ensign Pastor and the young man in civilian dress with him. A tall man on the far end of the bar stood up and addressed Ensign Pastor. "Danny Boy, where ya been. We were just about to write you off tonight. Thought the Navy might have thrown ya in the brig."

"Grab your drink and join us at the table. My buddy has some info for you."

They squeezed into a booth, Danny and Gaston on one side and Major on the other. Danny introduced them. "My friend in the civvies pretends he's nobody, but we all know he's secret service or some other shit he doesn't like to talk about. Gaston, meet Major."

"Major," Gaston said, "are you in the service?"

Major laughed a deep belly laugh. "Hell, no. I was once. Flew with the First Air Squadron in the Big War. Now I fly for fun."

"I understand you head up CAP here in the area?"

"Got our own air force," Major said proudly. "Three biplanes and four of the newer single-wing jobs. All at your service around the clock, weather permitting, of course." Major raised his hand, "Sarah," his voice boomed across the room. "Whisky for my friends." He looked at Gaston. "You're old enough to drink, aren't you?"

Gaston smiled and shook his head. "I drink on occasion."

"Well, damn, this is an occasion. What's on your mind?"

Gaston related what the Commander had told him about the sighting in the Aleutian Islands. He finished with, "What would it take to have the planes in the air dusk to dawn from here to Tillamook?"

"It sounds like your Commander is a little behind the times. We had a regional CAP meeting last week. In fact, the day after the Japs attacked Pearl Harbor. We've got a plan laid out for the northern coastline, from the Canadian border to the Navy base in Eureka. What it will take is lots of aviation fuel and mechanics. All our mechanics have been volunteering for active duty and we can't keep the planes flying without anyone to service them." Major looked around, "Where the hell is Sarah? Sarah! What does it take to get a drink around here?"

Sarah Knots was a short chubby woman with graying hair done up in a bun. She came over with three shot glasses and a bottle of bourbon. "I'll take that as a rhetorical question," she said putting the glasses on the table. "I hope you're not planning on me putting this on your tab?"

Gaston looked at her.

"The old fart is married to me. I should have kicked him out the day I won this place. A word of advice, young man. Don't get tangled up with these two. It'll only bring you pain."

"What was that about?" Gaston asked, after she had left.

"Twenty years ago she was head of the women suffrage movement for the town. When Roosevelt repealed Prohibition, I opened a bar. She won it from me in a poker game."

Gaston looked at Danny. "He's pulling my leg, right?"

"True story," Major said.

"Come on, Major. Tell him the rest of the story."

"Jesus, Danny. You never did know when to keep your mouth shut."

"It's okay. I don't really need to know," Gaston said, sheepishly.

"It was a strip poker game," Danny said. "Major was buck naked and Sarah was down to her bloomers. She poured Major another glass of whisky and said, 'Major, you're at the end of your rope. You haven't got anything else to bet." Danny looked over at Major. "You want to tell him, or do I?"

"Oh hell," Major said. "I was holding three deuces. I thought that was a pretty good hand seeing she drew four cards. So I said, 'woman, just to watch you parade around here in your birthday suit, I'll bet the *Blue Whale*. I laid my cards on the table and reached for my britches and she said, 'Hold on there. You bet the *Blue Whale* and I intend to hold you to it.' She laid three queens on the table. Dumbest thing I ever did in my life."

"After that, I guess the drinks are on me," Gaston said. He stood up. "I'll let the Commander know you need mechanics and gas. Good to meet you Major."

Danny was still sitting. "We're not going so soon. We've only had one drink."

"Give me the keys. My car is going back to the base."

Danny put the keys on the table. "I'll find my own way home."

Chapter 7

Christmas Eve morning started with breakfast in the mess hall. As Gaston walked across the white gravel road separating the mess hall from Officer's Quarters, he was surprised to see a number of others apparently hadn't obtained leave for the holiday. The base was alive with seamen and civilians alike going to and fro. The weather had cleared and it was a rare sunny day for late December. A cold breeze was blowing offshore. He pulled up the collar on his double-breasted suit. He was still a novelty on the base and was asked for his identification as he made his way to the back of the mess where the officers dined. There was a seaman standing at the door. "Would you like to start with coffee, sir?" he asked, as Gaston approached.

"Yes. Is the Commander dining in today?"

"Yes, sir. He's already ordered."

"Thanks. I'll be joining him." He walked through the door and greeted the Commander. "Good morning, sir. I'm sorry I'm late." He wasn't really late, but with the Commander there and apparently starting without him, he thought it an appropriate comment.

"Good morning, Mr. Carson. You're not late, I'm early. I thought I'd wrap up things here and get home for an early dinner. Grab a seat."

Gaston sat down. They were the only ones in the room.

"I understand you met with the local CAP."

Gaston stifled a smile. "Major says he needs a good mechanic and aviation fuel just to go dawn to dusk, seven days a week."

"I figured as much. How soon can they start?"

"As soon as he has what he needs. He has pilots for seven planes total. Three biplanes and four single-wing. He also said they have a plan that covers the coast from Canada to Eureka, California. I looked at the plan yesterday and it seemed doable.

Major's men would cover from Tillamook south to Brookings. Navy planes out of Eureka would handle the California stretch."

"Before I forget, I got a call from the FBI Director in Portland. I take it you already met Frank Billings?"

"He's the nicer one. His boss is an ass, if you don't mind me saying it, sir."

"You mean Will Manfred. He's under a lot of pressure from Washington. Hoover is a taskmaster. He keeps his men on edge all the time."

"You know I'm carrying special orders. They want to know who is calling the shots. I can't tell them."

"Everyone's on edge these days. No one trusts anyone."

"You trust me don't you?"

"I've been told by the brass to watch over you. You're a young man with the freedom to do whatever it is you do. I'm going to take advantage of it where I can. If you think I'm stepping on anyone's toes I'll expect you to tell me. Until then I can use all the help I can get. Hence the CAP. They have some good aviators, but they are an undisciplined group. If you can help with that, I'm sure it's in the best interest of the Country. We have 300 miles of coastline, mostly unpopulated. Our enemies could land anywhere and we might not find out for days."

"How likely is it that we could have an invasion on our coastline?" Gaston asked.

"I wish I knew the answer to that. Tactically, I can't see where it would be any more than a propaganda advantage to Japan. They come from a different background. Nearly every citizen out here has a gun for protection."

"If they invaded the West Coast, we would have to divert our forces from the Pacific. That would be a real win for them," Gaston said.

"I'm glad you see the importance in what we are charged with. It was only a few weeks ago when our attention was on keeping fishermen from getting into trouble in foul weather. Now we're using them as our eyes on the sea, so to speak. I saw the dummy periscope you brought in. Quite a lucky find. I'm interested in your thoughts."

Gaston sat back and let the mess attendant fill his coffee cup. He hadn't eaten anything. He took a fork of cold scrambled eggs and washed it down with hot coffee. "I think the Japs are trying to panic the public. If we have fishermen reporting they are spotting submarines off the coast, the citizens will demand we increase our forces for protection. We need everyone we can spare fighting the Japs in the Pacific."

Commander Goodman smiled. "I'm beginning to realize why you are out here. You understand what's going on better than most." He took a sip of coffee. "Do you have any plans for Christmas?"

"Hardly, sir. My family is, well, the Navy, or it was until I left the Academy. My girl is in Maryland and my parents are both dead."

"I want you to join my family for Christmas Eve dinner and bring a change of clothes. You'll be spending the night and celebrating Christmas with Margaret, me, and the kids."

"Sir, I don't want to impose on your family time."

"It's not an order, but I won't take no for an answer." Goodman smiled. He removed a notepad and wrote the address for him. "Be there by 1600 hrs. Any later and you'll never find it in the dark."

The Commander slid back from the table and removed the white linen napkin from his lap. "If it makes you feel any better, after dinner we can discuss how we're going to win the war, over a hot buttered rum of, course, and a piece of Margaret's famous bourbon fruitcake."

"Sir, you drive a hard bargain. I look forward to meeting the family."

Over Christmas, Gaston had planned on attending church and catching up on some reading during the quiet hours at the base. He had purchased *Grapes of Wrath* by John Steinbeck. He didn't know much about the book, but he'd heard it was going to be made into a movie. He liked the gritty style of Steinbeck's writing and his no-holds-barred approach to bringing attention to the plight of the less fortunate in society. There was a part of Gaston that wondered what his plight would have been, had fate not dealt him a better hand. People were still struggling to get out of The Depression, although they seemed to be doing better than most here on the West Coast. For the most part the general population had little, but they had enough, didn't want for much, and were thankful. But there was another side to the people that was beginning to show. Fear can do strange things to normally peaceful, law-abiding citizens. Fear could turn them into monsters. He had forgotten to mention the hanging of the man in Toledo. "Sir, one more thing before you go."

The Commander had started to get up, but sat back down.

"A man was murdered in Toledo the other day. I know it's not in your jurisdiction, but I heard he was a Japanese American. I thought you would want to know."

"How was he killed?"

"He was hanged. I don't know for certain, but I think the sheriff is trying to keep it quiet. The paper didn't have any information."

"How did you find out about it?"

"A teacher at the grade school was an eyewitness. He was trying to find someone to tell about it. I guess I had an honest face."

The Commander put his hand to his face and massaged it in thought. "I'll make some inquiries. You didn't happen to get the name of the victim."

"Yes, sir, I did." Gaston pulled a piece of paper from his inside pocket. "I wrote down the witness's story." He checked his notes. "Terry Nakamura."

"May I have your notes?" Goodman asked.

"I took them for you, sir."

The Commander stood. Gaston started to get up.

"As you were, Mr. Carson," the Commander smiled. "I'm afraid I ruined your breakfast. I hope I can make it up with a good dinner."

"No bother, sir."

"Oh, Mr. Carson, you might want to bring a suit. We'll be attending midnight mass at St. Anthony's."

"Sir," Gaston spoke, but thought better of it. As a guest, he would not be expected to bring gifts, would he? "Never mind. I'll see you in a few hours."

Gaston rushed around his room putting a change of clothes in his duffle bag. He dressed in his dark blue double-breasted suit, white shirt, green and red tie, and black felt fedora. His shoes were government-issue black leather with a mirror-like spit shine. It seemed like he had a thousand things to do. The question haunted him. Should he bring presents for Mrs. Goodman and the children? He pondered this a minute. No, they certainly wouldn't expect that from him. What the heck, he had enough time to do a little shopping. He would surprise them.

He hadn't counted on the stores being closed early on Christmas Eve. The clothing store would be closing at 3:00 p.m., the sign on the door read. He checked his watch. Less than an hour to shop. Fortunately, he had seen a picture of the Commander's family. In the picture his wife, Margaret, was wearing a stylish coat with a fox fur collar. The Commander was in his dress uniform, the kids in more casual attire. The boy appeared to be in his mid-teens. He wore a letterman's sweater with a large "T". The girl was wearing a cardigan sweater over a blouse with a small, curved collar. Her skirt extended below her knees, was plaid with long pleats. On her feet were bobby socks and penny loafers. Gaston remembered these things because he thought it odd that the Commander had children this old. He remembered thinking he must have gotten an early start in life.

"I need a present for a woman, a teenage girl, and a teenage boy," Gaston said to the elderly woman at the cash register.

"I'll need to know more than that to help you, young man," the woman said.

"But that's all I know," Gaston said.

After a few questions, the woman picked out some gifts and wrapped them.

"Thank you, so much," Gaston said. "I'm not very good at this."

"How come a young man like you isn't in the service?" the woman asked.

"Actually," Gaston said, and then he whispered, "I'm working undercover."

"Oh, my," the woman said. "Cloak and dagger stuff. You take care of yourself."

"I'll be sure and do that," Gaston said, picking up the large shopping bag of gifts. He had one more stop before heading out to the Commander's house.

Chapter 8

Gaston pulled in to the circular driveway of Commander Goodman's house. It was a two-story brick structure in a park-like setting, with a large, inviting, covered porch. Beyond the house, Gaston could see the mighty Pacific Ocean, bluer today than he had seen it since his arrival. There were a few other cars parked on the lawn, next to the drive, so Gaston pulled the loaner car alongside a sleek black Lincoln Cabriolet convertible. *This should be interesting*, he thought. *I thought I was a dinner guest and he's having a party.* He grabbed the presents and climbed the stairs. The door was ajar, so he nudged it open with his foot. "Hello!"

A young woman, the girl he had seen in the picture came running. "You must be... aren't you supposed to be in uniform?"

"Gaston Carson. And you are Commander Goodman's daughter. I recognize you from the picture in his office."

"Sharon." She held out her hand and he shook it.

"Here, these should go under the tree."

Sharon took the bag and looked him up and down approvingly. "Aunt Alice will sure be surprised."

"Alice?"

"My aunt, Alice Fitzpatrick. She's single, you know."

"Alice Fitzpatrick is your aunt?"

"On my mom's side. Boy, will she be surprised."

"I wish you'd quit saying that."

"They say on Christmas, anything can happen."

"Maybe I should just go find the others," Gaston said.

Sharon set the bag on the floor. "Oh, my gosh. Hold on, or Mom will kill me. Mr. Carson, may I take your overcoat?"

Gaston removed his overcoat and handed it to her. She opened the entry closet and put it on a hanger. She picked up the shopping bag. "Give me your arm; I'll escort you to the living room."

Gaston was impressed with the house. It had rich, hand-carved wooden pillars, high ceilings with ornate molding, and textured wallpaper. The floors were white marble. In the living room there were several people he hadn't seen before. He saw there were no servicemen other than the Commander, and he out of uniform. As it turned out he fit right in. He let out a sigh. Social events were difficult for him, even though he had been raised by a wealthy family in New York. Ever since his rescue from the streets, he had never been comfortable in formal social settings. He locked eyes with Commander Goodman, who excused himself from the guests and walked over to him. Sharon was still clinging to his arm.

"I see you've met my daughter," the Commander said. "Sharon, honey, would you go find your mother and let her know Mr. Carson has arrived. And tell your brother to come out of his room. He can listen to his records another time."

"He brought presents," Sharon said. "I'll put them under the tree."

"There was no need for you to bring presents," Goodman said. "That was very thoughtful."

Gaston was introduced to the other guests. He thought it strange they were all non-military. There was a doctor who practiced family medicine, the President of Coast Bank and Trust, the editor of the *Newport Times*, a local newspaper, and, of course, Alice, who he knew from the base. Billy Goodman, the boy in the picture, looked older, but was wearing the same letterman's sweater he'd been wearing in the picture.

Margaret took Gaston's arm. "Gaston, I believe you know my sister Alice."

Gaston couldn't help the burning that rose to his cheeks. He was certain everyone in the room could see it. He cleared his throat, but the words caught, anyway. "You're Commander Goodman's sister-in-law?"

"If you know what's good for you, you won't go advertising it. I'm doing my bit for the war effort, like everybody else. I don't want anyone to think I'm getting favors."

"I never..." He turned to Margaret. "Mrs. Goodman. Thank you for inviting me to spend Christmas with your family. I hope I'm not intruding."

"We're happy to have you, Gaston. I need to check on dinner. Alice, will you keep Gaston company, and get him a drink? No one should be without a hot toddy this time of year."

As soon as Margaret was out of the room, Alice asked, "What are you doing here?"

Gaston shrugged, "I guess the Commander needed an orphan to adopt for the holidays. I didn't know I was coming until this morning, and I certainly didn't know you'd be here."

"Well, you're not with me. Is that clear?"

Gaston looked at her sideways. "It never entered my mind; was it on yours?"

"Most certainly not!"

"Good. I'm glad we got that put to bed, I mean, cleared up." He felt his cheeks turning red.

"Mr. Carson," Commander Goodman called above the din of the room.

"Thank, God," Alice said. "I was hoping I wouldn't have to entertain you all evening."

"Did I do something?" Gaston asked her.

"Thurston wants to see you. I'll get you a drink." She walked off.

I wonder who put the bee in her bonnet, Gaston thought, as he made his way to the Commander.

Alice went into the kitchen to find Margaret. She found her peeking in the oven, checking on the turkey. "Margaret, did you tell Thurston to invite Mr. Carson?"

"Now don't be getting all upset. I thought you should be seeing someone. It's been two years. I merely suggested that Thurston invite a nice young man to even out the dinner guests."

Had it really been two years? Alice closed her eyes. She could still see the infectious smile on Donald's face. His eyes were blue and intense, filled with intelligence. He removed his cap and kissed her on the lips. "Don't take any wooden nickels," he said.

Those were his last words. She was certain they were going to spend the rest of their lives together. She told him he drove too fast. *Why did he have to be such a rebel?*

"Alice?" Margaret went over and hugged her. "You still love him, don't you?"

"Oh, Margaret," her eyes filled with tears. "I wish I didn't. I wish I could move on."

"It's all right, dear. You be civil to Gaston. He looks like a perfectly decent young man."

"Right over here," Goodman said to Gaston. "I think I missed introducing you to Allen Rich. He's the head of the local Civil Defense. I was telling him about the incident you described to me earlier today."

"Nice to meet you, Allen," Gaston said, feeling the grip of the man's large hand. You could always tell a working man by his hands. Allen had a firm grip and rough hands.

"Allen runs the lumber mill in Toledo," Goodman said. "Gaston, tell him the story you heard. I think it would be better coming from you."

"Not much to tell," Gaston said. "A school teacher said he saw the whole thing. He was really shook up."

A man in a tweed jacket interrupted them. "I recognize you from the office the other day. You were inquiring about a Japanese man who you said was murdered." The man was balding. Thick horn-rimmed glasses covered dark eyes.

"*Newport Times*," Gaston said. "I saw you in the office, but I spoke with one of your assistants."

"The name's Jim Fairbanks, you know like the town in Alaska. I found out something after you left."

"Really, what?" Gaston asked.

The four, Goodman, Carson, Fairbanks and Rich formed a tight circle. "Terry Nakamura, the man you say was hung, was reported missing by his wife last night."

"I heard talk that he liked to pluck mussels off the rocks by the lighthouse at low tide," Allen Rich said. "Maybe he got caught by a freak wave."

"You knew him." Fairbanks said.

"Hard not to know most everybody in Toledo," Rich said.

"Plucking mussels off the rocks doesn't go with the story I heard," Fairbanks said.

"I thought you newsfolks were supposed to deal with facts." Rich said.

"What's that supposed to mean?" Fairbanks was clearly getting defensive.

"It means, the man was reported missing, not hanged like you first said."

"I didn't say he was hanged. I said, I got a report that he was hanged and the sheriff didn't follow up on it."

"Sam didn't follow up on it because there was no body. No body, no story."

Gaston listened to the banter between Rich and Fairbanks. Clearly, there was bad blood between them. He assumed Sam was the name of the sheriff. *Rich is on a first name basis with the sheriff. Interesting,* he thought, *but it's a small community.* He dismissed his conspiracy theories for the moment.

"Excuse us a minute," Goodman said, pulling Gaston aside. Gaston followed him to the kitchen. There was a woman in an apron milling around. "Hired help," Goodman said, "don't worry about her. Did that conversation sound strange to you?"

"If I didn't know better, I'd say Rich knows something he's not telling. Good thing the tide's coming in."

"Why do you say that?"

"Nakamura's body could have been dumped off the rocks by the lighthouse."

Goodman thought it over for a moment. "I'm going to send a search party. If Nakamura washes up on the beach, I just might have a hand in the investigation."

"You want me to join them?" Gaston asked.

"The search party? No, Ensign Pastor is OD this week. He can handle it."

When they came back to the room, Allen Rich was putting an arm in his overcoat. "Sorry Thurston, I've got to get home to the family. Thanks for the drinks."

Goodman shook Rich's hand. "Merry Christmas, Allen."

"Yeah, that too," Rich said, going out the door.

The cocktail party wound down with the departing guests wishing the Goodman's Merry Christmas. Of the guests, only Gaston and Alice were left. Gaston figured Alice didn't count since she was family. He was feeling a little like a fifth wheel.

In the dining room, Sharon was placing ornate calligraphy name cards where each should sit. There were only the six of them left. Gaston was beginning to feel like this was a set-up for a blind date. He wondered if Alice felt the same. She was avoiding him like the plague. Maybe she knew about his girl back home. The Commander should have known. *No, it was coincidence, not a blind date.* He cornered her in the hallway. "Alice."

"What!" Alice whispered.

"Why are you whispering?" Gaston asked, whispering.

"Because you're whispering."

"Oh, I figured it out." Gaston's voice was normal.

"Figured what out?"

"Why we are here."

"I know why I'm here," Alice said. "I'm just trying to figure out how you sweet talked Thurston into inviting you to Christmas dinner."

"That's what I figured out. It was spur of the moment. He didn't give it a second thought. Don't you see, he just wanted me to have a nice family Christmas."

Sharon called from the end of the hall, "we're ready to sit down when you two lovebirds are ready."

"I'm going to kill you," Alice said, running toward Sharon.

"You girls settle down and take your seats. Alice, you're acting like a teenager. Quit encouraging her. She's impossible to control as it is."

Chapter 9

They were seated at the dinner table, Thurston Goodman at one end, Margaret at the other, Alice and Gaston on one side, Billy and Sharon on the other. Thurston led them in grace.

"Did you hear the Americans surrendered to the Japs on Wake Island?" Billy said. "If I was there, I'd give those bastards something to think about."

"Billy, you don't use that kind of language. Am I going to have to wash your mouth out with soap again?" Margaret glared at her husband.

"You're mother's right," Thurston said. "You're not too old to have your mouth washed out."

"I'm sorry," Billy said, "I just can't stand to be here while a lot of kids my age are already fighting. Dad, let me quit school and join the Navy."

"There are plenty of volunteers right now. The war is just beginning. You'll get your chance." The Commander glanced over at Gaston, to see his reaction. "Respect our guests. We can have this conversation another time. Let's get into the Christmas spirit." He raised his wine glass. "A toast to Alice and Gaston, two people who have set aside their dreams to help the Home Front."

Sharon saw her aunt's eyes water up. "Auntie Alice, I'm glad you moved back. I missed you."

"How about those Chicago Bears," Thurston said, in an obvious effort to change the subject."

"NFL champions. No easy feat," Gaston said.

"That drop kick for the extra point by McLean was the best play of the season," Billy said.

The three females started to laugh.

"What?" Thurston asked.

"I swear, you boys start talking about football and you'll forget to eat."

"Billy hand the mashed potatoes to your sister and let's eat before the turkey is cold," Thurston said.

"Guests should be served first," Sharon said.

"I think our guests will forgive us if we just pass the food around. This isn't a formal dinner," Margaret said. "You don't mind do you, Gaston?"

"No problem. I missed lunch and the sooner the food gets here the better."

"Thurston tells me you're on special assignment," Margaret said. "If I'm not prying too much, can you tell us how you came about such an assignment?"

Thurston glanced at his wife and shook his head. "Mr. Carson is under special orders. His mission is top secret. Even I'm not privy to all the details."

"It's okay, Margaret, I'm getting used to being asked that question. I'll tell you what I tell everyone else. There is a lot of concern in Washington over reports coming in from the West Coast. They thought a civilian would be better received by the public in the verification of the reports."

"But you were a midshipman," Billy said. "You could have been an officer."

"That would have been my first choice," Gaston said. "I'm not working for the Navy in this assignment; therefore, I had to forgo my commission."

"Mom's question was how did you get chosen. You must have done something special?" Billy asked.

"This is really a swell meal," Gaston said. "I don't think I've ever had better turkey dressing than this. Is it a special recipe?"

"That's so kind of you to notice, Gaston. It's my mother's recipe. When my family first came to the United States from Ireland, my mother took a job as a cook in the kitchen of the Biltmore Hotel in New York City. She started bringing home the recipes and trying them on the family. She made her own changes to them through the years. I'm afraid I'm not that clever, so I asked for her receipt file when she retired. I haven't found any need to change them."

"Your mother would roll over in her grave if you did," Thurston said. "I was terrified the first time I ate at her parent's house. We had meatloaf, and this is the honest truth, I looked around the table and asked if she had any ketchup." He started to laugh. "Honestly, you would have thought I'd set her hair on fire. She went into the kitchen and brought out a bottle of ketchup and set it down, rather hard in front of me. 'Here is your ketchup. Please take a bite of the meatloaf before you destroy it,' she said. I didn't dare put ketchup on it after that."

"Gaston?" Margaret asked, "Did your family ever have special Christmas traditions?"

"Well, one year when I was about 5, I remember one of the tenants in our boardinghouse brought over a large apple pie. My mother sliced it into thin slices so we would have enough for a piece at every meal over Christmas. I had apple pie for breakfast, lunch, and dinner. It was the best Christmas I ever had, up until this one."

"You had me going there," Alice said looking at him. She saw the water in his eyes. "My God, were you telling the truth?"

"We were pretty poor, when I was a child," Gaston said. "I was saved by a miracle."

Everyone had stopped eating. The room was silent. All eyes were on Gaston.

Margaret broke the silence. "I'm so sorry, Gaston. I thought we were poor, but you never had a traditional Christmas?"

"This will be my first," Gaston said. "I really appreciate the opportunity to spend it with you." He fidgeted in his chair, not really wanting to share too much of his past with strangers. "I don't mean I didn't celebrate Christmas as a child. There were a group of kids who spent the holidays at the school. We had a tree and presents, but not a family gathering, at least nothing like this. When I was older I used to travel," he pondered for a moment. I would reach a strange town and look up people with my last name in the phone book. Sometimes I would be invited over, but not knowing my father or anything about him, I don't know what I was looking for. Sorry, I got a little carried away."

The Commander cleared his throat. "Let's save dessert until after church," he said. "Everyone get enough to eat?"

"I'm stuffed," Gaston said. "Thank you, again."

"Then it's settled, let's gather around the tree for the present shaking." Thurston slid his chair back.

A large, fully decorated Douglas fir Christmas tree dominated the room. Around the tree were stacks of presents of every shape and size. Thurston put his hand on Gaston's shoulder. "This is my favorite part of the evening. Everyone gets to pick one of their presents, shake it, and try and guess what's in it. We don't open them until Christmas morning."

Sharon put on a record of Christmas carols. "Silent Night" softly filled the room.

Gaston sat back in an overstuffed chair. The tree nearly touched the ceiling. It was covered with brightly colored balls and electric lights, something he had only seen in the big department stores, back east. On the top of the tree was an angel with white feather wings. There were more presents than he had ever seen around one tree. He watched, fascinated by the scene, as Billy and Sharon each grabbed a present and started to shake it.

Sharon was very methodical in her approach to guessing the contents of her package. She weighed it in her hands, tilted it sideways, rattled it close to her ear. "It's clothes," she finally announced. "From the shape of the box and the weight, I'm guessing it's that skirt I've been admiring in the apparel shop in Depot Bay." She looked at her mother. "Am I right?"

"Now, you know the rules. You don't get to find out until tomorrow morning."

Billy looked at his box. "I don't even need to open it. It's obvious it's a basketball." He smugly looked at his father, and gave him a knowing smile.

Margret got up from her chair and picked out a small package and handed it to Gaston. "Your turn, Gaston."

She caught him by surprise. "I've never done this before, but I'll give it a try." He held the small package to his ear. "It's not ticking, so I'll rule out a time bomb."

"Gaston!" Alice exclaimed.

"Just kidding. I saw your name on the package and just thought..." He shook it back and forth. "It sounds like there might be liquid. I got it, a bottle of pancake syrup."

"You are hopeless," Alice said.

"You're up next, Alice," Margaret said. "Your turn to get even. This is from Gaston."

Gaston looked at Margaret and started to speak. She immediately put her finger over her lips and Gaston understood. She had purchased the present for Alice and put Gaston's name on it.

Alice took the package and held it in front of her. It was a thin box, very light. "It feels like a pair of nylons." She eyed Gaston. "You wouldn't buy me nylons. I wouldn't mind it if you did. They are almost impossible to get. No, more likely it's a pair of socks. I'm guessing a pair of socks."

"Dad, your turn," Sharon said, handing him a small package.

He took it and studied it. "I'll bet it's a pipe. Maybe one of those corncob things like MacArthur smokes. I can't imagine anything else in a box this shape."

"Okay, now for the grand finale," Billy said. "Mother this is from me." He handed her a large box.

Gaston could tell from the grin on Billy's face that he had done something to trick his mother.

"It's kind of heavy," Margaret said. She shook it. "It sounds like a rattle snake. Billy if there's a snake in here, you're going to be grounded for the rest of your life." She shook it again. "Okay, I give up. I can't think of anything that would make that sound. I'll just have to wait until tomorrow."

"It's getting late and we have to get to Midnight Mass," Thurston said, checking his watch. "Everyone do what you have to do and I'll bring the car around front."

Thurston brought around the family car, a Chrysler New Yorker with two-tone black and maroon paint. Thurston got out and opened the back door. "Margaret, you and the girls in back, Billy, you in front by me, Gaston can have the door."

The six squeezed into the large car. Three in the front, three in the back.

"Is this new?" Gaston asked. "I haven't seen one before."

"I bought it last year. I only drive it on special occasions. Rarely, Margaret uses it for shopping and whatever she does when I'm out keeping the Country safe." He smiled. "I had to tell her it was hers; otherwise we'd be cramming into the Ford. She thought it was extravagant to have two vehicles, but it only makes sense with her taking care of the kids' school activities and my hours at the base."

Gaston wasn't sure he knew anyone with two cars, unless it was the Roosevelts. They probably had a car for every occasion. He felt the plush upholstery. It was a fine car. "This is a swell car, Commander. I doubt they'll be making any more of these during the war."

"What did you think of the service?" Margaret asked, as they walked out of the crowded church.

"I liked the songs," Gaston said. "To be quite honest, I wasn't following the service very well. My mind has been on other things."

Alice came up from behind and locked her arm in Gaston's. "I was going to tell you, you clean up pretty well," Alice said. "I may have pegged you all wrong."

Back at the Goodman house Margaret served fruitcake and coffee in the room with the Christmas tree. "This is a wonderful Christmas," she announced. "Before we turn in for the night I want to get a picture of all of us around the tree. Thurston will you get the camera set up? Be sure to get that contraption that lets us take a family portrait."

"She means the remote shutter trip, the latest gadget Kodak has to offer," he said to Gaston.

They gathered around the tree. He jabbed Alice in the ribs and she let out a scream, just before the light flashed and the shutter snapped. "Gaston, stop that!" She pretended to be upset. "Thurston, we need to take another one. I'm sure I'll look like a freak in that one."

The last thing Gaston thought before he fell asleep that night was how wonderful it would be to be part of a family.

Chapter 10

It was 0647 hrs. Christmas morning when Ensign Pastor got the report from the beach detail. He immediately phoned Commander Goodman, who had been asleep less than four hours.

Commander Goodman took the call in his bedroom. "Who is it, dear?" Margaret asked from the other side of the bed.

Thurston hung up. "Go back to sleep, Gaston and I will be gone for awhile. Wait to open the presents until we get back, okay?" He slipped on a robe and went down the hall to Gaston's room. He knocked and opened the door. "Sorry to disturb you, Mr. Carson, but they found a body. I think we should be there when the sheriff shows up."

Gaston sat up in bed. "Right, sir. I'll get dressed."

The Yaquina Bay Light as it was known was built in 1871, soon after the city of Newport, Oregon was founded. The lighthouse was one of only a few lighthouses that had the crew's living quarters built into the structure. It had been decommissioned when another lighthouse had been built at Yaquina Head, three miles north. The decommissioned lighthouse was located on the north side of Yaquina Bay. For awhile, before the present Coast Guard Station was built, the lighthouse served as the living quarters of the Coast Guard, at which time an eight-story observation tower had been built. In 1934, the lighthouse, including the observation tower, was sold to the Oregon State Highway Division and was turned into a park. On Christmas Day 1941, hanging by a rope from the eight-story tower was a man identified as Terry Nakamura, a citizen of Toledo, a mill town ten miles up the river from the lighthouse. When Gaston and Commander Goodman arrived his crew was waiting for the sheriff to arrive, before removing the body.

Seeing the hanging body from a distance, Gaston choked back tears. "He can't have been hanging there two days," Gaston said. He followed Goodman to the base of the tower. "Sir, this doesn't make sense. From our conversation with Mr. Rich, I expected we'd find the body in the water or at least on the rocks."

"Unfortunately this puts it out of my jurisdiction," Goodman said. "The State of Oregon owns this property."

Sheriff Johnson was a man in his late forties. He had red hair and freckled red cheeks. He arrived at the scene driving a dark-green Ford Model A pick-up with *sheriff* written in white letters on the door. He wore a plaid wool shirt, tan pants, and brown ankle-high boots. "I'll take it from here," he said. "This is not the Coast Guard's concern."

"Commander Goodman. We've met before," Goodman said to the sheriff.

"Right," the sheriff said. "One of your men raped that high school girl last year. I understand you let him off." The sheriff's tone made it clear he had no use for the Commander.

"There was no proof. No criminal charges were brought. My investigation showed the girl's father put her up to it. They later ran off and got married."

"Like I said, I got this from here. You can call off your men."

"Mr. Pastor," Goodman called out. "Have your men return to base. I'll expect a full report on my desk Friday morning."

"Yes, sir." Pastor winked at Gaston as he walked past.

Gaston turned. "Excuse me, sir. I need a word with Mr. Pastor."

"Make it short. I'll meet you at the car."

Gaston caught up with Pastor. "What was that about?"

"Looks like you stumbled into a full-fledged murder. There's no way that body hanging there is a coincidence. You got the name right and the death-by-hanging right. My guess is you got the location right, too. Seems the only question remaining is how the body ended up here?"

"I've got a lot more questions than that," Gaston said. "I think there is an element in the area that's hostile to the Japanese around here."

"No shit. Good luck on solving this one."

"You and Mr. Pastor seemed to be going at it," Goodman said to Gaston.

"It's not that. I told him about the hanging when I got back to our quarters and the facts don't line up with the location of the body. He was just pointing that out in his own colorful way."

"It's pretty obvious someone moved the body here."

"And Allen Rich knew about the location," Gaston added.

"The question is, did he know before or after he was talking to us?"

"He's wrapped up in this, someway. I'm betting the body was on his property and when he found out we knew about the hanging, he had it moved."

"I think you're right. One thing is certain..."

"What's that, sir?"

"Terry Nakamura is no longer missing."

They arrived back at the Goodman house a little before 1000 hrs. "I've got breakfast on the table," Margaret said, as soon as they came through the door. "Wash up and join us."

"You didn't open the presents yet?" Thurston asked.

"Of course not. We wouldn't open them without you."

After breakfast they took their coffee into the living room and gathered around the tree again. "Let's start with Mother," Sharon said. "She couldn't figure hers out." She handed the present to her mother. All leaned forward as she tore the wrapping from the box. She slowly lifted the lid, reached in and pulled out a jar. "Billy, you gave Mother a jar of popcorn! You're such a fathead."

"Mom, that was just to throw you off. Look inside." Billy got up from his chair. "Here, give it to me, I'll take the lid off." He unscrewed the lid and reached inside the gallon wide-mouth jar.

"Here." He handed her a small box. "Precious things come in small packages."

Margaret opened the box and removed a large costume jewelry brooch. It was a gaudy looking peacock with tiny colored jewels placed around its fanned tail. "Thank you Billy. I'll wear it on my winter coat." She pulled him down and kissed him on the cheek.

Each opened their present. Billy got a baseball glove, not the basketball he was expecting. Sharon was spot on. The box contained a pleated skirt.

Alice didn't get nylons or a pair of socks. The box contained a silk scarf. "I hope it's not from Japan," she quipped.

Thurston didn't get the corncob pipe he'd imagined; instead it was an intricate Inuit scrimshaw carving, depicting hunters of polar bears and seals in the Arctic. "I smoke too much, anyway," he said.

Gaston examined the package one last time before carefully removing the wrapper. He wanted to cherish this moment. It was truly the best Christmas he'd ever had. The wrapper fell to the floor and revealed a bottle of Old Spice aftershave lotion. "Thank you, Alice, I'll be sure to wear it."

"Put some on now, I want to see how it fits you," Alice said.

Billy looked at Sharon and raised his eyebrows.

Gaston pulled out the small stopper and sprinkled a few drops on his hand. He rubbed his hands together and patted his face. It was then he realized he hadn't shaved. "I think it's supposed to be used after I shave. I'd forgotten. I must look a mess."

Alice came over and leaned down and put her face next to his. "It fits you well, even when you have a five-o'clock shadow."

"Anyone else want a sniff," Gaston said.

Finally after an hour of opening presents, they came to the few Gaston had brought with him. There was an imported Australian wool scarf for Margaret, a smoking jacket for Thurston, a silver charm bracelet for Sharon and Billy got his basketball.

As Gaston was getting ready to leave, Margaret gave him a hug. "The gifts were very thoughtful. You went way too far."

Gaston was at a loss for words.

"You're invited back anytime," Margaret said. "We enjoyed having you."

Gaston walked down the stairs of the house and out to his car. He had a lump in his throat. The Country might be entering a tragic war, but it hadn't spoiled the Christmas in the Goodman home. Suddenly, sadness came over him. There was a Japanese family in Toledo who must have had the worst Christmas of their life. He resolved that he wouldn't let the persons responsible for killing Terry Nakamura get away with it.

Chapter 11

Gaston heard a knock on the door to his room. "Be right there." He opened the door to Ensign Pastor's grinning face. He was holding a letter.

"Looks like your Christmas present came late." He handed the letter to Gaston.

"Thanks, I've been expecting this for the past week." He took the letter.

"Hey, if you don't have any plans for New Year's Eve, a bunch of us are going down to the *Blue Whale*. You're invited."

"Thanks, I'll keep that in mind." Gaston closed the door, turned on the desk lamp, sat down, and ripped open the letter. *It's pretty thin*, he thought. *Cheryl should have a lot to say about things that are going on back home.* He pulled the single sheet of paper from the envelop.

> *December 21, 1941*
> *Dear Gaston,*
> *I've given myself an early Christmas present. I've decided I need to do something to fight for our Country. Okay, I might want revenge for the Japs killing my dad, but they won't let me fight on the front lines. The best I could do was join the Army Nurse Corps. It looks like I'll be making it to sea before you. I've been assigned to a hospital ship in the Mediterranean. I'm so excited. Of course, Mom was furious when she found out, but I'm almost 20 and can make these decisions on my own now.*
> *Gaston, I know this may upset you, but there is no reason I shouldn't be able to serve my Country, just like you.*
> *I also know there is no way that we can carry on a relationship by mail. I was foolish to*

think I could do that. I don't consider this breaking up, just going in different directions. The war has changed everybody, even me. I don't want you to expect any more letters as I'll be terribly busy getting ready for battle, ha ha. I wish they would issue me a gun!

Sincerely, Cheryl

PS: Thanks for the pearl earrings. My ears aren't pierced yet, but I'm considering having it done.

Gaston wadded the letter up and threw it across the room. *She'll never make it. She's been so protected, she won't know what hit her.* He walked around the bed and retrieved the ball of paper. He flopped back on the bed and unraveled the letter. He read it again. *She dumped me. She could just as well have started with Dear John.* He thought about how he and Cheryl had met. *Maybe it wasn't meant to be, but she was my first love, at least the first one I cared seriously about.* He found a fountain pen and some stationery, and started writing; not to Cheryl, to her mother.

Gaston sealed the letter and put a stamp on it. He dropped it in the mailroom. On the way back to Officer's Quarters he wondered why he wasn't more upset. He had been around midshipmen who had gone AWOL after getting a *Dear John* letter. He'd even seen a classmate commit suicide. He examined his feelings. He was sad, but not angry; certainly not suicidal or even heartbroken. Maybe he hadn't really been in love, or maybe it just hadn't hit him yet.

The days between Christmas and the New Year were scheduled work days on the base, but the rest of the coastline had pretty much shut down. Gaston had tried to follow up on the hanging with Jim Fairbanks, but the paper was closed for the holidays. He checked with the Sheriff's Department, but there was only one person on duty and he was no help at all. He decided if he wanted to find out what was going on he'd have to speak with Terry Nakamura's family. Back on the base, he borrowed a phonebook from communications and looked up Terry Nakamura. There were three Nakamura's listed, but none of them were Terry. He started calling from the first listing.

The first call was answered by an elderly man. He spoke broken English. "Terry not here." The person hung up.

Great! Now I don't know if he lived there and wasn't home, they knew he was dead, or they don't understand I'm trying to contact family members. He called the second number. A woman answered and, in broken English, gave him the number he was looking for. He called the number and a woman answered. She seemed very distraught. He made an appointment to speak with her. She said Terry's funeral was scheduled for December 31st, New Years Eve day. She agreed to meet with him on December 30, at their home in the little town of Siletz, bordering an Indian reservation in the foothills of the Coast Range Mountains.

December 30 was a stormy day and he had to weave around downed trees and branches as he made his way up the narrow road to the town. Siletz consisted of a general store, a Catholic church, and a school. The few houses Gaston could see were nothing more than one-room shacks with tar paper roofs and clapboard or metal siding. Indoor plumbing would have been an odd luxury to the people. As he drove by, he noticed even the one room school had an outhouse. He stopped at the store and inquired about the location of the Nakamura home and was directed through town about a mile. The general store also served as the post office and he got the box number from the clerk. Most everyone he saw appeared to be American Indian. The directions were easy to follow and he had no problem locating the rusty mailbox on the end of the dirt road leading to the house. He drove several hundred feet down a rutted dirt road. A sign with Japanese symbols was posted at the end of the driveway. He guessed it was the Japanese spelling of their name or a welcome sign. The modest house was set in a clearing surrounded by a lawn in front, a small fruit orchard on one side, and forest on the other. He stopped and honked the horn twice as he had been instructed by Mrs. Nakamura.

She came out of the house carrying an umbrella. "You must be Mr. Carson," she greeted him. "Come in, I will keep you from getting wet."

After introductions, Gaston sat at an ornate enameled wooden table. Mrs. Nakamura poured steaming tea into small bowls and handed one to him.

She was a beautiful young woman. Her jet-black hair was in a tight bun on her head. She was wearing an ornate teal-colored silk dress with Japanese characters embroidered on one sleeve.

"Has the sheriff come to see you?" Gaston asked.

She nodded, "Sheriff Sam Johnson." She spoke perfect English.

"Did he tell you what happened?"

"He told me my husband hanged himself."

"Do you believe him?"

She shook her head. "He would not do that."

"Do you know if your husband had enemies?"

"You don't understand." She pointed at herself. "We are the enemy. Everybody hates us."

"I'm sure not everybody, but you're right, I don't understand. Can you tell me what led up to his death?"

"First, you need to understand. There are many types of Japanese in America."

"Different types?"

"Oh, yes, a big difference. There are Japanese who have immigrated from Japan, who swear loyalty to the Emperor. There are Japanese immigrants who are not citizens, but have a loyalty to America. There are also some Japanese who wish to return to Japan to fight for the Emperor. There are second generation Japanese Americans who are American citizens by birth. There are also second generation Japanese Americans who are born to interracial families. You know, a Japanese and a Caucasian are married and have a child. It is very complex, but I know my husband. He was a loyal American. He sent our children to public school, and taught them English as his parents taught him. I don't understand why we are treated like the enemy."

Gaston sipped his tea and listened. She was right, it was very complex. "Mrs. Nakamura, did these hostilities start after the bombing of Pearl Harbor?"

"Oh, yes. It started the day Pearl Harbor was bombed. We moved here with the American Indians, because we feel safe here. Until a week ago we lived in Toledo, but our house was burned. They said it was an accident, but we knew it was on purpose. Not long afterward, my husband lost his job. The day he went missing he had an appointment with his old boss, Allen Rich. I told him not to go, but he thought he might be able to get his job back. He worked in the office as a shipping clerk." She pursed her lips trying to stifle her emotions, but tears streamed down her cheeks.

"Tell me more about the Japanese community. I saw there are two others named Nakamura in the telephone book."

"My husband's grandfather and his parents still live in Toledo. His grandparents immigrated from Japan before the Great War."

"Have there been any instances of aggression against them?"

"I prefer you talk to them. I am not aware of any, although I suspected something might have happened."

"I'll talk to them. What was it that caused your suspicions?"

"Terry's father had bruises on his face and a black eye, when we were at the family dinner last week. He said it was nothing, he took a fall."

*****

New Year's Eve day was crisp and cold. It was easily the coldest day he had seen since coming out West. The trees were covered with frost and the mud puddles had a thin layer of ice, something that rarely happened this close to the ocean, he was told. He was in the kitchen of Officer's Quarters pouring a cup of coffee when Alice walked in.

"It's been so quiet this past week, I don't know why they have me come to work," Alice said, getting a cup out of the cupboard. She set it on the counter next to his.

"You never know," Gaston said, pouring the coffee for her.

She poured sugar from the glass container and stirred it in. "Sugar?" she asked.

"I know I'm sweet, but you're the first one ever to call me sugar."

"Seriously? You think...never mind. You got me again." She laughed. "What have you got going? I'm going crazy with the quiet. I feel like something bad is about to happen."

Gaston moved his cup to the table and sat down. "Join me for coffee and tell me about it."

She sat across from him and blew the steam from her cup. She took a sip, then set it down. "Still too hot," she said.

He watched her puckered red lips and smiled. "You were saying you expect something bad to happen. I didn't know you were superstitious."

"Superstitious, no, that's not me. I've just been antsy lately. The talk about the war. People are afraid the Japs will attack the West Coast. We have almost no soldiers to stop them. It just has me nervous."

"We have the CAP and CD; you should join Civil Defense, you'd keep better informed. I doubt the Japs will mount a full-scale attack."

"Better informed! You don't think I know what's going on? I answer the phones and a lot of people talk to me, and not just Coast Guard personnel."

"Still, you're buying into the panic. Logistically, there is almost no advantage to the Japs attacking Oregon, or California, for that matter."

"They attacked Alaska. What's to prevent them from coming here?"

"They took an island that had no population with the exception of a few Eskimos. There was no defense, no communication. It was a bold move, but we'll get them off the island. As far as the mainland, we have radar, physical spotters, beach patrols, some air spotters—weather permitting—the United States Coast Guard. What I worry about is panic from our own people. Every person of Asian descent is suspected of being a spy in the public's eye. We don't have a means of policing a wide-scale uprising against our Japanese citizens."

"So you're saying I should be more worried about attacks on the Japanese in this country, not the ones attacking our ships in the Pacific."

Gaston drained his cup, got up, and picked up the percolator from the stove. He topped off Alice's cup and refilled his. He put the pot back and brought the sugar to the table. "I don't want you to put words in my mouth. Obviously, the Coast Guard is here to protect against an invasion. I'm just hoping we are as concerned prejudice and bigotry don't result in mob rule against law-abiding Japanese descendants."

"Personally, I feel uncomfortable every time I see one."

"A Japanese American?"

"How do I know it's a Japanese American? It could be a spy for all I know."

"Good point. If I wanted to get someone to spy here on the West Coast, I'd make sure he didn't look like a Jap. Think about that. That bald headed man named Jones may be a spy. That's what I'm talking about paranoia."

"I get upset every time I talk about it. Do you mind if I change the subject?" Alice stirred more sugar into her coffee. "It's New Years Eve. Do you have big plans?"

Gaston welcomed the change of subject. "No plans. Danny Pastor invited me to the *Blue Whale*, but I don't fit in with that crowd...You?"

"I might, if I could find a date."

Gaston looked at her and grinned.

"You're giving me a look," Alice said.

"I'm not giving you a look. It sounds like you want me to accompany you on a date."

"I don't go out on dates with encumbered men, and I certainly don't ask men on dates."

"Encumbered! You think I'm encumbered?"

"Well, I don't know what you call it. You…you're engaged…or going steady, or what?"

"None of those. Cheryl has joined the Army Nurse Corps. She thinks it's better if we are not *encumbered,* as you put it."

"Your girl broke up with you, when were you going to tell me?"

"It's not the kind of thing a guy likes to advertise."

"Well, you don't seem to be very upset."

"Maybe it will hit me later."

"You want to celebrate?"

"With you?"

"Of course, with me. Who do you think I was talking about?"

Gaston rubbed his forehead and didn't answer. He wasn't sure if a headache was coming on. "I thought you didn't ask guys out on a date?"

"What, you don't want to go to a New Years Eve party with me?" She turned and started to walk away.

"Whoa, don't flip your lid, it's just…I thought it was the guy's job to ask a girl out."

She stopped and turned back to face him. "Oh, you think I was being forward."

"Can we start over? Since I'm recently *unencumbered,* would you be so kind as to allow me to escort you to a New Years Eve party at an undisclosed location?"

"I'd love to. Pick me up at 2100 hrs." She grinned, showing mischievous eyes and those cute dimples again.

"Thank God, we got through that. You don't have a father, or a chaperone I need to get approval from, do you?"

Alice laughed. "Stop by my desk and I'll give you my address and my phone number."

The party was at the local Grange Hall, a vacant single-room school building that had been purchased for Grange social activities. Servicemen were let in free. Gaston showed his I.D. card.

"I'm sorry sir, Grange members only."

Alice pulled out her card. "He's my guest."

He escorted Alice to the coat room. "I like your hair that way. It brings out your freckles."

"You really know how to compliment a girl. Remind me to teach you some manners. You do know how to dance, don't you?"

"I've been known to cut a rug or two. Do you like to swing?"

"Gaston Carson, I may have completely misjudged you."

"It happens a lot. This is a party, let's go get some punch."

Alice opened her clutch and pulled out a flask and handed it to Gaston. "This might help give the punch a little more punch." She raised her eyebrows.

"I'm glad you thought of it. I didn't know where we were going."

"I'll bet that happens a lot," Alice said, grinning again.

The band did their best to play all the latest big-band hits. They danced to almost all of them. Swing, jitterbug, and then the band played "Stardust".

Alice snuggled close to him. "You know when we were at my sister's house, I saw you standing under the mistletoe. I wanted to kiss you so bad."

"Why didn't you?"

"Because, I thought you were taken. A girl doesn't make a move on another girl's man."

"Sorry, I didn't know the rules." He pulled her closer to him and they almost stopped moving. He looked into her eyes.

The countdown for the New Year began. They stopped and got their horns ready. "Ten, nine, eight, seven, six..." Alice stood on her tip toes and kissed him in the lips. "Three, two, one, Happy New Year!" He grabbed her around the waist and lifted her off her feet. "You were supposed to wait for the count down," Gaston said. He could hardly contain the grin on his face.

"Sorry, I didn't know the rules," she said. They kissed again, this time it was a long and passionate one. The din of the crowd faded away, they were caught up in the moment, in their own little world. When they stopped to take a breath, Gaston said, "Happy 1942."

"What's going on?" Alice asked, turning to see people running for the door.

"Stay here," Gaston said. "I'll check it out." He ran for the door, but Alice was close behind.

In the parking area, there was a big circle of people. Three men were beating up on a man in the center. Gaston jumped from the porch and broke through the circle. He didn't make it to the man on the ground before he was blindsided by a wild punch. He responded by decking the man. He bent down to pull another man off the person on the ground. That man was much larger than Gaston and wasn't about to get off the man he was pummeling. Gaston got him in a choke hold and yanked him free. The man on the ground was able to get up, fight off the remaining attacker, and escape through the crowd. Gaston let go of the man he was holding. The man turned and was about to punch Gaston, when Gaston realized who it was. He blocked the punch. "You don't want to do that, do you Allen? I thought you just picked on poor defenseless Japanese."

"Why, you little shit, I'll have you thrown in jail for this!"

"Last I heard, it was a crime to attack defenseless Americans."

"Americans! That yellow, slant-eyed, bastard would just as soon kill us as look at us."

"Are we cool, Allen?" Gaston eyed the big man. "You're not going to try and hit me, are you?"

"Get the hell out of my sight. The sheriff will be paying you a visit. God help the United States if you're here to protect us."

Gaston rubbed his jaw as he walked back through the crowd to where Alice was watching. "Let's get your coat," Gaston said. "I think we'd better go."

"Are you hurt?"

"I'll be fine. Do you know anywhere we can get something to eat?"

"My place, if you promise to behave."

"I think I've made enough enemies for the night. I promise I'll be on my best behavior."

Chapter 12

On the second of January, 1942, Yaquina Bay Coast Guard Station was bustling with activity. The Japanese invasion of the Philippines had begun a mere ten hours after the attack on Pearl Harbor. Nearly all the American aircraft were destroyed in the initial attack, leaving insufficient air cover to protect the country. Now Manila was occupied by Japanese troops.

It was as if the New Year had arrived and brought the war with it, but the West Coast was so far away from the action, they went about preparing for war in the only way they knew how. This was the day the Civil Air Patrol was to put their plan into action. Goodman had delivered on his promise to send a mechanic from the Coast Guard motor pool to work with the airplane pilots on a daily basis.

Gaston had been invited to act as a spotter with Major, in his single-engine biplane. He was excited to be able to see what the coastline they were protecting looked like from the air. He arrived at the airfield three miles south of the Coast Guard Station. There was a blanket of fog covering the grass runway. Gaston pulled up to the hangar, a large wooden building with a rusting metal roof. He parked outside and walked through the man door on the side of the building. This early in the war, there hadn't been any provisions to keep the public from the airfield, something Gaston took note of. Inside the hangar he saw Major checking out his plane. "Good morning, Major," Gaston said, walking up to him. "Is this the equipment we'll be going up in?"

"If this goddamned fog doesn't ground us," Major said. "Let me show you this beauty. It's a Boeing Stearman 75, built just after Boeing bought out Stearman. You sit in front and I'll fly it from behind. There are two sets of controls so if something goes wrong, you can fly it. Keep your damn hands off the stick unless I tell you. This baby cost me nearly $12,000. It has the higher horsepower Lycoming engine. She'll do 180 knots if I give her the juice. One thing you'll learn is always look for a landing spot, just in case we get into trouble. We don't need to worry much about that, the tide will be out and there's plenty of beach. We're going to be making a run to Brookings. That's right on the California border. They have an airfield there. We'll top off the fuel and head back home. The trip to Brookings will be about two hours and we'll cover 160 miles as the crow flies."

"I thought you said this thing will fly at 180 miles per hour. That would make the trip less than an hour," Gaston said.

"We'll only be flying about two-thirds throttle. Our objective is to watch the beach and ocean close in to spot any suspicious activity. We can't do that very well at full throttle. We're not in a race; we want to see what's going on."

"I understand. Am I dressed warm enough?"

"I've got a leather cap and goggles for you. I see you brought a pair of gloves, you'll be glad you did."

Major yelled for two other men to assist him turning the plane around and rolling it out for take off. He went over to an office area and spent a few minutes talking to a radio operator. "We can go now. Get your ass inside and buckle up. I don't want you falling out when we fly upside down."

Gaston laughed. He had seen barnstorming events where pilots did stunts like that, but also knew it was against regulations to perform stunts on Uncle Sam's nickel. At least he hoped that was the case.

"One more thing. If you need to take a leak, now's the time to do it. You wouldn't be the first passenger who wet his pants because he didn't heed my advice.

"Guess I'll go whether I need to or not," Gaston said, heading for the latrine.

Ten minutes later they were buckled in and Major motioned for a man to turn over the prop. The man gave it a spin and it fired. Gaston could see the fog was still as heavy as before. Once he had heard fog was a killer to land in, but as long as the layer was thin, takeoff was reasonably safe. He hoped that was the case. The cockpit was equipped with a radio and a mic, but Gaston hadn't been briefed on how to use them.

The engine revved and the noise was deafening. He felt the plane bump and bounce along the grassy strip and before he knew it everything was smooth. He felt the stick between his legs move back and saw the floor pedals move, but didn't have a clue what was happening. After a few seconds of flying blind, they broke out of the fog and banked toward the ocean. The cockpit compass showed they were headed south. Below him, all he saw was a gray blanket. In the distance to the east he could see the trees atop the slopes of the Siuslaw National Forest. Within five minutes they were out of the fog and Major took them down to within a hundred feet of the beach. They stayed on a southerly route with the breakers and sandy beach on their port and the blue Pacific on their starboard. He wondered if nautical terms applied to aircraft. He recalled the difficulty midshipmen had learning the language of the sea. Some even went to the extreme of writing "S" for starboard on their right palm, so they wouldn't make the cardinal sin of calling out the wrong instructions. After the novelty of the first few minutes had worn off, he felt the biting cold, damp wind in his face. He was sure his lips were turning blue. He had to remind himself why he was up there. They didn't expect to see anything, but he'd better keep an eye out, just in case.

About an hour into the flight he felt the plane bank sharply and they were flying out to sea. He wondered what was going on. Before long the plane went into a shallow dive, then he saw what Major must have been checking out. It was a fishing boat. Major banked sharply and dipped low enough that he could read the name and numbers on the bow. Gaston wrote them down in a small notebook. It was one of ours out of Bandon. The three men aboard waved and yelled. *I'll bet they don't get many visitors out here,* Gaston thought. They continued down the coast and Gaston checked off the small towns as he could see them. It was a bird's-eye view and an incredible advantage over ground transportation to check the hundreds of miles of coastline. Just as Gaston checked off Port Orford on his map, he caught sight of something out to sea. He raised his hand and pointed. Major immediately banked the plane to investigate. It was big and black, *maybe a submarine*, he thought. In the few seconds it took to get to the area the object disappeared. Then he saw it again, several huge blue whales headed south. He could see how they may be mistaken for a submarine by an untrained observer.

Brookings was surrounded by clear skies and typical winter temperatures in the upper fifties. The field, located a little over a mile north of the town had a single dirt runway stretching 1500 feet north to south. Major circled once to check out the wind sock on a pole. A slight breeze coming from the south was perfect for a landing from the north.

Gaston was impressed with his skill when Major put the plane down.

Major taxied to a weathered building on the south end of the runway and killed the engine. Except for the hangar and another small house next to a fuel tank on a stand, the airport looked deserted.

When Gaston's feet hit the ground, he could still feel the vibration of the engine tingling through his legs. "It's good to be on the ground again. What do we do now?"

"See that fuel tank; we're going to fill a couple of those jerry cans with gas and top off the tank. After that we're going to see if we can find Talbot Miller, he was supposed to meet us here. He pulled a pocket watch from his pants pocket and flipped open the cover. "Must be something going on, he's always been here when he said he'd be. He's our link to Eureka."

Gaston was up on a ladder pouring the second can of fuel down the funnel when he heard an engine rev up, sputter, and backfire. He watched as a biplane attempted to land, but the engine went silent. "He's too far out!" Major shouted. "Jesus Christ, that's Talbot!"

They watched as the plane took a steep dive, gained air speed, then glided to a perfect landing. The plane rolled to a stop halfway down the runway. "Finish topping off that tank," Major said. "I'm going to see what that crazy son-of-a-bitch is up to."

Gaston finished his job, tightened the fuel cap and descended the ladder. He stood with the empty can in his hand watching Major and Talbot whoop and holler and hug each other in the middle of the runway. *Are all pilots this crazy?* he wondered.

They came walking back, arm in arm, like two lovers on a stroll. They were laughing and cheering and having a good time. When they got to Gaston, Major introduced Talbot Miller to him. "This son-of-a-bitch thought he'd hop over to Crescent City and bring back lunch for us. The idiot forgot to put fuel in his tank."

"I thought I had enough," Talbot said, holding up a paper bag. "It's only a fifteen-minute flight."

"You damned near killed yourself over a couple of sandwiches," Major said. "I thought I'd have to shovel you off the runway."

"Come on in the shack and we'll have lunch," Talbot said, to Gaston. "He keeps on giving me shit, we'll eat his lunch."

The shack was a one-room house with a stove and sink in one corner, a painted table with four chairs, a small desk with a radio set, and a back door that he learned was the shortest distance to the outhouse.

"I've got to use the head," Talbot said. "That little incident nearly scared the shit out of me." He laughed as he left.

Major went to the sink and washed his hands. Gaston did the same and Major handed him a towel that looked like it hadn't been washed in a year. "He had a close call," Gaston said.

Major pulled out a chair and sat down. "Hell, that wasn't close. You should have been with us when we flew under the Waldport Bridge. We clipped the tail and crashed in the middle of Alsea Bay. Lucky for us the tide was out."

"You called my trip stupid," Talbot said, coming through the back door. "At least I didn't spend time in the hoosegow." He went over and washed his hands and dried them on the same dirty towel. "It took my life savings at the time to go his bail." He joined them at the table. "Anyone hungry for one of Mom's deli sandwiches?" He reached in the bag. "There's one for each of us, as long as you like oven roasted turkey." He handed Major a sandwich. "Don't go telling anymore stories about our flying escapades; you'll scare the lad half to death." He got up and brought back a coffeepot and three mugs. He poured lukewarm coffee and sat down again.

"You can tell me," Gaston said. "I need to know how scared I should be."

"Some other time," Major said, "we've got to get back up the coast. Any activity to report down this way?" He took a bite of sandwich.

Talbot finished chewing and washed it down with a big gulp of coffee. "We've had three reports of a submarine sighting, all early morning or late afternoon. Some of the crab boats stay out overnight. They catch activity we can't verify. I know these men and they may spin a yarn or two about their catch, but they're honest as the day is long. I think their reports are authentic."

"Have they got any solid evidence, like a photo or debris?" Gaston asked.

"I doubt it, but subs have been reported in several areas. I don't think it's a hoax."

Gaston took a drink of coffee and grimaced. It was bitter. "Major, any chance you could leave me here for a few days? Maybe I could catch a ride with one of the crab boats. Maybe I'll get lucky and see one of those subs for myself."

"What do you think, Tal? Can you set up an overnight tour for Gaston?"

Chapter 13

The boat was thirty feet with a wooden hull. Her name was *Matilda* after the owner's wife. Like the only other crab boat he'd been on, the rear and side decks were stacked high in rusty wire crab traps. Gaston stood on the dock and wondered if his entire stint in the war would be on fishing boats rather than the ships he had imagined. As a midshipman, he had dreamed of serving on a battleship, or one of the new aircraft carriers. Several years earlier, on a trip to Newport News, he saw firsthand the construction of the USS Enterprise, a Yorktown Class aircraft carrier. His dreams at the Academy had him serving on such a grand ship and maybe even serving as Commander as she sailed to far away ports displaying the might of the United States Navy.

"You coming aboard or are you going to stand there with your feet glued to the dock?"

Gaston snapped back to reality and glanced up at a man with a large drooping pipe in his mouth. The part of his face that wasn't hidden behind a white beard was beet red. In another setting he could have been Santa Claus himself. "I'm supposed to meet Captain Jack on *Matilda*. Are you Captain Jack?"

"Mr. Carson. I expected someone much older. You sure you can handle the sea?"

"I'll manage. Permission to come aboard?"

"I'll be damned. You're a Navy bloke. No civilian uses that protocol. Get your butt in gear; we're going to miss the tide at the bar if we don't cast off in the next few minutes."

The fishing ports in Oregon were mostly close to the mouth of a river. Tidal effect caused the trip from the river to the ocean to be quite rough. If they could catch the current on the outgoing tide, the ride would be much smoother. Gaston had heard most small craft lost in the Pacific were in the critical minutes when they crossed from the river to the ocean, or the return. To attempt the trip at the wrong time could mean the loss of the boat and the crew. Gaston hurried up the ramp. He didn't have any luggage, but had managed to borrow a box camera from Talbot. Gaston reached out his hand, "Gaston Carson. I'll try and stay out of your way."

Captain Jack gripped Gaston's hand. He had the roughest hand Gaston had ever felt. He looked into Captain Jack's eyes. They were clear as crystal. Crow's feet fanned out on each side of the man's face. He guessed the captain would have a wrinkled, weathered face behind the white beard. The captain smiled and removed the pipe from his mouth. Gaston saw a mouthful of yellowed teeth, worn on one side from holding the pipe between them. Immediately the other two crew members cast off the bowline and the captain eased the boat out of the harbor. The trip to the bar was a short one. They reached the ocean, and Gaston grabbed the rail. The waves breaking over the bar were as tall as the cabin of the boat. The captain eased the engine for a moment and the boat started drifting backward, then he gunned it full throttle and rode the swell of the incoming wave. The bow dropped like a rollercoaster into the trough and the captain steadied his feet as they crashed through the next wave. After that it was relatively smooth sailing. They plowed through four foot swells, but without wind there were only occasional whitecaps out to sea.

"You think we'll see a submarine?" Gaston asked.

"It don't matter what I think, either we will or we won't. If you get a picture with that contraption, though, it'll be a miracle."

Gaston thought the same, but he had to try.

The day on the boat was the same routine he'd seen before. He helped out tying bait, mostly dead bottom fish, inside the traps. It was a smelly job, but one of the crew had loaned him a rubber apron and boots to keep him from getting too stinky. Near nightfall the captain turned on the mast light. It lit up the boat and the water around it. They weighed anchor in 200 feet of water and waited for dawn. Sleeping quarters on the *Matilda* were cramped. Gaston took an upper bunk and closed his eyes. Soon the rocking of the boat put him to sleep.

"He hasn't got a family or home." The woman was speaking to her husband. Gaston overheard the conversation from the kitchen of the mansion. He was eating a sandwich and finishing a bottle of Coca-Cola. A young black woman wearing an apron and white cap put another Coca-Cola in front of him and removed the empty bottle. "Thank you. I ain't never had two in the same day."

"Drink up, you little ragamuffin. You'll be out on the street again. You may never get another one."

"The kids are mostly gone. The least we can do is get him into a school. He seems pretty smart." It was the woman speaking again.

"I'll see what I can do," the man said. The woman pushed the man in a wheelchair into the kitchen. "What do you think about going to school?" he asked Gaston.

"I already been through grade five. I thought I'd get a job. A man's got to support himself," Gaston said. "How come you're in a wheelchair?"

Roosevelt ignored the question. "If you didn't have to go to work, and could go to school, what would you do with your life?"

Gaston's eyes got large. "You wouldn't be kidding me, would you? Only kids from means gets to go to school past the fifth grade. My mom said there ain't nothin' gained for nothin'. She said I had to go to work so we could eat."

"Would you rather go to school?"

"Sure, who wouldn't? You sure you're not kidding?"

"You're a bright boy, Gaston," the woman said. "If we sent you to get an education you'd do good with it, wouldn't you?"

"I'd be eternally thankful. An education is nothing to be wasted."

"Come with me, you're going to spend the night with us."

He found out that evening he was spending the night in James', the governor's son's, room. "James is about your age. He's away at school." Mrs. Roosevelt said. She gave him a pair of boy's pajamas.

In his dream, Gaston was about to drift off to sleep when a loud crash sent the boat into a tilt that knocked him out of bed. Seconds later he was standing in ice cold water up to his ankles. "Gaston, get the hell out of there!" It was the captain at the top of the cabin stairs.

Gaston was bunking in his clothes, but had only socks on his feet. On deck, the captain was shouting directions to the crew on how to launch the small dingy that served as a life boat. *Matilda* was listing badly. "She won't make it," the captain shouted. "Grab a Mae West, put it on and as soon as you get it in the water grab onto anything that will float."

Gaston grabbed a life vest and cinched it tight around him. *Matilda* was slipping rapidly into the water, bow first. The crew was holding on to anything they could to keep from sliding into the ocean, as they struggled to get the dingy free of *Matilda*. Another minute passed and the railing Gaston was holding onto was underwater, dragging him with it. He let go and a large wave swallowed him. The cold water was gripping his lungs so hard he was nearly paralyzed. When he managed to get his head above water for an instant, he took a breath. His life preserver didn't seem to be doing much good. Every time a swell would come, it seemed to break over him. *Matilda* had a hold of his left leg and was taking him down with her. He struggled to free himself, but couldn't figure out what was holding him. He put his right foot on the submerged railing and pushed up with all his might. He felt his pants rip and he was free. He kicked away until his head was above water. The mast light was still blazing overhead. Like a spotlight in an otherwise black night, it illuminated a large circular area. Then he saw it— a large, dark object silently moving away from him. Just before it slipped beneath the sea, he read the number painted in large letters on the conning tower, *I-26*. In another instant the mast light disappeared beneath the water in an eerie glow. A minute later everything was black, and he was freezing cold.

"Gaston, are you there?" The voice sounded far off and he couldn't tell which direction it was coming from.

"Help!" Gaston patted his life vest trying to find the pocket containing a flare. He lit it and held it up, but the rise and fall of the ocean swells caused him to bob like a cork. One moment he was on top of the mountain, the next in the deepest valley. He could hear voices calling, but couldn't see a thing. The voices calling his name were drifting away, then they were gone. At the top of the next swell, he got his bearings. He spun around until he saw lights. He didn't know whether they were on land or at sea, but he did the only thing he knew to do. He swam as hard as he could toward the lights. As it turned out, the lights he was swimming toward were on the dingy with the captain and two crew members. He waved the flare and finally they saw him. They had been rowing toward shore, away from him. "Captain Jack, is that you." A flashlight beam dancing over the water passed over him, then came back and rested on him. The captain extended an oar. "You damn well better not swamp us," the captain said. "Go around to the stern and the boys will pull you in."

On the small boat, Gaston, completely exhausted, lay face up, gasping for breath. "I guess it's my lucky day," Gaston said. "I thought I was a goner."

"Another ten minutes in that frigid water and you would have been paying Davy Jones a visit." The captain looked at a hand-held compass to get his bearings again. "Head that way." He pointed due east. "With the drift of the currents we'll likely end up in Gold Beach. You boys row harder, or we'll all die of exposure out here." He took off his heavy coat and laid it over Gaston who was shivering violently. "We don't get to shore soon, he won't make it."

*****

Gaston woke to sunshine coming through a bedroom window. For a moment he thought he was dreaming. "Where am I?" he asked.

There was a man standing by the door talking to another person. "Damn, Gaston, don't you know that water's too cold to swim in?" Ensign Pastor said, entering the room.

"I do now," Gaston said. "What are you doing here?"

"The Commander wanted me to come over and check on you. Seems he got a call from the White House asking about you."

"White House? What day is it?"

"Monday, January 5th."

Gaston scooted up in bed. "I've been here since Saturday?"

"Technically, since Sunday," Pastor said. "The crew of the *Matilda* hit shore shortly after midnight."

"I'm still groggy. What town are we in? I don't remember anything after the boat sank."

"You're back in Newport. They brought you back up here by ambulance."

"Really, why'd they do that?"

"Because they were afraid you were going to die. They thought you'd have a chance if they could get you into a hospital." Pastor turned toward the door. "Alice, he's awake."

Alice came in and stood by the bed. Her eyes were red. "I leave you alone for a day and look what you do," she scolded.

Gaston grinned. "It's coming back to me. We may have been the first fishing boat sunk by a Jap sub."

"I think you're still delirious," Alice said. "I just called Commander Goodman and he's on his way over. Do me a favor and stay in bed until he gets here."

Gaston nodded. "I don't think I'll be going anywhere in the next hour."

News traveled fast and people were lined up in the hall to see Gaston. Ensign Pastor was making sure no one got in before the Commander got to debrief him. When the Commander arrived Ensign Pastor closed the door. Goodman and Gaston were alone in the room.

"The White House has called three times already today wanting to know your condition."

"Glad to see they miss me," Gaston said, making light of the situation.

"I need to know what happened. Thirty-foot fishing boats don't go down in relatively calm water without good cause."

"Commander, does *"I-26"* mean anything to you?"

"Jap subs use 'I' designations on their conning towers."

"*I-26* was the number the kid in Winchester Bay had on the drawing he made," Gaston said. "We were sunk by the same sub, but I don't think it was intentional."

"I wouldn't be so sure. According to the newspaper *I-26* was the sub that sank *Cynthia Olson* on the day Pearl Harbor was attacked. She's been operating off the Oregon and California coast for months."

"I think she surfaced and pierced the hull by mistake. There is no doubt in my mind it was I-26," Gaston said, "I saw the conning tower number clearly just as our boat was going under."

"That makes me feel a little better," Goodman said.

"Sir?" Gaston said, confused.

"We're dealing with a lone submarine, not a fleet. They've been putting those fake periscopes in the water to scare us. Chances are there's only one sub causing all the ruckus."

"One submarine against the entire US Coast Guard. I like the odds," Gaston said.

"So do I." Goodman said, getting up. "Drop in my office as soon as you feel better." He opened the door. "There's a line of people out here to see you. You remember Fairbanks from the *Newport Times*?"

"Yes, sir."

"Better think about what you are going to tell him...loose lips."

Gaston mulled it over in his mind. *Loose lips sink ships;* it was all over the place, on posters tacked in virtually every government building in the country. How much about what was going on could they keep from the public?

Fairbanks knocked on the door casing. "I heard you were awake. Can I get a scoop?

"Have you found out anything else about Terry Nakamura?" Gaston asked, trying to divert the subject from his ordeal.

"I was talking about how you ended up nearly drowning in the ocean." Fairbanks pulled out his pad and flipped it to a clean page.

"Oh, that," Gaston said. "Really there's not too much to tell. The boat went down for reasons unknown. We all barely escaped with our lives."

"There's a rumor that you were torpedoed by a Japanese submarine."

Gaston smiled. "You know what they say about rumors."

"What?"

"Exactly."

Chapter 14

"Mr. Carson," Commander Goodman said as soon as Gaston walked through the Headquarters entrance.

"Commander, you wanted to see me?"

"I was visited by Allen Rich. He seems to think you are a troublemaker."

"*I'm* a troublemaker? Somebody needs to step on his toes. I'm almost certain he's involved in the Nakamura murder, and New Year's Eve, he and another man were beating up a Japanese man at the Grange dance. We couldn't have a worse person in charge of Civil Defense."

"Then there is something to it."

"What should I have done? They were beating the shit out of that poor guy. Excuse my language. It upsets me to think we would consider everyone with dark skin and slanted eyes our enemy."

"You need to stay away from Rich. He's been around the area a long time and he packs a lot of influence."

"Come on, Commander. You're not buying into his bullshit."

"Mr. Carson, just because you were invited to my house doesn't mean you can use that kind of language around me. Stay away from Allen Rich."

"But, sir."

"Regardless of your connections in Washington, you are still under my care. Right now you're walking on very thin ice. I'd suggest you walk softly. Get out of my office. You're dismissed."

Gaston turned and left the building. *What the hell was that all about?* he wondered. He went back to Officer's Quarters, stormed past Alice, and went in the kitchen. He found a clean cup and filled it with stale coffee. He sat down and shook his head back and forth. Something was going on and he wasn't privy to it.

Alice came in. "You want to talk about it?"

"No!" He stared at the black liquid. "To tell you the truth, I don't know what's going on."

"Then you want to talk about it," Alice said, sitting down.

"Not here," Gaston said. "What are you doing after work?"

"We're having a USO meeting at the new grade school. We're planning a St. Patrick's Day party."

"How long will that take?"

"Until 2000 hrs, I guess. What's with all the secrecy?"

"Can I come by your place around 2030?"

"Gaston, should I be worried?"

"Not about me. If you're not home, I'll wait in the parking lot."

"I'll be home."

Gaston left the station and drove to the *Blue Whale*, hoping to catch Major on his favorite stool. He hadn't talked to him since the incident in Brookings. He wasn't surprised to see Ensign Pastor sitting right next to him at the bar. When Major saw Gaston he raised his hand to get his wife's attention. "Sarah, look who walked in. Bring him a cool one."

Sarah sat a mug of beer on the bar. "Don't have too much fun tonight, you've got to fly in the morning," she said to Major.

"Gaston, what's on your mind?" Major asked.

"I'm not certain; I thought I'd pick your brain about night flying."

"Night flying?" Major took a drink of his beer and wiped the suds from his upper lip. "Doesn't make much sense. It's darker than the inside of a well digger's ass out there at night."

"There must be a way of equipping the planes with a spotlight," Gaston persisted.

"You've got to give me more information. What are you looking for?"

"Jap submarines," Gaston said. "I think they surface at night and recharge their batteries, take in fresh air, and dispose of whatever waste they produce. Our coastline is so remote, they do it without fear."

"Jap subs at night," Danny said, "that would be like trying to find a needle in a haystack."

"Maybe," Gaston said, "but if they are out there and we can find them, then we can send a Coast Guard cutter with depth charges after them. We need to let the Japs know we're not letting them spy on our towns without repercussions."

"I don't know," Major protested. "The guys are tired already, what are they going to say if I ask them to fly at night?"

"For crying out loud, Major," Gaston said, "you're not going to find anything on the beaches during the daytime anyway. If you switch the crew to night flying you might just help us fight the war." Gaston tipped back his head and downed his beer. "Think about it and let me know what you need."

"Hold on, you're not going to drop a bomb on me and walk out. I already know what I need, and there's not a snowballs chance in hell we're going to get it. We need a lighted airfield. Did you hear me, an airfield with runway lights so we can see where to land. We need forward looking radar, so we don't crash into the cliffs or the trees and can spot things in the water, lighted cockpits; hell, only three of our planes have enclosed cockpits; and Radio Direction Finders for each plane. I can give you a list, but you're pissing up a rope if you think you'll get those items."

"Give me the list," Gaston said, slipping off his barstool. "We won't know unless we ask. I've got to go."

Gaston drove to the duplex where Alice rented the upper floor apartment. Her light was on, so he went up the outside stairs and knocked lightly on the door. The glass pane in the door rattled. He saw the curtain swing back. She opened the door.

"Gaston, a girl could get a tarnished reputation inviting a handsome guy like you in at all hours of the night." She kissed him on the lips. "I've been concerned. Something's happened since you were dumped in the water."

"I'll tell you what happened, but you need to keep it to yourself. Can you do that?"

She pulled her forefinger and thumb across her lips. "My lips are sealed. I was so worried when I found out you were in the hospital."

"What I told you in the hospital was true. Only you and the Commander know."

"You were sunk by a Jap sub?"

"Not intentionally. They probably don't even know they hit us. The sub surfaced and we happened to be in the wrong place. They put a large hole in the hull and we went down fast. I was asleep in the cabin when it happened."

The teapot started whistling and Alice took it off the hot plate that served as her stove. She removed a perforated metal tea basket from the pot and placed it in the sink, poured hot tea into cups, and offered him sugar.

"No, thanks." He watched her stir two spoonfuls of sugar into her tea. "Remember what happened New Year's Eve?"

She smiled and started to blush.

"Not that," he said. "The fight outside; you know Allen Rich was in the middle of it."

"Of course, but you don't know who started it."

"I know a Japanese American was being bloodied by a bunch of thugs. If I wouldn't have come along we may have had another death."

"Another death? What do you mean?"

"A Japanese American was found hanging from the observation tower at the lighthouse Christmas Day. That was why the Commander and I had to leave."

"Why didn't I see it in the paper?"

"Because the paper was told to bury it."

"Our paper is censored?"

"You need to keep this quiet. I don't want to tell you something that will get you all riled up and have you tell someone else. If all that's going on was published, it would only make things worse. The public is on the verge of panic already. You said as much, yourself."

"But how can they keep the death of anyone quiet. The families, the funeral, it's not possible."

"That's what I thought, but it gets worse."

"God help us," Alice said, putting her hand over her mouth.

"I took it upon myself to do some digging and visited the wife of the man who was hanging from the tower. His name was Terry Nakamura, a second generation Japanese American. He was born in a house ten miles up the river from here. He worked at the Toledo forest products plant as a shipping clerk. His boss was Allen Rich."

"Allen Rich, the man at the Christmas party?"

"Allen Rich, who was beating on the guy at the New Year's Eve party and the same man who is the head of Civil Defense."

"Gaston, why are you telling me this? I don't see how me knowing these awful things is going to help!"

"Alice, I'll tell you why you need to know this as soon as you calm down." He reached across and held her hand.

After several minutes, Alice pulled her hand away and took a sip of tea.

Gaston blew on his tea and sipped it. It was already getting cold, so he emptied the cup.

"Okay, I'm calm," Alice said. "This is terrible. You don't know how this makes me feel."

"I feel the same way. I need for you to keep your ears open for any strange conversations that involve doing harm to any Japanese descendents. Let me know if you hear about any Japanese citizens being tormented. I think there is an organized effort to bully them. Just as bad, there is an equally organized effort to keep it quiet."

"There aren't many Japanese in the area. I've heard some talk that there may be spies among them, coordinating a Japanese attack on the mainland."

"Where did you here that?"

"At the USO meeting, just tonight."

"I'm telling you, this kind of talk will only breed discrimination. Most of the Japanese are just as loyal to the United

States as we are. We can't molest them just because their skin is a different color or their eyes are different. What if we started identifying every German and put a swastika on them. That's what Hitler is doing to the Jews. It makes us no better than our enemy. We have to protect our citizens, all of them."

She had never seen Gaston so passionate. "Is that why you were sent out here, to make sure the people don't do something crazy?"

"I don't know," Gaston said, hanging his head. "I'm not certain I can do much about it. There aren't many who see it the way I do."

"That's what I like about you, Gaston. You know exactly where you stand."

"You know what I like about you?"

"No, what?"

"You're a good listener. I feel better after talking to you." He checked his wristwatch. "I've got to go. I have a phone call to make."

"Who are you calling this time of the night?"

"That, I can't tell you," Gaston said. "Someday I will, but not now."

"That's a new wristwatch."

"A late present to myself. My other one stopped when I took it for a swim. The jeweler said it was a total loss." He checked his watch again. "I really do have to make that call."

He kissed her goodnight. "I'll see you tomorrow?"

She smiled, and nodded. "Goodnight."

Chapter 15

In the midnight call Gaston filled Roosevelt in on the activities of the Japanese submarine, including his recommendations for night flights and lighted fields for night landings. He reiterated his belief that the Japanese presence was only harassment and not the start of a full-scale invasion. Then he told the President of the plight of the Japanese citizens and their need for protection.

He signed off and headed to Officer's Quarters to try and get some much needed sleep. As he walked the gravel road from Headquarters, he saw Ensign Pastor parking his car.

Danny Pastor saw Gaston and called out to him, "Gaston, you're out kind of late for a kid your age."

"I could say the same for you, old man." Gaston caught up with him. "I don't know how you do it. You drink too much, smoke too much, sleep too little, and do it day after day. Don't you get tired of it?"

"What are you, my mother?"

"Sorry," Gaston said, "I'm just speaking as a friend."

"Let me tell you about friends." Danny stopped on the steps of Officer's Quarters. "Friends let you down. Friends can't be counted on. Friends die and leave you all alone."

Gaston knew it was the beer talking, but still, Danny must have experienced the traumatic loss of a friend at some point in his life. "I'd like to think we're friends, just the same."

"Let me tell you, you've got a lot to learn about friendship," Danny said, slurring his words.

"Why don't you tell me?"

"Not now, I'm drunk. Catch me when I'm sober."

"That's nearly impossible," Gaston said.

Danny laughed. "I like it. You have a since of humor. We could be friends." He opened the door. "Age before beauty." He walked in, in front of Gaston.

"I couldn't have said it better myself," Gaston said. They walked up the stairs toward their rooms. "You're not going to be banging the walls again tonight are you?"

"I already took care of that," Danny said, smiling.

Gaston awoke only seconds before the post bugler blasted reveille over the loud speakers. He showered and made his way to the Officer's Mess for breakfast. There were three officers already at the table.

"It's all over the morning news," one of the officers said. "Navy flier, Don Mason, operating off the coast of Newfoundland sent the message, 'Sighted sub, sank same.' How's that for keeping it simple and to the point."

"Go Navy," Pastor said, looking over at Gaston. "Our civilian says he's going to get us equipped to spot subs at night. Isn't that right, Gaston?"

"How are you going to do that?" a junior officer asked. "We don't even have a naval flying force present."

"I think Mr. Pastor stretched the truth a little," Gaston said. "I was just inquiring as to the requirements for CAP to spot subs if they show up along our coast at night. I said I'd ask for the equipment."

"I heard there were subs already here. We can't get Washington to do anything about it. And how about the rioting against the Japanese already here in the country? You'd think Washington would be a little more aware of our problems out here."

"Maybe there is a sub or two," Gaston said. "What if they were just harassing us enough to get us to pull ships from the Pacific Fleet. We'd play right into their hands."

"On the other hand," Pastor said, "what if they are just testing our resolve and if we don't retaliate, they see it's okay to invade."

The junior officer sitting next to Pastor had been quiet, but he put down his toast and took advantage of a short break in the discussion. "There's talk of an underground Jap spy ring; Jap sympathizers feeding information to the Japanese subs. We need to clear the coast of all the Japanese Americans, citizens or not."

"And how are you going to do that?" Gaston asked. "It's not practical nor is it moral to remove them just because they have Japanese ancestry."

"Civil Defense is working on a plan right now that would do just that," the officer retaliated.

"What?" Gaston was visibly upset. "Where did you hear that?"

"It isn't a secret. If you attend CD meetings you will hear talk about it."

"You're talking incarcerating American citizens." Gaston was incredulous.

"Not really, only the Japanese."

"What are you going to do about the Germans? We're at war with them, too. Oh my gosh Lt. Weber over at supplies. Boatswain's Mate Ludwig. I could go on; a quarter of our base is German ancestry. Are we going to incarcerate them? Do you see how ridiculous this is?"

"Don't kill the messenger, I'm just telling you what went on in the meeting the other day."

"I think every one of us needs to oppose any incarceration of Japanese citizens," Gaston said.

"It's all right to talk like that among friends, but you say that on the street and you'll be pegged a Jap lover. That could get you killed."

"God help us if the Japs land on our beaches," Pastor said. "How are we going to tell the Japanese Americans from the real Japs? I don't see where that's ridiculous."

"I don't see any way around it. If we let them roam freely, we're inviting an invasion. They could assimilate into our society and wipe us out at night, just like the Greeks did to the citizens of Troy, when they delivered the Trojan horse. It didn't take that many to wipe out the whole city."

"Thanks for the history lesson, Lieutenant." Gaston said. "Forgive me if I don't buy into all the fear mongering." Gaston returned to Officer's Quarters and stopped at Alice's desk. She had just arrived and was removing her coat. "Good morning, sunshine," he said, putting on his best face.

"Have you seen the morning paper?" Alice asked, handing it to him.

"Thanks," he said, taking it. He read the headlines. *62 U-BOATS SUNK!* "That's great; we can't even get the equipment to sink one."

"I'm not talking about the U-boats, look at the article on the thing we were talking about last night." She lowered her voice to a whisper. "I think the newspaper is preparing the people to accept internment camps for the Japanese Americans."

MOB BURNS ASIAN MARKET Gaston, read the entire article. "This reads more like an opinion piece than news. They are arguing, it's best to move the Asians into internment camps for their own safety. What about enforcing the laws of the Country?"

Alice looked up from her desk. "I hear many are leaving voluntarily. There are a number of Japanese-owned houses and farms in the area that have been put up for sale in the last month. I agree it's tragic, but it's not our fault. We didn't start this war."

"Neither did they. Most of them came here to be free. This will be a blight on our country for years to come."

The phone rang, Alice answered. "Officer's Quarters, may I help you?" She raised a finger for Gaston to see. "He's right here; would you like to speak with him?" She handed Gaston the phone. "He's asking for Mr. Carson."

"Carson speaking."

"Mr. Carson, this is Seaman 1st class Andrews at the front gate. There's an Army vehicle here with a delivery that requires a signature from you."

"There must be some mistake. I didn't order anything."

"Okay, sir, I'll send him away."

"Andrews, hold on. Ask the driver for the invoice and read me the items on it."

"Yes, sir."

Gaston put his hand over the phone. "Some kind of mix up," he said to Alice.

"Mr. Carson?" It was Andrews again. "Item 1, Quantity 200, incandescent bulbs with weather tight insulated sockets. Item 2, Quantity 10, sealed beam 24 V headlamps with mounting brackets. Item 3, Quantity 10, auxiliary portable direction finding RF devices."

"I'll be right out Andrews," Gaston said. He handed Alice the phone and started out the door.

"What's happening, Gaston?" Alice asked.

"Our ship has just come in." He disappeared out the door.

At the gate he talked to the driver. Then went back to Officer's Quarters for his car. He motioned for the truck driver to follow him. "You can unload it in that hangar." He said, pointing to the only building in sight.

Major was with three other civilian pilots inspecting their equipment, checking off items on a clip board.

"Major," Gaston called across the open bay.

"Hey, Gaston."

"I've got a delivery for you. Where do you want it?"

Major came over to Gaston, the clipboard still in his hand. "What's up?"

"I've got runway lights, spotlights for your planes and direction finders, plus a bunch of other stuff you can use for night flying."

"Holy shit, you were serious."

"That Jap sub nearly killed me. The Commander says the same sub sank a merchant ship off California less than ten hours after Pearl Harbor was bombed. You bet I'm serious."

A week later Gaston got a call from Major and met him at the Newport airstrip hangar.

"I thought you might want to check out the new equipment. The guys are having a ball with this stuff. We can now tap into the radio tower, and find our way back if we get lost in fog. We strung the lights along the runway. I'm going up tonight to check them out. You up for a night flight?"

"You bet. Name the time."

"How about 2200? It should be plenty dark by then. We need to give this a good test."

That day word traveled like wildfire across the Coast Guard Station and around town. The closest the town had ever come to runway lights was when ten vehicles lined up along the side of the runway one night when the Governor of the State had arrived late and the town fathers thought he would turn around if they couldn't find the airstrip. It was such a novelty that it seemed like the whole town turned out for the occasion of the lighting of the field.

When Gaston arrived at the airport, a crowd had gathered. Nearly a hundred people were standing along the runway. The runway lights were turning on and off, as they tested how well they marked the landing strip. Major was explaining the procedure to a young volunteer. The volunteer also had a radio and headphones to take instructions from Major as he was coming in.

The hangar had been equipped with a radio tower and antenna for the direction finders to pinpoint their location.

Gaston donned new leather flight gear, including a leather cap and goggles. When he got in the cockpit he noticed the spotlight addition, a metal handle that could move the light in a sweeping arc. In addition, the cockpit radio was operating and he could hear everything Major was saying. "Testing," Gaston said. "Can you hear me, Major?"

"You need to push the button on the side of the headset, if you want to talk to me," Major said. "Check list complete, ready for contact."

The prop man cranked the propeller a quarter turn. "Contact," Major said. He spun the prop and the engine fired. They taxied along the lighted runway. It looked like a well-lit street with the string of lights staked only six inches off the ground. About 300 yards down the runway the biplane lifted off into the night. Gaston looked down to see the runway lights strung out like a string of pearls. They went out and there was nothing but a black void where they had been. He figured they were still testing the system. In another minute they were over the ocean looking at a star studded sky. Gaston flipped the toggle on the spotlight and moved the handle. To his delight he could see a round beam the size of a baseball diamond catching the swells on the ocean. "You see that," he said, tripping the headphone mic. "We have eyes at night."

"Roger, that," Major said. "I'm going to test our Radio Direction Finder."

"Roger," Gaston replied.

Ten minutes into the flight Gaston thought he saw something in the ocean. He keyed the mic. "Did you get a look at that?"

"Negative."

"Circle around. I thought I saw something in the water."

"Roger."

The plane did a sweeping turn and Gaston saw it again. "There it is, can you take it a little lower?"

The plane slid down until the crests of the swells looked like they were going to touch the wheels. "Low enough," Gaston said. "Dead ahead." There it was an I-class Japanese submarine on the surface. "Are you looking at this?" Gaston asked.

"What the shit! Gaston turn out the light, he has a machine gun!"

The warning came too late. Bullets strafed the plane and the fabric of the bottom wing was badly torn. The wind had whipped it into a V-shaped tear that was flapping like a flag in a wind storm. Gaston turned out the light. "Are you okay, Major?"

"I'm okay, but I'm not sure about the plane. I'm heading back." He banked the plane. In the distance Gaston could see the glow of the town from the lights reflecting off the clouds. *Shit, they hadn't implemented blackout instructions for the town, there had been no reason, but there is now,* he thought. As they approached Newport, Major banked to the south and started descending toward the airport. The runway lights were glowing dead ahead. Then everything went black.

"Randy, what the hell happened, I need lights!" Gaston was listening to the one-sided conversation between Major and his ground control. There was nothing but silence on the other end. Major banked the plane and nosed up making a pass to give them time to fix the lights. Again Gaston could see a million stars and a black void where the ocean was below them. The plane circled around toward the city lights again and then headed south to where the airfield was, but there was nothing but black. "I can't take a chance without the runway lights. I can't raise anyone at the hangar. You want to ditch in the ocean or the beach?"

"I don't like either choice. Take it around again, they'll get the lights fixed."

"Sorry, Gaston. I'm having a bitch of a time with the controls. The wing is too far gone. We're going to land this thing or crash, your choice."

"Let's try the sand, I've been in the water and I didn't like it."

"Pretty rocky along here, have you got any ideas?"

"Go south, just south of Seal Rocks is about five miles of flat beach."

Gaston saw a huge patch of fabric rip from the wing. "I'm going to turn on the spotlight and point it forward. Did you get the landing lights installed?"

"Landing lights. Oh, shit, I forgot." He flipped a toggle and they had headlights. They cleared Seal Rock by a hundred feet. They could see waves crashing below. "Where's that beach? We need it now," Major said.

"Hang on, it's coming up."

"Shit, you didn't check the tide tables did you?" Major took the plane away from the cliffs. There wasn't a wide enough stretch to set the plane down safely.

"Don't put it down here," Gaston yelled. "Hop over that hill and set her down."

Major gunned the engine and the plane rose slightly, but not enough to clear the treetops. Gaston heard a loud crack as a wheel snapped a limb from a tall fir.

"We're going down. Hold on!" The plane cleared the hill and dropped rapidly toward the beach.

"Get over those rocks!" Gaston yelled.

Just beyond, the rocks disappeared and a fifty-foot wide stretch of wet sand stretched out. To their left were another fifty feet of loose sand and a high cliff. He was out of options. Major set the wheels on the wet sand and taxied along the surf line. Eventually he turned toward the soft sand and the cliff that bordered it. He didn't want the ocean claiming his plane when the tide came back in. "Lucky at flying, unlucky at love," Major said, turning off the engine.

"You keep this up, I'm going to stop flying with you," Gaston said.

"What do you mean? Lady Luck was with us."

"I've flown with you twice. You fly me to Brookings and I end up freezing my ass off in the ocean and now we're stranded on the beach. I'm beginning to think the only luck you have is bad luck."

"You're going to blame your dunk in the ocean on me? I just saved your ass and you better appreciate it."

Gaston took a deep breath. "I apologize; I guess this is really my fault. Have you got a frequency on your radio that can raise the Coast Guard? I think they could come and rescue us."

"Already done," Major said. "You've gotta admit, it was pretty exciting, though. Made me feel like I was in the Great War again."

The cliff along the beach rose about fifty feet. The outgoing tide had made the beach stretch out about a hundred yards where the plane finally came to a stop. "Here, take this flare and see if you can start a fire in that driftwood over there," Major said, handing Gaston a ten-inch long red stick.

"Are you sure this isn't dynamite," Gaston said, joking.

Major took the flare back from Gaston. "It's a flare, but it sure looks like dynamite. You've just given me an idea." He handed the stick back to Gaston. "On second thought, I'll gather some of the driftwood and we'll build the fire closer to the surf, so they can spot us easier from the highway."

"A fire will feel good, that fog is rolling in pretty fast," Gaston said, touching the flare to a stack of twigs and debris they had gathered. In a few minutes the fire was burning brightly and they moved back because it was too hot for them.

It was over an hour later when a brand new Willy MB, better known as a Jeep, with canvas-covered top and doors pulled to the west side of the Pacific Coast Highway, just south of Seal Rock. Two men got out and stood looking along the beach.

"Does that look like a bonfire to you?" Commander Goodman asked Ensign Pastor.

"It's about a mile away; can't be certain, but it would be in the right spot." Pastor jumped in the driver seat, the Commander got in the passenger seat. "Let's see if we can find access to the beach along here," the Commander said.

"I know a place, but it's a pretty rugged access.'

"Let's go. They didn't say there were any injuries, but we don't know."

Pastor cruised down the highway another half-mile and took a rutted dirt road that wandered through thick brush, Coastal pine and Rhododendron bushes. He stopped at the beach access road. "I'll get out and see if we dare try it," Pastor said, opening the door.

"I'll join you," Goodman said. He removed a flashlight from the glove box and they walked in the beam of the headlights the few feet to the edge of the cliff.

Goodman scanned the terrain. "You call this a road? It looks pretty risky."

"If you want to climb down, I'll take the Jeep." Pastor said. "It might be safer that way."

"I think we should find a better access road. We go down *that*, we'll have to get another rescue crew out of bed tonight. Let's try the beach access at Waldport."

"That's another three miles south."

"It's a better option, don't you think?" the Commander asked.

"Yes, sir."

Major dragged a heavy piece of driftwood to the fire and let it fall. The crash sent embers flying in all directions.

"You planning on being here all night?" Gaston asked, brushing a burning coal from his shoulder.

"No fun having a beach party without a bonfire. This will burn all night, if we need it."

"I want to be in my bunk, not out here tending a fire," Gaston said, frustrated. "We could have walked to Waldport by now."

"You want to walk on a dark beach, no moon and a heavy fog rolling in, be my guest. I'm going to stay with my plane and make sure no one decides it's abandoned and up for salvage."

"We've been here over an hour. There should have been a hundred people here by now."

"I doubt that," Major said. "As far as I know, the Coast Guard is the only one who got my transmission. Technically, we're not lost at sea, just stranded in a sparsely populated stretch of the beach. Worse comes to worse, we will be arrested for being on the beach after dark."

Gaston rolled a log closer to the fire and sat on it. "You and that fellow in Brookings, Talbot, sound like you go back a long ways."

Major sat down on the log next to Gaston. "Back in the day he had the nickname, Crash. I knew him five years before I knew his first name was Talbot. It seemed like he was always experimenting with airplanes, trying new things. He's walked away from more perfect landings than I can count on both hands."

"Perfect landings?" Gaston questioned.

"He calls them perfect landings. We all called them crashes." He laughed. "To Talbot a perfect landing is any that you can walk away from." He picked up a stick and stirred the fire. "Of course there, were a few he didn't walk away from."

"I gathered that," Gaston said. "How about you. How'd you get a handle like Major?"

Major adjusted his feet and played with the stick in his hand, scribbling in the soft sand. "Major was a battlefield commission given to me by my men. It never stuck with the Big Brass. I only made it to Captain, but my men preferred Major and it stuck."

"You fought in the Great War; did you fly?"

"Damn right, I did. Dropped bombs by hand on German convoys while they peppered us with rifle fire. I was shot down twice, once behind enemy lines. Now that's a story..."

"Over here!" Gaston stood up waving.

Major caught the stick on fire and started waving it above his head. The headlights bounced along the surf and then angled straight toward them.

Commander Goodman was the first out of the Jeep. He looked at Gaston and Major. "You boys need a lift?"

"Boy am I glad to see you, sir," Gaston said.

"Major, I have a truck with a hoist on the way. They can load your plane and get it back to the hangar. Ensign Pastor, get on the radio and contact the flatbed and tell them where we are."

"I'd better stick around until they load it," Major said. "I can ride back with them."

"Mr. Carson, I want to hear about this...what do you call it?" the Commander asked.

"Trial flight," Gaston offered.

"Trial flight. What the hell were you thinking, going out at night, and lighting up the airfield like a Christmas tree? There's a war going on and we're supposed to be observing blackout rules after dark."

"I can explain, sir."

"We have the trip back, and I'm all ears." The Commander held the door open for Gaston.

Before getting in, Gaston pointed down the beach, "Looks like your ride is coming Major. I'll be talking to you later." He climbed in the back of the Jeep.

Ensign Pastor was driving, Goodman was in the passenger seat, and Gaston was in the back. They were on their way back to the highway access when Commander Goodman said, "Ensign Pastor, any conversation you hear in this vehicle is classified information and any mention of it to anyone outside of Carson and myself will get you court martialed, do you understand?"

"Yes, sir."

The Commander turned sideways, "Well, Mr. Carson, You need to tell me your story, all of it."

Gaston figured the Commander knew most of the story already. "Where do you want me to start?"

"You can start with your seemingly impulsive desire to get yourself killed. You put a light on an airplane and you are a sitting duck for a submarine. You do realize they can see you long before you'll be able to see them."

"I wanted to be able to spot a sub, so you could send a Coast Guard cutter after it and sink it. I'm concerned that the Japs will think our coastline is not patrolled and they will attempt a landing."

"Really, Mr. Carson? Did it ever occur to you that we have an Army, a Navy and the Coast Guard already concerned about the same thing? I know whoever is directing you is classified, but you have to give me more information. Right now we are stepping on each other's toes. Special assignment or not, you are rapidly overstaying you welcome, and I'm not the only one. The CAP and CD both have complained to me. The last thing we need is a loose cannon running around in the middle of a war. You're smart enough to get my drift."

"Commander, I understand clearly. We spotted a Jap submarine tonight and he fired on us. At least the Commander of that sub knows we know he's here. We caught him by surprise. He's going to think twice before he surfaces next time."

"I'm not angry with the results you got, only in the way you went about it. For instance, if you would have told me you had access to lights for the runway, I could have prevented the disaster we had tonight. You do know the Newport airstrip is under my command, as well as the Port of Newport. It was a civilian operation until we declared war. Under the War Powers Act, the President put it under my command."

"I'm sorry, sir. I didn't realize..."

"Don't be too concerned, I only got the word a week ago myself and haven't had time to put a plan together on how we are going to secure the site and control the traffic. But you will see some changes, mark my words."

"Sir, the runway lights, who turned them out?"

"Nobody. They were wired into the existing fuse box that wasn't equipped to handle the load. Shortly after testing them, every fuse in the hangar blew and the wiring caught on fire. Along with the lights everything else went down. That's why you lost communication and your RDF. You guys were on your own out there. Frankly, I'm surprised you were able to land safely. I hate to think of who would be on my ass if you were killed. The last time you pulled one of your stunts, I got a rash of calls from Washington. Do you blame me for wanting to know what's going on?"

"No, sir."

"Good, I'm glad we got that settled. Now, what can you tell me?"

"Sir, I can tell you that we need to equip our air cover so that they can search for the enemy day and night. That's what I was trying to do. I could use your help in meeting that objective."

"Let me get this straight, you're telling me you have orders to search for Jap subs along our beaches?"

"No sir, not exactly."

"Then what, exactly?"

"Sir, it's complicated."

The Commander sounded frustrated. "I don't give a shit how complicated it is, I need to know what you are doing in areas of my command."

"I'm trying to tell you. The best I can do is let you in on any other plans I have."

"You have to do better than that. I want to know before you even think about doing something on your own again. If it's in the best interest of the war, I'll help you. Anything short of that, I'll throw your ass in the brig and deal with the consequences later. Are we clear?"

"Perfectly, sir."

Chapter 16

A week went by without the incident being mentioned by either Gaston or the Commander. Gaston had only talked to Major once, when he made a trip out to the airport to see how repairs were coming on Major's plane. It looked like it would be another week, before he would attempt another night flight. In the meantime the Commander had requisitioned an electrician to install enough power to upgrade the lighting. Also, Gaston noted, a chain link fence was being erected along the western perimeter of the airport, limiting access to the hangar and runway. In another week there would be a guard shack, a gate and a Coast Guard MP assigned to keep unauthorized people out. *Great*, Gaston thought. *Now I'll have to get permission from the Commander to fly with Major.*

Back at the base, Gaston caught Alice leaving Officer's Quarters for the day. He checked his watch. "You're skipping out a little early. Got a heavy date?"

"What day is it?" Alice said, walking up to him. She adjusted the kelly-green scarf around her neck.

Gaston cocked his head. "St. Patrick's Day?"

Alice pinched him. "What kind of an Irishman are you? You're not wearing green!"

Gaston grabbed his head with both hands in an exaggerated gesture. "Oh, my gosh. Oh, that's right, I'm not Irish."

"I should hit you, Gaston Carson. Everybody is a little Irish, especially on St. Patty's day."

"Well, if the wee lass will forgive me, I'll pick her up in an hour and we'll join the Leprechauns for the best corn beef and cabbage in the country."

"And don't forget the green beer...and, Gaston, find something green to wear, I don't want you embarrassing me. I am Irish, 100% and proud of it."

"I'm 100% American. Okay if I ware red, white and blue?" Gaston kidded.

"Wear green or you'll be wearing black and blue," she chided. "See you at 1800 hrs and don't be late, they tend to run out of corned beef early."

Gaston had completely forgotten about the St. Patrick's Day party. Alice had been working on it for the past several weeks. He'd better find something green in his wardrobe or he'd be the brunt of the ball.

Alice lived in the upstairs apartment of a two-story house that had been modified into a duplex. To get to her house, Gaston needed to drive less than ten minutes inland from the base. When Gaston walked down the stairs of Officer's Quarters, it had been dark for about an hour, but with the blackout restrictions in full force, it was pitch black outside. Added to the darkness was a heavy cloud layer that was dropping a steady stream of rain over everything. With time to spare he left the base, wound through the narrow streets along the bay, and headed upriver. He noticed headlights behind him, but thought little of it. It was still early, but darkness was setting in. The car behind had its headlights covered, allowing only a narrow beam to show through the slit. The car continued to follow him. He stopped before turning onto Yaquina River Road. The vehicle that had been following pulled around and cut him off. Three men, their faces covered and baseball bats in their hands, rushed Gaston before he could react. They pulled him from his car. Two men held him, while a huge man slugged him in the face and body repeatedly. Gaston slumped over and the men let him crumple to the ground. Two men began kicking him.

Gaston, nearly unconscious, heard the men yelling. "That'll teach you, Jap lover."

"Maybe next time you'll think before you start meddling in other people's business."

The big man kicked Gaston one more time and the other men picked up their bats and started hitting him, like they were trying to kill a snake or an unwanted pest.

"That's enough," the huge man said. "We're just teaching him a lesson, not trying to kill him."

Gaston was unconscious, lying motionless on the shoulder of the road. The three men pushed Gaston's car off the road and down a ravine into a mass of blackberry briars.

"That should make him a little harder to find," the big man said, as the car sunk down into the briars and disappeared into the night.

When Gaston didn't arrive on time, Alice became miffed. She had told him to be on time because the food would run out. After waiting half an hour, her anger turned to concern. Maybe he had something come up at the post? She waited an hour more, and not hearing anything decided to call the guard shack at the Coast Guard Station to see if he had left. According to the man on duty, he had left two hours earlier. Now, Alice was very concerned.

She called her sister. "Margaret, I'm worried. Gaston was supposed to pick me up nearly two hours ago and he hasn't shown up. Before you say it's probably nothing, I checked and he left the Coast Guard Station on time, but he never arrived."

"Alice, any number of things could have happened. He could have had a flat tire. You know how bad the tires are, and these roads, I could go on."

"Margaret, please! I know Gaston well enough that he would have found a way to call me. I'm going to go into town and see if I can retrace his route. I thought Thurston might want to know."

"Thurston just came in. We're about to have dinner. I'll put him on."

After listening to Alice's story, Thurston agreed to drive back into town and see if he could find Gaston. "Alice, you drive the route you think he would have taken and wait under the bridge. I'll go to the station and drive the route from that other direction. It'll take me about half an hour to get there."

Alice left her house and drove slowly past the Bay Front shops. The rain was coming down in torrents, and the wind was beginning to pick up. She could smell the fish processing plant as she eased her car along the narrow street. She had rolled her windows down so she could see and the rain was blowing into the car. There were very few lights. She passed a tavern and saw two men arguing out front. She could hear the bark of sea lions as they gathered around the fishing boats hoping to get a free meal from the fish filleting station, one of the few activities that were still going on in spite of the war. Her route took her under the Yaquina Bay Bridge where she waited for her brother-in-law. Parked below the bridge, she was sheltered from the rain. While she waited she took a towel from the trunk of her car and started wiping down the leather seats and the inside windows. Everything was soaking wet, including her. *I don't know why I'm doing this,* she thought, *it will all get wet again*, but she decided it was better to be doing something. She couldn't just sit. In about fifteen minutes Thurston showed up as promised.

"Any luck?" Thurston asked.

"I traced the route I think he would have traveled, but there are several others he could have taken. I'm going to drive them all. It's so dark out you could easily miss him."

"He's driving a motor pool car. I think I would recognize it."

"Look on the side of the road, he may have driven off. If he did, he'll be almost impossible to find in the dark."

Thurston drove the route Alice had driven, but in the opposite direction. Alice took a route that went farther north and then turned inland. If Gaston had to do some late shopping he may have gone that way. They agreed to meet under the bridge after the next loop if they didn't find anything. If they didn't show up, then they would know the other had found him. Alice drove her loop, came back through the Bay Front, passed the smelly fish processing plant and stopped in the shelter under the bridge. The wind had continued to pick up and was flying sideways past her headlights. She waited an anxious few minutes until Thurston showed up again. Neither had seen any evidence of Gaston.

"Were you and Gaston headed for the USO dance?" Thurston asked. Alice started crying. She nodded. Her hair was stringy and dripping wet. Her mascara was running in streaks down her face. "Park your car and come with me. We should be able to organize a search party from there."

On the way to the USO Alice tried to straighten out her hair. She removed a compact from her purse and a handkerchief and started wiping her face.

Thurston was putting together a plan in his head. He knew there would be many eager young bodies willing to help, and he wanted to get the most mileage he could out of them.

Chapter 17

Gaston was soaked to skin when he awoke, disoriented and shivering. He tried to get up, but stumbled and fell back down. He rolled over to his side and tried to get up on one knee. He slipped again, and this time when he fell he hit the edge of the gravel shoulder, and rolled down the ravine. He passed out again.

When Commander Goodman showed up at the St. Patrick's Day dance he noticed nearly half of the room was under his command. The men looked nervous. The Commander rarely showed up for such events. The women, mostly young girls who attended the local high school, waitresses, local shopkeepers, bartenders and secretaries, went right on dancing to the band, even though the men cleared the floor immediately.

Without a word being said, they sensed something was wrong. They saw the Commander go to the stage and the band stopped playing.

Goodman took the mic from the woman singer and spoke into it. "At ease, gentlemen. I'm sorry to interrupt your dance, but I could use some help. Many of you know Mr. Carson. You may know him as Gaston. He has gone missing, and we haven't a clue as to where or why. Has anyone seen him this evening?"

No one responded. He motioned for Alice to join him on stage. "Alice is the secretary at Officer's Quarters at the Coast Guard Station. Mr. Carson was supposed to pick her up and bring her here to join you. The route from her house to where Gaston is known to have left the base is three...four miles at the most. Alice and I have driven it twice tonight and haven't seen any evidence he was there, but you all know it's raining like hell, and it's darker than a Japs asshole out there."

The crowd laughed. "I need volunteers to walk the route with flashlights in an organized fashion. If he's out there and he's hurt, he could be in serious trouble. Who wants to help?"

Nearly all the men in attendance came forward. They were divided into three groups, about fifteen men in each group. The Commander called the base and requisitioned fifty flashlights with fresh dry cell batteries to be brought to the Grange. Alice met with each group and explained on a map the three possible routes Gaston could have traveled. By midnight the Bay Front and the outskirts of Newport looked like it had been invaded by a swarm of fireflies. People in houses along the streets came to their porches and asked what was going on. Some of them grabbed their rain gear and joined in. Alice walked the route she had originally driven, this time with a flashlight in hand. She scanned the areas where Gaston could have driven off the road. When she came to Yaquina River Road, she scanned the ravine with her flashlight. She saw a red flash, and scanned the beam on it again. She grabbed the man next to her. "Right there, is that a taillight lens?" The man shined his light beside hers. "Could be, people push abandoned cars into the blackberries to get rid of them." He started to move away.

"Wait just a minute. You need to check it out." Alice was furious that he would dismiss such a possible clue.

"You want me to go down there? Lady, you're nuts. That would be suicide this time of night, in this rain, without the proper gear. Most likely an abandoned car."

"Either you're going down there or I am."

The man thought it over for a minute. "Hey, we may have found something!" he yelled. "Someone fetch a rope."

Immediately there were fifteen flashlights scouring the brush from the side of the road. "There's only one way we're going to find out if it's an abandoned car or Gaston," Alice said. "Someone has to climb down there."

"Those are blackberry vines," someone said. "They have thorns enough to cut you to pieces."

"I get it. It isn't going to be pleasant, but we need to check it out." Alice was emphatic. "Will someone see if they can find Commander Goodman? Maybe he'll have some resources he can lend."

"I'm a volunteer fireman," a young man said. He was dressed in a rain slicker and wore a pair of knee-high rubber boots. "Our station has equipment that could help."

"Good," Alice said, "see if you can get us some rope and whatever clothing someone would need to go into that mess."

Goodman showed up. He was drenched. "What have you found, Alice?"

"This is the most likely route Gaston would have taken and we found what we think is a taillight of a car." She shined her light down and stopped on the faint red spot. She noticed her flashlight was getting dimmer by the minute.

"We need to get some better equipment over here, if we're going to check this out," Goodman said.

"I take it the other two parties didn't find anything," Alice said.

"Nothing," he said. "I'm going to go back to the base and get some better equipment. We need auxiliary lights and a winch so we can let someone down and pull that car out if we need to."

"There's a volunteer fireman going for some equipment. Would that help?"

The crowd moved back from the shoulder when they heard the fire engine's siren. The truck was massive and the young man driving stopped alongside the road. He got out. "If you fellas can shine your light down there I'll let out some fire hose and climb down. At least we'll know if it's been there awhile or is the rig we're looking for."

He let out some hose from a reel on the side of the truck. He grabbed the large brass nozzle and hung onto it. "Someone get up there and only let out enough for me to get down there." He went over the edge and slowly descended into the dark. "We need more light," he shouted up. Those holding flashlights pounded them on their hand trying to keep them lit. "There are some lamps in the toolbox. I can't see a thing, if you don't do something." He stopped descending and leaned back with his feet resting on wet grass, just short of the thorny briers. His canvas coveralls would protect him from the thorns, if he had to go deeper into the vines.

Someone lit a gas lantern and lowered it down to the fireman on a rope. When the lamp hit a wet leaf or a clump of grass it would sizzle and send up a plume of steam. The white-hot mantel cast a bright light, making the darkness disappear in its small circle, but the area around it seemed to be even darker than before.

The fireman grabbed the lantern by the handle and looked around. "Keep the rope on the lantern tight, I've got to go farther down." The lantern glowed like a white flare, blinding those who were trying to see past it. Then they saw the light rise up and illuminate the scene. The fireman was standing on the rear bumper of the car. He maneuvered the lantern trying to see inside. "I think this is the car," he yelled. "It has a government license plate." He removed a hand ax from a tool belt on his waist. With the lantern in one hand and the ax in the other, he smashed the rear window, and lowered the lantern inside. He smelled gasoline. "Get me out of here," he screamed dropping the lantern and grabbing the fire hose with both hands. The car burst into flames. The fireman frantically climbed the hose, trying to free himself from the blackberry thorns. It seemed they were grabbing him, holding him in place. Flames licked at his boots, as he yelled for help. Two men cranked the hose reel and the fireman started to move away from the flames. At the top of the ravine, as the fireman scrambled to get footing, the car exploded, sending a huge fireball into the sky. Glass and metal fragments showered the area. The flash lit up the ravine. The fireman was still holding onto the hose searching for a foothold when the blast propelled him into the crowd. He landed on half a dozen other people, who were knocked off their feet. The scene was total chaos. Alice and the Commander received flash burns from the explosion, but were otherwise uninjured. Others were not so lucky. Shrapnel from the explosion hit some people, knocking them unconscious, cutting them and breaking limbs. People were down all over the road.

Alice broke down, hysterical. She pounded the Commander's chest. "How could this happen? Every time, this happens!"

The Commander pulled her to him. She had lost her fiancé to an automobile accident two years earlier. That was what brought her to the West Coast to be near her sister. To Alice it was all too clear. It was happening again.

He held her tightly to him. "We don't know that he was in the car. Don't give up. I need you to help me." He patted her back and her hysteria melted to sobs. "Come on; let's finish what we came to do." His voice was calm, even though his face was burning from the blast. The blowing rain actually felt comforting to him right now.

A vehicle pulling a huge spotlight on a trailer arrived from the base. The Commander directed it to be placed at the edge of the ravine. The spotlight was originally designed to help with searches at sea, but was easily adapted and shined brightly into the ravine. The powerful beam cut through the driving rain and made the gully light up as if it were the middle of a summer day. What they saw was the mangled hull of the car, still burning. Several small fires were around, but there was little concern, because everything was so wet.

An ambulance pulled up and emergency technicians started checking the injured. They loaded the fireman on a stretcher.

"Don't take me yet, I need to speak to the Commander," the fireman said.

The Commander and Alice were summoned. They saw the fireman covered with black, charred residue, head to toe.

"Commander, I saw him. He's only a quarter way down the ravine," the fireman said.

"He wasn't in the car?" Alice asked,

"He's on the ground; I saw him just before the explosion."

Alice screamed, "He's down there!" She stood pointing down the ravine. "Shine the light down there. Everybody, Gaston is somewhere on the slope, he wasn't in the car." She was screaming out orders in a steady stream of commands. She ran to the edge where the fire hose was still dangling over the edge. She grabbed the hose. "I'm going down," she said.

"Alice, let one of the men do that," the Commander yelled, but she was already over the edge.

Alice hung onto the hose with both hands and dug the toes of her high heels into the wet grassy slope to keep her stable. Fire was still burning in places, but the rain had put most of them out. She looked to the left and then to her right. She saw an unusual lump; the color of green didn't quite fit the rest of the terrain. She looked at it closely. It was Gaston. She remembered telling him he needed to wear green. His overcoat was torn open and she could see a pale green sweater. He was too far away for her to reach. He wasn't moving. "He's down here and he's going to need an ambulance. Pull me up, and get him help!"

Chapter 18

Gaston was suffering from hypothermia and multiple injuries, a concussion, several broken ribs, and so many bruises the nurse stopped counting. "I can't believe this was all from the automobile accident," the doctor said. "He's lucky to be alive."

"When do you expect him to be awake enough to talk?" the Commander asked.

"I gave him some morphine to ease the pain. He's going to be out of it for a few days. If you want, I'll have a nurse call you when he's able to talk."

"That'll be fine. I'll leave my number at the desk." The Commander was tired. He was still soaking wet and wanted to go home, take a hot shower and get some much needed sleep. He looked over at Alice, who was equally tired, wet, and miserable. "We need to go. I can drop you off at your car, or you can come home with me."

"You go ahead. I want to stay with Gaston for awhile."

"Alice, you're exhausted, and in need of sleep. You heard the doctor. He won't be awake for at least a day."

"Okay, Thurston, but can I have a few days off?" She had no intention of leaving Gaston alone. She let the Commander drop her off at her car, went home, cleaned up, and returned to the hospital.

Back at the hospital, she inquired about the fireman that was admitted. "He was a lucky man," the night nurse said. "He was treated for minor burns and released."

"You don't happen to know his name; I'd like to send him a 'Thank You' card. He risked his life to save Mr. Carson."

"I can't give out that information, but you know where he works, I'll bet they'll make sure he gets it."

"Thank you. May I go in and sit with Mr. Carson. He was on his way to pick me up when he had the accident."

"Are you family, miss?"

"Alice Fitzpatrick. We were dating."

"I guess I can make an exception considering you are...sweethearts. Like I told the Commander, he won't be holding any conversations soon."

*****

I-26 was a B1-type submarine commanded by Yokota Minoru. It had been commissioned November 6, 1941, almost one month to the day before the attack on Pearl Harbor. As soon as the submarine had completed her maiden voyage, Commander Minoru opened his orders and headed for the West Coast of the United States. On December 6, while his countrymen were preparing to attack Pearl Harbor, he had another target in his periscope. The problem was the war hadn't officially started, so he waited 350 miles off the coast of California with the lumber freighter *Cynthia Olson* in his sights. His orders were to wait until 0300 Tokyo time before attacking. At 0330 Tokyo time or 0800 Hawaiian time he surfaced and fired a warning shot over the bow of the merchant ship. The crew of the *Cynthia Olson* radioed they were being attacked and the crew abandoned ship in lifeboats. Commander Minoru proceeded to shell the ship with its 16 cm deck gun until the *Cynthia Olson* slipped beneath the sea. The distress call was heard by the steamship *Lauraline*, but the simultaneous attack on Pearl Harbor was getting all the attention, and no one came to the crew's rescue. The entire crew of the *Cynthia Olson* perished at sea.

Learning that the aircraft carrier, *USS Lexington*, was not in Pearl Harbor during the attack, Commander Minoru was given orders to search the Pacific for her. He finally gave up and headed for the Strait of Juan de Fuca for a scheduled bombardment of the American coastal cities. On Christmas Eve 1941, he raised his periscope and scanned the city of Seattle, but the air traffic was constant and the surface patrols frequent. Commander Minoru thought an attack would be too risky. He headed south to carry out information gathering missions along the Oregon Coast. His chance encounters with fishing boats and the surprise spotting by a night flying biplane on that night in late February, caught him completely off guard. Needing repairs, he headed to Japan, putting in at Yokosuka dry dock. He was there on April 18 when Doolittle made his famous raid. *I-26* escaped damage from the raid, and with the latest upgrades, was sent back out to patrol the coasts of Washington and Oregon. For Commander Minoru, it had been a quiet war.

*****

Major knocked on the hospital door to Gaston's room. "I see you are doing much better. Guess you won't need these." He held a couple of magazines up. "You getting out?"

"As soon as Alice gets here." He hobbled over to the table where Major had dropped the magazines. He picked them up. "I'm going to her place to recuperate, and in a week or so, I'll be back as good as new, at least that's what they tell me."

"It'll be good to have you back. We have the airport rewired and have been making night flights for the past week. Haven't seen a thing. I'm thinking I need you as a spotter, you're like a Jap sub magnet."

Gaston laughed. "Did they get the RDF working?"

"Radio Direction Finders are working swell. I could find my way back blindfolded."

"I'll take your word for it. Give me a couple of weeks and I'll be glad to take another ride with you."

There was a knock on the door casing and Alice walked in. "Hey Major, you're not trying to talk this guy into doing anything dangerous."

Major raised his hands. "Not me, I wouldn't do anything like that."

"Come on, Gaston." She slipped her arm in his. "Stay away from that guy." She grinned at Major. "At least for a little while."

A week went by, then two. Gaston was growing stronger every day, but he was going nuts sitting around nursing his wounds. He took up running to get his strength back and before long was running from Alice's apartment to the Coast Guard Station, having lunch with Alice and running back.

On April 18, he arrived at the base early and went to see the Commander. "Sir, I thought I'd tell you. I'm ready to return."

"Close the door, Mr. Carson. Remember our talk before you had the accident?"

"Of course, sir. You asked to be brought up to date on what I was doing."

"When you return to duty, what is your plan?"

"Well, I thought I might catch up on some of the sightings that have come in. Major said he'd like to have me join him on a night run along the coast. He thinks he has the bugs worked out of the system."

"Good," the Commander said. "You may want to check this one out." He handed Gaston a telegram. "Just let me know if you decide to investigate it."

Gaston took the telegram, folded it, and put it in the breast pocket of his shirt. "Sir, did you ever figure out what happened the night I got hurt?"

"What do you mean, you were in an auto accident? Do you remember why you ran off the road?"

"Things have been coming back to me. I haven't told anyone else, but I was attacked by three men. I was driving through town and a car was following me. I remember, it had its headlights taped off, per blackout instructions. I stopped before turning onto Yaquina River Road. Before I knew what was happening, I was pulled from the car, and they beat the crap out of me. The last thing I remember, I was on the ground and these guys were smacking me with baseball bats."

"You need to talk to the sheriff. If you were attacked, it would be as a civilian. I'll call Sam, if you want."

"So much time has passed, I doubt he could do anything, and their faces were covered. I guess I'll drop it."

"That does explain one thing," the Commander said. "You know the fireman who first spotted you?"

Gaston shook his head. "I heard the story, but I can't remember him."

"Well, he said all the windows were rolled up and intact before the car blew up. That fits with your story. You couldn't have been thrown from the car. You think they threw you into the ravine before pushing the car over the edge?"

"I don't have a memory of that. You wouldn't happen to still have the car, would you?"

"It's in the motor pool on a trailer. I've been waiting for you to get well, so you could make one of your midnight calls and get it replaced."

Gaston grimaced. "I'm not sure it works that way, but I'll try. You don't mind if I take a look at it?"

"Go ahead, there's not much to look at but burned, twisted sheet metal. It was a total loss. You're not getting another one until this one is replaced."

"Yes, sir." Gaston left and ran over to the motor pool. He checked his wristwatch. He'd have just enough time to check it out, before meeting Alice.

Gaston found the car as the Commander had said. It was in several pieces, all piled on a trailer parked in the corner of the building. He looked through the wreckage, but didn't find the piece he was looking for. He thought a moment, then left to meet Alice for lunch.

"What's the occasion, you want to take me to a restaurant?" Alice asked, handing Gaston the keys to her car. "With gas rationing, we can't go far. I need enough to get to work."

"I thought we could stop by the place where I had the accident, then we could go to the *Seafood Grotto*."

"Wait a minute. You want me to take you to where you were almost killed? What is this, some kind of therapy?"

"Just a hunch. I went by the motor pool to see the wreckage and a piece of the car was missing."

"Gaston Carson, you are beginning to worry me."

Gaston stopped the car and pulled the emergency brake. "I won't be a minute." He got out and stood on the edge of the road looking down the ravine. The blast had blown all the leaves off the berry vines, and what remained was a patch of burned bushes without leaves. Then a hundred feet away from him, almost on the edge of the road, he saw the trunk lid. It was completely intact and had no sign of being burned. He walked down the road, reached down and picked up the heavy piece of gray painted metal from the shoulder.

"You're not going to put that dirty old thing in my car," Alice said.

"How else am I going to get it back to the base?"

"I don't understand why you want it." She removed a towel from the trunk of her car. "Make sure you don't get the upholstery dirty."

"I'll tell you why I need it over lunch." He covered the piece with the towel and carefully slid it behind the driver's seat.

They both ordered coffee and enjoyed a cup before ordering their meal. Gaston ordered a fresh baked salmon fillet, and Alice ordered a halibut steak. They both came with mashed potatoes and a choice of vegetables, green beans or broccoli. Both ordered the green beans.

"You remember," Gaston said, "I told you I was attacked by some men on the night I ended up in the ravine?" He continued without giving her a chance to respond. He knew she thought he was delusional. "I've been racking my brain trying to figure out how I could prove it."

"That's what that thing is going to do?" Alice seemed amused.

"If I'm right, whoever attacked me pushed my car over the cliff. They would have left handprints and fingerprints all over the trunk lid."

"But it's been over a month and it's been raining every day. You have to be the most optimistic man in the world, if you think finger prints survived all that."

"You may be surprised. You know how dirty your car gets in the winter. That road grime surface is as good as a fingerprint kit to my way of thinking."

"Okay, you seem to have an answer for everything. Once you lift fingerprints, how are you going to find the guys who did this? It's not like you can fingerprint everyone in town."

"Maybe not, but I know where I can get a good start."

"Somehow, I don't think you're going to let this rest until you get your answers."

"Now, you're beginning to understand me," Gaston said, smiling.

That night Gaston made a midnight call to the President, the first in over a month. He already knew the White House had checked on his condition. Not having anything to share, he had let the calls to the White House go. He made his request for a car replacement, let the President know there was a growing concern for the safety of the Japanese Americans and that he was on top of the investigation on who had attacked him. The President requested, he contact Frank Billings at the Portland office of the FBI and seek their help in solving who his attackers were.

The next day Commander Goodman received a Western Union wire transfer for $928, the cost of the car Gaston had wrecked.

Gaston met up with Major at the *Blue Whale*. He grabbed him and his wife and pulled them off in a corner. What he requested caused Major to break out laughing, and Sarah to curse. "I'm running a bar, not a police station. You want fingerprints; you'll have to collect them yourself."

"Fair enough. What time do they usually come in here?"

"Almost every night around seven," Sarah said.

"Plan on me hanging out in your kitchen," Gaston said.

Sarah seemed genuinely perturbed, but finally agreed to help. "If you get Major to hang out with you, I'll collect the glasses for you."

"Major, how about it?"

"Hold on a minute. If I'm hanging out in the kitchen everyone will suspect something. I think this clandestine operation needs to take place without raising suspicion."

Sarah glared at Gaston. "You're collecting your own glasses and you better not break any."

"Dually noted," Gaston said.

*****

The *Blue Whale* was one of the more popular bars for the younger crowd along the Central Oregon Coast, but with the war and young men enlisting, it became an after-work hangout for those who were not eligible for the draft and older men who worked in timber and fishing. Both timber and fishing were considered essential to the war effort, but those ineligible for the draft were a different story. Some were petty thieves, criminals of varying degrees or just incompetent. There also was an element of society that had medical issues including mental issues. All came in contact with one another at the *Blue Whale*. Saturday nights were especially rowdy, and when you mixed in the members from the Coast Guard and a few local Indians, it sometimes became a dangerous place to hang out. However, no one messed with Major or Sarah. They had the power to ban you from the premises forever, if they wished.

The back corner of the *Blue Whale* had two pocket pool tables and a large billiard table. Often teams from other taverns would compete in a pool league or tournament. On the night that Gaston chose to collect his fingerprints, a pool tournament was underway. Toledo Mill Workers were pitted against the *Blue Whale*, of which Major was a player.

It was an eclectic mix of people, all ages and backgrounds. Fights had broken out in the past and Major was on scene to make certain those in from the neighboring town would be on their best behavior. It was customary to consume many pitchers of beer, the reason the taverns sponsored the events in the first place.

When Gaston came through the back door into the kitchen, Sarah told him the tournament was underway, and his primary suspect, Allen Rich, was present and drinking. With Allen were his minions, also suspects in Gaston's eyes. Gaston waited, peeking through the door. It was time for his plan to unfold.

Major brought a pitcher of beer to the table where Allen was sitting, waiting for his next turn. "Allen, you boys are playing so well, I thought I'd buy you one on the house." As soon as Allen got up, Major set the pitcher down on the table and accidently bumped the pitcher against Allen's glass of beer. "What the hell, Major," Allen said. "You going to buy me another one?"

"Sorry, man. I'll clean this up and bring another round for the table." The two other men got up and moved out of the way to avoid getting wet. Major wiped the table down with a bar towel and picked up the glasses, being careful to preserve the prints. He replaced all the glasses with clean ones.

"What the hell, my beer was getting stale, anyway," one of the men said. "I think we're going to need two pitchers, since you're buying."

Major, still apologizing, gritted his teeth and nodded. He carried the tray back to the kitchen. "Damn, I'm good. I got the whole table in one try." He handed the tray to Gaston. "Better leave through the back door."

Gaston had brought clean paper bags to wrap the glasses. He was out the back door and nearing his new motor pool car when one of the men who had been sitting at the table with Allen approached him. Gaston turned just as the man was taking a swing at him. Instinctively, Gaston held up the bag for protection. The attacker smashed his fist into the bag of glasses breaking them and causing the bag and shards of broken glass to scatter across the ground.

Not waiting for the man to take another shot at him, Gaston cold-cocked him with a single punch. "Damn, you sure have a way of screwing up a man's plans," he said, staring at the broken bag. The man was sprawled out on the wet sand of the parking area, his fist bleeding. Gaston picked up the broken bag, carefully gathered the glass fragments, and put them back in the bag, loosely wrapping them again. He made a note of the man's face. He was certain he was one of those who attacked him, but he was away from the table where Major had gathered the glasses. *Maybe he ducked out for a smoke,* Gaston thought. He put the bag of glass fragments on the seat, went back into the kitchen, got a clean glass from the cupboard, brought it out, and wrapped the hand of the unconscious man around it. He carefully placed it on the seat next to the other specimens. He then slapped the man on the face. "Hey, wake up. You need to be alert when the FBI comes for you."

FBI Agent, Frank Billings, had arrived earlier that afternoon and had processed the trunk lid for prints. There were four sets of prints on the surface of the paint. One was from Gaston, the other three were unknown. Gaston was amazed at the quality of the photographs Agent Billings had developed using the portable photo lab he had set up in the office of the motor pool. Now, Gaston hoped he could solve the rest of the puzzle. He handed the wet and torn bag full of glass fragments to the agent.

"I expected whole specimens," Billings said.

Gaston handed him the unbroken glass. "I saved one." He left the agent to his work.

The next morning Gaston caught up with Agent Billings in his makeshift dark room. "Don't come in," Billings said. "I'll be done in a minute." When Billings emerged from his darkroom, he had a smile on his face. "I'll show you what we got. I can have the local police pick up the men."

"Three of them," Gaston said.

"No, all four. We had evidence from a hate crime against a businessman a while back. All four of the men appear to be involved in that one, too."

"He didn't happen to be a Japanese American shop owner?"

"He was." Billings pulled several pictures that had been enlarged and put them side by side. "We got perfect matches, only we won't be able to put names to them until we pick these guys up."

"I think at least one of them was involved in a murder," Gaston said.

"Now that's quite an accusation," Billing said. "I hope you have proof."

"How about an eyewitness?"

"You?"

"No, a school teacher from Toledo. The man who was murdered was Terry Nakamura, a second generation American of Japanese ancestry."

Billings shook his head. "All unusual deaths of Asian Americans are being reported to our office. I already checked into the Nakamura case. Suicide, according to the sheriff's office."

Gaston grabbed his arm. "You need to talk to the teacher. I spoke with him the day before Nakamura was found hanging. He told me the man was hung in Toledo by several men, and we found him hanging in Newport. Doesn't that sound strange enough to see if these guys are involved?"

"How do you explain the sheriff's report?"

"You may want to look into him, also. I understand he and Allen Rich are pretty close. If people can't go to the sheriff, what's next?" Gaston let go of Billing's arm. "We've got a pretty good brig on the base here. If you want, I'll check with the Commander and see if he can supply some MPs to help with the arrest."

"I thought this was a boondoggle. I had plans to spend tomorrow checking out the scenery."

"It's better in the summertime, anyway," Gaston said.

Six MPs, Gaston and Billings raided the *Blue Whale*. Another raid occurred at the same time in Toledo. Gaston had called Fairbanks and given him a heads-up about the raid. He was there with the *Newport Times* photographer. "I can't wait to see the the front page in the morning," he said. "This is a pretty big scoop for this town."

"Thanks, Gaston. Do you want to give me your take on this?"

"Sorry," Gaston said. "I may be called as a witness, and I don't want to compromise my testimony. I'm sure you'll get a pretty colorful take from Major, though. He's right over there." He pointed to the tall man.

"Everybody knows Major," Fairbanks said.

Chapter 19

April 27, 1942

Gaston had scheduled another trip to Westminster Bay. The *Guppy* had had another encounter with a submarine, and this story was more unbelievable than the first. Gaston packed a duffle bag of clothes and a brand new Argus AF 35 mm camera. The camera came with the latest autofocus technology and a leather case with shoulder strap. This time he didn't want to be caught with his pants down, if they could find the submarine again. Of course, the whole thing could be a hoax. Mitchell Williams sure did like free beer, but if this story was true, it could change the way they would be fighting the war in the Northwest.

As he cruised down the highway he noticed traffic was much lighter than it had been. He met the occasional log truck, but not many cars. The new gas rationing was having the desired effect.

He paid particular attention to the terrain when he got to Seal Rocks. He stopped and took a picture. Looking at the huge rocks and the number of them strung out along the beach, he wondered how Major had missed crashing into them. As he continued south, he tried to picture where they had actually landed. Between the highway and the beach were a few hundred feet of trees and undergrowth. He couldn't see the ocean. He decided, on another trip he might return to the scene of the landing and determine just how lucky they were, but for now he had a sub sighting to investigate.

As he started to climb the steep, winding road at Cape Perpetua, it started to rain. He climbed into the clouds and was in fog so thick he slowed to a crawl. It was daylight, but the sharp turns and the sheer drop off into the ocean made it a scary trip in perfect weather. Gaston slowed, taking extra caution. He wasn't about to miss his appointment in Westminster Bay because of a reckless move. He was in the dense fog for ten minutes before dropping down the other side into steady rain again.

Next time he would consider asking Major to fly him. From his association with Major he had found out most of the small towns along the coast had dirt runways that would accommodate the short takeoff and landing of a biwing. "You're becoming spoiled with the luxuries of life," he said, breaking the silence.

As he entered Winchester Bay, he went straight to Mable's and inquired about a room. He then drove to the tavern where he was to meet Mitchell Williams. J.P. was at the bar and walked over and greeted him. "Good to see you, old man," Gaston said, "you're still alive?"

"Buy me a beer and I'll tell you all about Mitch's latest encounter. Not that I believe him, though. That lad's got a fisherman's imagination."

"I'll buy you a beer, but I think I want to hear the story directly from Mitch." Gaston checked his watch. He hoped Mitch would be there soon. It was already beginning to turn dark outside. Gaston ordered a beer and caught up on the latest gossip. Three Japanese families were forced to sell out and move for fear of their lives. One of the lumber company owners was offering to buy out Japanese land owners for the timber—at a discounted price, of course.

Gaston tried to keep a neutral face, but inside he was becoming very troubled. What he had witnessed first hand in the Newport area appeared to be widespread.

"It's a damn shame those Japs are holed up on those islands off Alaska," J.P. said, setting down his empty mug. "When I was younger, we would have got a bunch of us together and given them a run for their money."

"There ain't nothing but frozen ground up there, anyway. What do you suppose they want with it?" the man next to J.P. said. He had a long face covered with white stubble and no front teeth.

J.P. glanced at Gaston, then at the bartender. "My generous friend is going to buy me a refill." He turned to the toothless man. "You ain't got a brain in your head, if you don't know the answer to that. Them there Japs want to prevent us from using those islands to launch an attack on the Jap mainland. I heard that on the radio."

Gaston was amazed that J.P. was away from the bar long enough to listen to the radio, much less, sober enough to understand the news. He had heard exactly the same thing, and it was precisely the reason the US was preparing to regain the islands.

Mitch came through the door wearing his rain slicker over canvas coveralls and rubber boots. He noticed Gaston right away, broke into a wide grin, and stated the obvious, "Gaston, you made it all the way down here again."

"You left a message at the Coast Guard Station. I thought it warranted a trip. Grab a beer and let's go somewhere we can talk in private."

"You be that way," J.P. said. "Long as you're buying, I can take a hint."

"Manny, have you got coffee on? I'd like a cup and a beer for Mitch."

"Ahem." J.P. held up his mug for Gaston to see.

"And one for, J.P. I should buy stock in this place, as much as it costs me every time I come in." He found a table in a dark corner and pulled out a chair for Mitch.

As soon as Gaston had his coffee and Mitch took the first drink of his beer, Gaston pulled out his notebook. "You're a pretty good artist. Draw a picture of what you saw."

"It was dark, but I could make out some details 'cause the sub had lights on it. Strangest thing I ever saw, an airplane launching from a submarine."

"You're sure it was an airplane?" Gaston watched as the sketch took shape. *This is one I need to see for myself,* he thought. *I doubt the President himself will believe it.*

The next day he played fisherman again, and spent a fruitless day on the *Guppy.* When they came back in, he drove back north to the Coast Guard Station, not certain he should include the incident in his call to the White House. *Was it a real sighting, or the overactive imagination of a teenager craving attention?*

*****

On March 22, 1778, Captain James Cook encountered a small opening along the westernmost part of what is now the state of Washington. He named the point of land to the north of *Cape Flattery*. In 1857 a lighthouse was constructed on the nearby island of Tatoosh. On June 20, 1942 the Japanese submarine *I-25* rose to periscope depth and viewed the two bright flashes every twenty seconds from the lighthouse. Commander Meiji Tagami was under orders to search for ships that may be headed to Attu and Kiska Islands in the Aleutian chain which the Japanese had invaded and now occupied. Just after midnight, approximately seventy miles off the cape, the *I-25* encountered the *SS Fort Camosun,* a newly built, coal fired freighter on her maiden voyage from Victoria to England. The freighter was laden down with plywood, lead, zinc and other materials to aid the war effort in Europe. Again Commander Tagami brought the submarine up to periscope depth, checked his range, and fired a torpedo striking the freighter. The Commander then surfaced and began shelling the disabled vessel. The *SS Fort Camosun* was still afloat, but low in the water. Commander Tagami assured himself the freighter was sinking and left the scene before the distress calls were answered.

The crew abandoned the ship, not knowing that the cargo of plywood was providing enough buoyancy to keep the ship afloat. The Royal Canadian Navy corvette *Quesnel* heard the distress call of *SS Fort Camosun* and arrived on the scene six hours later. No lives were lost and the *SS Fort Camosun* was eventually towed to Seattle, where it was repaired and put back into service.

At the same time *I-26*, under the command of Yokota Minoru was operating to the north, off the coast of Vancouver Island. Off Estevan Point, Commander Minoru brought his submarine to the surface and started shelling the lighthouse. Gaston heard news of the two events the next day and contacted Goodman.

Commander Thurston Goodman's office was modestly decorated in a nautical theme. The many citations the Commander had received in his twelve years of service in the Coast Guard were displayed on the wall behind his desk. Throughout the office were photographs of ships he had captained, and crew members who had served with him. On his desk was a studio picture taken with his wife, son, and daughter, and the scrimshaw carving he had received for Christmas. Tensions were high with the latest news of submarine attacks.

"What do you think, Commander, are the Japs bringing the war to the mainland?" Gaston asked.

"This one's got me puzzled. Sinking merchant ships is one thing, but what's the reason for shelling a lighthouse? Seems like a waste of ammunition to me."

"I've had this theory," Gaston said, from his seat across the desk from the Commander. "We know there are at least two submarines, there may be more, but it hardly makes an invasion force. I think they're trying to scare the population into demanding protection. How many armed forces would have to be shifted to the coastline to make certain the mainland wasn't invaded?"

The Commander packed some Red Chief tobacco into his pipe and lit it. He drew in a deep breath and exhaled, filling the room with the aroma of fresh tobacco. He leaned back and watched the blue cloud rise over his head. "Other than the big cities, Seattle, San Francisco and Los Angeles, the entire coast is nearly unpopulated. We have all kinds of forces patrolling the coastline in populated areas. I could buy into your theory. It is so sparsely populated between the cities; it would take a hundred soldiers to every citizen to secure the entire coastline. That would take a huge force from the rest of the war."

"We're thinking alike, but how do we keep the public from panicking?"

"We could inform the public. Tell them what the Japs are trying to do," the Commander said.

"I thought of that, sir, but the first shell that explodes in someone's backyard is going to cause all hell to break loose. At that point, I doubt anyone will care what the Japs are trying to do, and they will have been successful."

"Then we have to find another way."

"I agree. Certainly the sightings we've had so far have been questionable enough. The papers haven't given them much credence."

"I guess we can deny, deny, deny." The Commander took another long drag on his pipe.

"I've got to make a call, Commander. I'll check in with you again tomorrow."

*****

Commander Meiji Tagami ordered his men to observe silence as the *I-25* hovered just above the ocean floor off the coast of Astoria, Oregon. He had been patiently waiting for several hours. Japanese intelligence had identified a submarine base inside the mouth of the Columbia River. He had devised a plan and was about to carry it out. He felt his heart race as the returning fishing fleet passed overhead. "Now," he said. He brought the submarine off the bottom and glided along, shadowing the fleet of fishing boats. They were heading through the minefield at the mouth of the Columbia. This tactic would make certain he would avoid the mines. As he silently maneuvered under the fleet, his crew remained quiet. Sweat dripped from Tagama's face. He wiped his brow. "All clear," he said, "set it on the bottom." He was safely inside the minefield. He had carefully documented the path of the fleet, making sure he had an escape route. As an extra precaution, he turned the submarine around with the bow facing open sea. Nighttime came before he gave the order to surface to periscope depth. He could clearly see the distant lights of his target nearly eight miles up the Columbia River. There was no activity on the river. He surfaced. His 13.2-cm gun on the rear deck of the submarine was facing his target. The bow of the sub was pointed toward the Pacific, to provide for a quick getaway. He started shelling the target from 1700 meters out. He had no idea if he was sinking any submarines, but he knew he was in the range of his target. His men fired a volley of seventeen rounds. Within a few minutes a spotlight from the shore lit up the deck of *I-25*. An A-29 Hudson bomber appeared out of nowhere. It started dropping bombs. Meiji ordered his men to cease fire and prepare for an immediate dive. He was able to avoid any damage from the bombs and carefully maneuvered back through the minefield to open sea. He had managed to attack a military base on the United States mainland and save his crew of ninety-seven.

*****

Commander Goodman called Gaston into his office for the second day in a row. "Well, it was all over the news; Fort Stephens was fired upon last night. I can't help thinking the Japs are headed our way. Can you go up to Fort Stephens and get me a firsthand account of what happened?"

"Sir, I'm not sure anyone up there will talk to me," Gaston said.

"Come on, Mr. Carson. I've seen you do some pretty remarkable things. I don't know who's pulling the strings for you, but I'll bet you can jerk a few to get an interview for me."

"I'll try, sir." Gaston decided to make an unscheduled call to the White House. It was certain they had heard of the shelling of an American military post. Maybe the President would want his take on it.

*****

Gaston checked his map. The Pacific Coast Highway roughly followed the Oregon Coastline up to the town of Astoria on the edge of the Columbia River. Northwest of Astoria a road led farther north, and, literally at the end of the road, was Fort Stevens. North of Fort Stevens was the wide mouth of the Columbia River, and across the river, Washington State. The drive would be long and tiring. In many ways the road to the north was more difficult to maneuver than the road south. He would need to talk Major into another flight, weather permitting.

As a member of the CAP, Major had a few privileges not shared with civilians. One was a larger gasoline ration. Aviation gas was in short supply and it was increasingly difficult to keep the airplanes flying. Major wondered if flying Gaston to Fort Stephens was a good use of his ration. "Gaston, I'd like to help you, but I barely have enough fuel to make my weekly submarine spotting flights."

"How much do you need?"

"A hundred gallons should do, but there is no way of you getting your hands on that. I was grounded one day last week because I couldn't get fuel. I would need to top off my tank at whatever airfield we're going to use."

"If I can get you the fuel, you'll do it then?"

Major shrugged. "Sure."

Gaston showed Major his ration book.

"What the hell is that?"

"I got this in the mail after meeting with the local ration board. The note said it's generally reserved for congressmen, governors and diplomats."

Major examined the book. A large "X" and the notation 'not restricted to quantity', was on the book under Gaston's name.

"What the hell? Gaston, you keep pulling tricks out of your hat, like a dime store magician."

"You think it'll work?" Gaston asked.

"You didn't steal it did you?"

"No, I didn't steal it! I told you it was issued by the local board."

"When do we leave?"

"Tomorrow morning."

Chapter 20

The flight to the Coast Guard Air Station in Warrenton, a few miles south of Fort Stevens took only an hour with a near constant southerly tailwind. Southerly winds generally brought a storm and the last thing Major wanted was to fly into a storm on the return trip.

Commander Goodman had arranged for Gaston to meet with US Army Captain Jack Wood. The Captain and his driver were waiting as Major touched down on the tarmac. Major immediately noticed the three fixed-wing airplanes and a new experimental craft called an auto-gyro, parked near a large hangar. Major secured his plane to tie downs anchored in the pavement.

Captain Wood introduced himself to Gaston and Major.

"Captain, do you mind if I take a look at that auto-gyro?" Major asked, "I've only read about them. Never seen one for real."

They walked over to the craft that looked more like a large mosquito than an airplane. "It's a strange looking craft," Major said. "I'd sure like to fly one of these someday. What's it used for?"

"We're testing it as a submarine spotter," Wood said. "It has incredibly short takeoff and landing distance and is quite maneuverable."

"What's its downside?" Major asked.

"I guess you could argue it's a victim of advancing technology. They are already working on a version where the rotating wing is powered and another version that doesn't require a rear facing propeller at all. They call it a helicopter and claim it will be able to take off and land vertically, and will even hover over a target. Can you imagine technology like that?" The captain was clearly excited about the future of the rotating winged aircraft.

"Come on, I'll show you the results of the shelling and you can ask questions as we travel." They climbed into the car: Captain Wood in the front with the driver, Major and Gaston in the back seat.

Their first stop was Battery Russell. "If we would have received permission to return fire, it would have been with these guns," Captain Wood said.

"But you didn't return fire." Gaston said.

"We were ready. We couldn't tell exactly where the shelling was originating from, so our plan was to target the flashes, hoping for a hit."

"There was some talk about your guns lacking range to the target?"

"I guess we'll never know. The Senior Duty Officer never gave an order to fire. We had the sub spotted for a moment, but the spotlight was extinguished immediately. That was also a direct order from the SDO."

"Were you concerned that you were under fire and the SDO refused to give the order to return fire?" Gaston asked.

"Damn right, I was peeved; but in retrospect, his decision was the correct one."

"Why do you say that?"

"It was evident it was a single submarine. Its shells were going all over the place. It was clear it didn't have a target. In the end we didn't have a single casualty."

Major was listening to the conversation and not participating. It was not his job on this trip, but he sure had a lot of comments he was saving for later.

"You agree with the decision, then?" Gaston asked again.

"I agree with Major Hudson's explanation. He was SDO that night and his decision was backed up by Colonel Doney. The submarine appeared to be out of the range of our guns. Their argument was, 'why give away our defensive positions by firing back if we couldn't destroy the target, anyway.'" Captain Wood thought a minute. "You know, we sent a Coast Guard plane out and he was able to drop a few bombs, but he said the sub had disappeared almost immediately and he had no way of tracking it."

They went on to tour the damage from the exploded shells. Men were still scouring the beach for shell fragments. There were several six-foot diameter craters on the beach and surrounding swampy area. "The closest we came to casualties was when one shell exploded near a house with three children inside," Wood said.

"What's your thought on overall readiness against an attack like this?" Gaston asked.

Wood chuckled. "I don't mean to make light of this, but the consensus of my superiors, before this incident happened, was it would never happen. Today they are reviewing our response should something similar happen again. They thought Japan was too busy fighting the war in the Pacific to attack the mainland. They admit they were wrong, and although the horse has left the stable, they are already issuing requests for upgrading our guns and improving civilian warning systems. You saw the men stringing barbed wire along the beach; that's a direct result of the post incident debriefing."

"I understand the newspapers got hold of the story," Gaston said. "It made headlines across the country."

"That wasn't my doing," Wood answered, in a defensive tone. "Something of this magnitude obviously can't be hidden from the public."

Gaston knew the attack was a wake-up call for the defenses on the West Coast. It added fuel to the fire of those wanting a full-fledged defense system set up along the entire coast. He feared such an undertaking would play into the Japanese plans.

Major had been correct in assessing a storm was on the way. It wasn't uncommon for an early summer storm to move in off the ocean and bring strong winds and rain. When he got the latest weather information from the Coast Guard Air Station, he was told it would be raining in Newport. The brunt of the storm was not due to hit until midnight. He should be safely in bed by that time.

"How's the weather?" Gaston inquired.

"We're going to encounter a strong headwind and rain. Other than being a little miserable, we should be fine. My motto is never fly into a storm. We should be well ahead of this one."

As they headed south, Gaston could see large thunderheads on the horizon. *Never fly into a storm? He probably meant, never fly into a hurricane. There was clearly a storm on the horizon.*

On the flight back, Gaston developed a new respect for Major's flying skills. The thunderclouds were isolated and Major was able to fly around them. The trip took an extra hour because of the diversions and the headwind. As they approach Cape Foulweather, Gaston thought how appropriate the name was. Cape Foulweather rose some 600 feet from the ocean and seemed to create its own weather patterns. They flew directly into a cloud so dense; Gaston was completely disoriented and couldn't tell direction. Everything was gray and wet—up, down, and sideways. The plane shook violently and Gaston thought they may lose the wings. To his relief it lasted only a minute before they broke out of the cloud into heavy rain again. As miserable as the cold raindrops were stinging his face, he was glad to see them again.

It was dusk when the Newport field came into view. Gaston had never been happier to set his feet on solid ground, even if it was soaking wet.

"Major, I'd like your take on the Fort Stevens visit when I report to Commander Goodman. Would you mind joining me?" Gaston asked.

"Be glad to," Major said, "but I'm going to tell him exactly what I think."

"You always, do," Gaston said. "You always do."

*****

That evening, Gaston had a dinner planned with Alice. She had promised to show off her domestic skills, even though she only had a hot plate for a stove. *This should be interesting,* he thought, as he knocked on her apartment door. As soon as the door opened,

Gaston smelled dinner. "What is that aroma?" he asked, after kissing her lightly on the lips.

"That's dinner, and it's ready to serve."

"I'm always hungry. Any time is good for me."

"First I thought you might like a beer." She went to the icebox and got a stubby bottle of Olympia. She handed him a bottle opener and he popped the top.

"I've got a funny story to tell you about Olympia beer," Gaston said. "I'll tell you another time." He saw the tiny table with a checkered red and white tablecloth, a lit candle, and two plates. A loaf of Franz bread and a butter dish were there also.

"I hope you don't mind eating in. I've nearly used up my four-gallon ration of gas for the month. I don't know how they expect us to get by on so little."

Gaston didn't dare tell her he could get as much gas as he wanted. "It isn't a shortage of gas the government is trying to protect," he said. "The Japs invaded Burma, where we get nearly 90% of our rubber. Rubber is in such tight supply the most practical way to ration it is to make sure anyone who owns a car doesn't have more than five tires, and to make certain those tires last, they ration the gas. The system has its flaws, but most people are embracing rationing as their way of helping with the war effort."

"You think I'm not being patriotic?"

Gaston lifted his hand in defense. "I didn't say that. It's only natural to want the freedom we had before the war."

"Maybe I am being selfish."

"You were able to gather enough to make a meal," Gaston said, lifting the lid on the kettle on the hotplate.

"Get out of there," Alice said. "I was able to trade some of my dairy ration stamps for meat. Margaret never seems to have enough milk."

"You've got our dinner in there," Gaston said, nodding to the kettle.

"Irish stew. I guarantee you'll like it."

"And if I don't?" Gaston said, kidding her.

"Then, you can go someplace else and eat. There'll be more for me," she said, saucily.

Alice got another beer from the icebox and opened it. She clicked her bottle against Gaston's. "Take a seat, dinner is about to be served."

Alice served the stew in soup bowls. She set a bowl in front of Gaston. "Be careful it's hot." She filled another bowl and placed it on her plate and sat down. "You always eat this with bread and butter, not crackers like soup."

"Okay," Gaston said. "Is this a dish you had often as a kid?"

"Almost every night," Alice said, "but we didn't get meat in it very often. Sometimes we'd get chicken, sometimes something indescribable."

"Indescribable?" Gaston repeated.

"It could have been rabbit or squirrel. My parents wouldn't tell us."

"But you ate it," Gaston said.

"We were kids, and hungry. You probably never had to experience that, but we were poor Irish immigrants."

Gaston hadn't discussed his past with Alice. He had never felt comfortable enough to do that until now. He took a spoonful of stew, chewed, swallowed, and touched his mouth with a cloth napkin. "You think I came from privilege, don't you?"

"You went to the best schools when the country was reeling in depression. You don't get into the Naval Academy in Annapolis without knowing someone who can pull strings. I'd say that amounts to privilege."

Gaston took a drink and looked into her eyes. "I've been blessed beyond anything I ever deserved, but that's not the whole story." He finished his beer. "I told you my mother died. I never knew my father because my mother was a prostitute. We lived in a boardinghouse. I didn't realize how bad we had it until my mother died and her john kicked me out on the street."

"Oh, my God, how old were you?'

"That was 1931. I was 12."

"Gaston, I'm so sorry. I never knew."

"It's okay, the story gets better from there." He told her how he'd been rescued by a very powerful man and removed from the streets of New York City.

"This is very good. I'm amazed." He said, taking another bite. He didn't like remembering his past, but thought any girl he might become serious with should know where he came from.

"You're amazed! You didn't think I could cook, did you?"

"No, it's not what you think. I didn't think you could manage a meal with so little. Your stew is fantastic."

"I'll accept that as an apology. How was your trip?"

"I'm not sure. The fort was bombarded with sixty-pound artillery shells and didn't, or couldn't return the fire. They were either completely caught off guard and unable to get their act together or very clever." He explained how they didn't return fire and blacked out the fort so they couldn't be seen.

"That sounds like what they did was effective."

"That's what they thought."

"But you don't think that?" She raised her eyebrows. Her green eyes sparkled in the candlelight.

"I think there's an enemy submarine still operating out there. Heaven only knows where it will turn up next." He paused to finish his stew. It was getting cold.

After dinner, Alice fixed tea and they retired to the living room, which also served as the bedroom by way of a Murphy bed. Across the room were two chairs on either side of a console radio with a built in phonograph player. A nearby bookcase served as a coffee table for one of the chairs. Near the radio was a record stand. "Would you like to hear some music?" Alice asked.

"I'll pick out something," Gaston said, shuffling through the large discs. "Bing Crosby, Artie Shaw, Count Basie, you're kidding me. You don't have any Dizzy Gillespie?"

"Records cost money. I can't buy everything."

He put on Bing Crosby, *They Say It's Wonderful.* "Would you like to dance?"

"Well, we have to be quiet. You know there are people downstairs."

"That's why I put on Bing Crosby."

As he held her close and they swayed to the music, Alice whispered in his ear. "Gaston, I'm scared."

They stopped dancing. "Would you like to sit and talk about it?"

"Oh, it won't do any good. I don't know what's the matter. This war, the news is filled with invasions and war stories. What if they do invade us?"

"You mean the Japs?"

"The Japs, the Nazis. I had to trade enough stamps to buy some beef so I could make dinner for you. I want things to go back to where they were."

"You mean the high unemployment, the food lines and the..."

"Don't make fun of me. I just don't want to worry that my windows might be letting out too much light at night, and we might be bombed, or my neighbors might be planning on killing someone just because they look a little different. If I had my way, I'd put Roosevelt and Churchill in a room with Hitler and Hirohito and have them all duke it out. Winner takes all!"

Gaston shook his head. "We'd all be speaking Japanese or German then. FDR can't stand more than a few minutes without help, and I swear as big as Churchill is, he'd have a heart attack if he had to exert the least amount of effort."

Alice laughed. "You know what I mean. Why do we have to fight wars? Why can't we all get along?"

Gaston sighed. "I wish we could."

Alice pushed away from Gaston. "Why did you say the President can't stand without help?"

Her question caught him by surprise. "Because he's paralyzed from the waist down."

"How do you know that?"

"I saw his leg braces and watched how much he needed help, just to get dressed. He moves around the White House in a wheelchair."

"How do you know all this?

"I saw them. He wears iron braces on both legs, just to help him stand."

"You've seen the President with his clothes off?"

"Only by accident. I was outside his bedroom at the White House when his aides were dressing him."

"You were at the White House?" Alice gave him an incredulous look. "You're beginning to frighten me, Gaston."

"I told you I'd tell you some day. I speak to the President directly every week."

"Oh my God. You're not kidding."

"Alice, don't go nuts on me. It's no big deal."

Alice swallowed hard. "Not to you maybe, but to me it's a very big deal!"

"I shouldn't have told you," Gaston said. "I promised the President I'd keep it a secret." Gaston looked worried. "You're not going to tell anyone, are you?"

Alice took a deep breath and forced herself to stop trembling. "I believe you are telling me the truth, Gaston, but if I told anyone, they would laugh me out of the room. If you are indeed talking to the President, I won't mention it to anyone. They might put you in the looney bin. If you are telling me a story just to impress me, you are doing just the opposite."

"I'd better go," Gaston said, checking his watch. "It's getting late and I have a big day tomorrow."

"When will I see you again?"

"I'll be at Officer's Quarters unless I get called out again."

"Then what's the rush?" She grabbed the lapels of his suit jacket and pulled herself close to him.

He leaned down and kissed her on the lips. "I'm trying to prevent a war on the West Coast."

"Gaston, I almost forgot," Alice said. "The paper said the FBI arrested some men who attacked you."

"No big deal. They were a bunch of thugs."

"Did they say why they did it?" Alice asked.

"I really do have to go. It's been a long day. I'll tell you what I know in the morning." He pecked her on the forehead. "I'll stop by your desk and we can have coffee." He grabbed his hat and overcoat from the coatrack and let himself out. She stood in the doorway for a moment. The wind was driving rain right in her face. She watched Gaston holding his hat so it wouldn't fly away. He got to his car. She closed the door. She was falling hard for him, but there were still things that bothered her. She decided to see if she could get more information from Thurston. If she was going to fall seriously for another man, this time she had to be certain.

In the back of the *Blue Whale*, beyond the last pool table, was a single table with three chairs. Beyond it was a short hallway that led to a restroom. Sam Johnson walked out of the restroom buttoning the fly on his trousers. He was not wearing his sheriff's uniform or his badge. He wasn't packing his gun. He pulled out a chair and sat down. Five minutes later a man with a pitcher of beer came toward him followed by another with three glasses.

"Hey, Sam. Sorry to call you so late." Don Johnson set the pitcher on the table. His brother Gene set the glasses down and filled all three. His hand was shaking to the point that he set the pitcher against the lip of the glasses to keep from spilling it.

"What did you boys do this time?" Sam asked.

Gene started to speak, but Don cut him off by raising his hand. "We were trying to convince this Jap that he'd be better off in another town, when he grabbed a machete from under the counter. Gene shot him. It was self defense, clear and simple."

"That's right. He would have killed Don if I didn't shoot him."

Sam took a long pull on his beer, nearly draining the glass. Don started to refill it, but Sam waved him off.

"Where did this happen?" Sam asked.

"At the Asian Market on Yaquina River Road."

"What did you do with the gun?"

"That's just it," Gene said. "I dropped it."

Major came into the back room. "You boys need anything else, we're about to close for the night."

Sam pushed out from the table. "We're fine, Major. We were just leaving."

"Where are we going?" Gene asked.

"You're going back home. I don't want you out there screwing things up."

"Don't be so hard on him," Don said. "The man was going to kill me."

"Really! What the hell were you two doing at the Asian Market anyway?"

Gene started to answer, "We were—"

Sam cut him off. "It was a rhetorical question, you idiot. Didn't you see what happened to Rich? The FBI is checking me out, and you pull a stunt like this. Get out of here and I don't want to see your ugly faces again. If you weren't my cousins, I'd throw you both in jail for stupidity."

Sam followed the two out into the parking lot. It was getting late and the storm was raging. He leaned into the wind and opened the car door. The wind jerked the door from his hand and nearly ripped it off the hinges. It took him three tries to get the door to latch after he got in. He headed at high speed to Yaquina River Road and the Asian Market. As he pulled into the parking lot, he saw all the lights were off and the door was closed. He opened it and walked inside. There were things scattered everywhere. He slipped on something and caught himself on the counter. He regained his footing and nearly tripped over the body. The man, lying in a pool of blood, was still holding the machete.

Sam grabbed the man by his feet and dragged him through the door, out into the rain. He opened the back door of his car and started to lift the body.

Gaston had taken a few minutes to let the windows clear of fog on the inside, but that didn't work. He grabbed a small towel he kept for wiping his windows and wiped all of them. As he was driving down Yaquina River Road away from Alice's he noticed a car parked at the Asian Market. He saw a man struggling with something and pulled in to see if he needed help. He caught Sam Johnson with the body in his hands. He immediately recognized the sheriff. He rolled down the window. "You need some help, Sheriff?"

Sam stared at Gaston with wide eyes. "He hurt himself; I'm taking him to the hospital."

"I'll help." Gaston started to get out of his car.

"I got it under control. You run along."

Gaston could see just enough that he knew the man was dead. The bullet hole in his head was unmistakable. Gaston got out and walked over to Sam. Sam let the man fall in a mud puddle. He instinctively went for his gun, which wasn't there. "Gaston, I know what this looks like, but I came across the market and the door was open. He was already dead. I need to get his body to the hospital for an autopsy."

Gaston knew he was lying. "It's pretty evident he died of a gunshot wound."

"Probably attempted robbery."

"Sheriff, none of what you are saying adds up. Tell me what's really going on?"

The sheriff was a muscular man. More than once he had subdued rowdy lumbermen with his bare hands. He took a swing at Gaston, but Gaston saw it coming and leaned back, letting the wild fist fly past his jaw.

He grabbed the sheriff's other arm and twisted it behind him. "Suppose we go inside and make a phone call." Gaston pushed the sheriff ahead of him through the open door. The narrow beam of his headlights cast long shadows across the scattered mess in the store. He could see blood on the floor where the body had been.

"You're going to pay for this, Gaston. I'm sheriff. I run this town. You'll never get away with this."

"Shut up!" Gaston found the phone and clicked the hanger. "Operator, get me the Newport Police Department."

When Police Chief Landon Myers arrived he was still in his nightshirt. He stopped short of the sheriff's car and glanced at the body. He drew his 1932 Model Infield service revolver and rushed the door. He saw the sheriff first. "Sam, what the hell are you doing? I got a call there was a murder." Then he saw Gaston. "You're that fella got Al Rich arrested. I read about you in the paper."

Gaston realized he may have made a fatal mistake. "The sheriff was trying to get rid of the body when I caught him off guard. He's trying to cover up a murder."

Myers leveled his revolver at Gaston. "Suppose that's not the way I see it. I see a desperate man in the act of committing homicide; the sheriff walks in on it, but gets caught off guard, right after he used the phone to call my office. Is that the way it happened, Sam?"

"Pretty close," Sam said. He struggled to get loose from Gaston.

"Let him go, Carson, I'm taking you in."

Gaston started to let the sheriff go, but saw another option. He shoved the sheriff at the police chief and dove for the gun on the floor. He grabbed it and fired, striking the Police Chief in the arm. The Police Chief dropped his gun. The sheriff went for it.

"Don't do it," Gaston said. He went over to the gun and kicked it away.

"I'm bleeding. I need a doctor," Chief Meyers cried.

"Over against the counter," Gaston said. "I don't know what the two of you think you are doing, but you're not going to get away with it."

"What are you going to do now, Carson?" the sheriff asked. "You can't arrest the law around here and expect to get away with it."

Gaston figured the only way to handle the situation was call the Commander and see if he could get some MPs over to diffuse the situation. The Police Chief did need attention for his wound and the sheriff wasn't going to be cooperative. He went to the phone.

Don and Gene were headed to their house in the country. Gene pulled the car over to the side of the road.

"What are you doing?" Don asked.

"I left the gun back there. It's got my fingerprints on it."

"Sam said he'd handle it."

"What do you think he's going to do?" Gene asked. "He's got the dead guy with the bullet from my gun in his head. They tie my fingerprints to the gun and I'll be hanged, just for killing a Jap."

"Let's do what Sam told us. He'll find the gun and dispose of it with the body."

"I'm not taking a chance; I'm going to make sure." Gene made a U-turn and headed toward Yaquina River Road. It took him two minutes to reach the Asian Market. He pulled the car into the lot and saw three cars. "This doesn't look good. Sam's in trouble."

Inside Gaston heard the car pull up. *That was quick*, he thought, thinking it was the MPs.

Suddenly two figures blocked the light in the doorway. "Drop your weapon, or I'll shoot," Gene demanded.

All Gaston could see was the silhouette of two men. He didn't see any guns. "Identify yourself." Gaston said.

The words were barely out of his mouth when the sheriff used the distraction to grab a carton of cigarettes from the counter and toss them at Gaston.

Gaston ducked and the two men and the sheriff rushed Gaston. They wrestled him to the ground. The sheriff put his knee on Gaston's arm and removed the gun. He held Gaston as Don and Gene bound his arms and legs with twine from under the counter. They stuffed his mouth with a rag. Gaston was tossed into the back of the sheriff's car. The sheriff was dragging the market's owner back into the shop when the MPs showed up.

"What's going on here? We got a call there was a murder."

"I'm Sheriff Johnson. The wounded man is Police Chief Meyers. This isn't Coast Guard jurisdiction. We've got it under control. I'm just moving the body inside until the coroner can examine it."

The MP shined his light around the scene and back into the sheriff's eyes. "Do you have some ID, sheriff?" After seeing the sheriff was who he said he was, the MPs left.

The sheriff placed the murder weapon into a clean paper bag. "Can you make it to the hospital or should I have one of the boys drive you?"

Landon Meyers eyed Don and Gene. "I'll manage."

"I thought I told you to go home," Sheriff Johnson said. "I said I'd take care of this!"

Gene grabbed the bag into which the sheriff had placed the gun. "I came back for my gun. It has my fingerprints on it."

"Don't take that, it's our ticket out of this mess."

"What do you mean?" Gene asked.

"It's the gun that shot the Jap and it's the same one that shot Chief Meyers."

"So?" Gene asked.

"So, it has Gaston Carson's fingerprints all over it. This couldn't have turned out better if we planned it. We have him firing the murder weapon at the cop. He had to be the one who killed the Jap, right?"

"Damn, you took care of everything," Don said. "Come on, Gene. We can go now."

The next morning, the sky was clear and the sun was shining. Offshore a bank of fog blocked the horizon. Alice smiled when she walked down the steps from her apartment. It was a beautiful day. She was looking forward to having coffee with Gaston. As she drove past the Asian Market she noticed Gaston's car and immediately dismissed it. *There must be two cars like that in town,* she thought. She continued on to work and put on a pot of coffee. When Gaston didn't show up she started to wonder if the car she saw was his. When Ensign Pastor came down, she called out, "hot coffee in the percolator."

Danny stopped by her desk. "You're in bright and early."

"I was supposed to meet Gaston for coffee. You haven't seen him, have you?"

Danny went into the kitchen and poured two cups of coffee and brought them out. He set one down in front of Alice. "So you won't be completely disappointed, I'll join you."

"Thanks, Danny, but I'm worried. Did he come in last night?"

"You're not going to let me enjoy my coffee until I go see if he's in, are you?"

She shook her head and gave him an innocent smile.

Pastor came back down the stairs in less than thirty seconds. "If he did, he's not here now."

"Last night was really stormy. I passed a car that looked like his parked at the Asian Market. Do you think he could have had car trouble and stayed there?"

"That's a stretch. He would have come back here. He probably got up early and headed out."

"He would have left me a note." Alice said, growing more concerned by the minute.

"You don't know that. He probably got called out and had to get someplace fast."

"Then it could be his car I saw. You're the only one here. Would it be all right if I went and checked? I'd only be gone half an hour or so."

"I don't have anything going. I'm headed over to the mess for breakfast. I think I'll survive."

"Thanks, Danny. Tell the Commander I said, hi."

"Sure," Danny said, not intending on speaking to the Commander if he could avoid it.

As Alice was putting on her coat, the phone rang. She answered it, "Officer's Quarters, may I help you?"

"Alice," it was Goodman's voice, "would you tell Mr. Carson I'd like to see him."

"Mr. Carson is not in, sir."

"Did he leave information of where he was going?"

"No, sir, I haven't seen him."

"All right, thanks."

She looked at Ensign Pastor. "The Commander is looking for Gaston. I'm going to check his parking space."

"Good luck," Pastor said. "You didn't touch your coffee."

Not seeing Gaston's car in his space, she got in her car. She cursed herself for not checking the Asian Market when she was driving by. As Alice pulled into the parking lot at the Asian Market, a grubby unshaven man was attaching Gaston's car to a tow truck. He began to lift the front end. She pulled her car up close and rolled down the window. "What are you doing with that car?"

"What does it look like, lady? I'm hauling it in."

"Where to?"

"Is this your car, lady?"

"No, I think it belongs to a friend."

"Well, if it does, your friend is in a heap of trouble. I'm taking it to the city police compound."

She went to the City of Newport Police Station. The brick building was constructed with a reception area in front and a desk blocking access to the area where prisoners were kept. It contained four cells which Alice could not see. She stood waiting for the clerk to acknowledge her.

"How may I help you?" the clerk asked, looking at Alice. She had her hair wrapped in a red bandana and wore thick glasses, but they were propped above her eyes, looking like they were held up by her unruly eyebrows. She picked up a piece of paper, slipped the glasses over her eyes and and examined it.

"Do you have a Gaston Carson here?"

"Do you know his middle name or initial?"

"I don't know it. There can't be that many people named Gaston." The frustration was beginning to show in her voice.

The clerk looked at the paper again. "Gaston Carson," she dragged out the words. "He murdered the owner of the Asian

Market by a gunshot to the head, shot the Chief of Police in the arm, and held Chief Larson and Sheriff Johnson hostage. Been a long time since we had the likes of one like him in here."

"There must be a mistake," Alice said.

"That's what they all say," the clerk said.

"Can I see him?"

"I have strict orders not to let him see anybody until the judge gets here for arraignment."

"Does he have a lawyer?"

The clerk shrugged. "I'm going to tell you something, because you look like a nice girl. This man is no good. Instead of joining the service and fighting the war like other young men his age, he's running around our streets killing people. If I were you, honey, I'd leave him be."

"When I want your advice, I'll ask for it," Alice said. She stormed out of the office.

Chapter 21

Gaston sat in his cell, shivering and still soaking wet. He had a wool blanket wrapped over his shoulders, but it didn't seem to help. As he waited to be charged, he thought about his predicament.

How did I get here? he asked himself. *Why did the President pick him to be his eyes and ears on the West Coast? I was trained to serve in the Navy, not be a spy for the President.* Roosevelt had chosen him because he spoke his mind. He'd like to tell the President a thing or two right now! He sat hunched over, shivering and mostly feeling sorry for himself, but in the back of his mind, he remembered how he was chosen.

It was May 18, 1932. Roosevelt was campaigning for his first run at the White House. At the time Roosevelt was still Governor of New York. Gaston was brought to the Roosevelt mansion in upstate New York. It was a birthday party, but Gaston didn't know for whom. There were other kids there his age, but he preferred hanging out with the adults and listening to them discuss the politics of the day and Roosevelt's decision to run for the White House.

There was a group of men standing around Roosevelt, who was sitting in his wheelchair. Some pulled up chairs and sat. "I believe the voters need to know that the candidate for president is in a wheelchair," Roosevelt said. "I will not deceive the American voter."

The men in the circle were discussing the ramifications of such an announcement, but it was clear to Gaston, they were worried more about disagreeing with Roosevelt than giving an honest opinion of the outcome of such a revelation. After several minutes of rocking back and forth, Gaston couldn't hold his tongue any longer. "Sir," he said, in a loud voice. "If you disclose that you are in a wheelchair, the public will see you as weak. An invalid.

They want a president who is a strong, dynamic leader. You must present that image, if you want to win."

Gaston backed up, expecting someone to backhand him for speaking out. He was just a kid. What did he know?

Roosevelt motioned for Gaston to come over. Gaston was trembling, expecting to be punished for such an outrageous outburst.

"Help me up," Roosevelt said.

Gaston took an arm and aided the Governor to his feet. Roosevelt took a cane and steadied himself while he retrieved the other cane. He stood tall. Looking almost regal to Gaston.

"Son," Roosevelt said, "I believe you are right. My strength is in my resolve to lead this Nation out of the Great Depression and into a world of hope and prosperity. I cannot project strength from a position of weakness. I shall stand and project strength."

Roosevelt never told Gaston that was a defining moment, but Gaston knew it. He never saw a picture in the paper showing Roosevelt in a wheelchair. When Roosevelt addressed the people he was standing. He won the nomination of the Democratic Party and the election. As Gaston reflected on that, he wondered at how that incident would define his life. Now he was on the West Coast, sitting in jail, most likely going to be charged with murdering one of the people he was trying to protect.

He cursed himself for not assessing the situation correctly as soon as he saw the sheriff. Then, when things escalated, he'd overreacted. There was no way he could have known the two men who showed up were with the sheriff. He let out a long sigh. *What's next?* he wondered.

Through the high, narrow window in his cell he could see daylight. He realized he already knew what was next. The sheriff had framed him and put him in jail without allowing him to call anyone. What was next could only be worse. He heard footsteps. The woman with the red bandana on her head brought a tray and slid it under the barred door.

Gaston wasn't hungry, but seeing the scrambled eggs, gravy over toast, and coffee in a tin cup changed his mind. He picked up the tray. He needed to eat for nourishment, if nothing else. With the sheriff and the police chief both witnesses against him, there was no way that this was going to be a short stay. As he ate, he started to put together a plan for his defense.

Alice returned to the base with the intention of finding a lawyer for Gaston. She picked up the phone. When Commander Goodman heard Gaston was in the city jail he cursed, something Alice had never heard him do.

"I'll call and see if there's anything I can do," Goodman said. "I'll let you know what's going on."

Commander Goodman was denied access to Gaston. He was told he could talk to him after his arraignment. Goodman, not being used to rude treatment, called the county prosecutor.

William Hill, the county prosecutor, had been in office less than three months, having been appointed after the former prosecutor was called to active duty. He was an elderly man who had previously served in the DA's office until his retirement. This was his first case after coming out of retirement. The Commander had met him once at a social gathering, but they were not friends.

"Bill, this is Thurston Goodman Remember, we met at the dedication of the new bridge back in '39?"

"Goodman? Yeah, I remember. You're the Commander at the Coast Guard Station."

"One and the same. I was hoping you could give me some information about a prisoner in the city jail."

"Gaston Leroy Carson," Hill said.

"What's he charged with?"

"I'm still preparing the charges for the Grand Jury hearing this afternoon. We had to get a judge assigned out of Taft, our judge recused himself."

"Judge Johnson isn't hearing the case?"

"It seems the sheriff is part of this case. The Judge and the sheriff are first cousins."

"What can you tell me?"

"It's pretty serious. There's a long list including murder," the prosecutor said. "Anything more will have to come from his attorney."

"He has an attorney?"

"Not that I know of. Good talking to you, Goodman."

The phone went dead. Goodman sat at his desk for a moment trying to wrap his head around Gaston being accused of murder. Nothing fit. His biggest problem wasn't that Gaston was in jail. His biggest problem, he knew, would be trying to explain it to whoever would be calling from Washington. *Gaston's stay in the hospital was bad enough, when the White House found out he was in jail*...he didn't want to think about it.

The Grand Jury hearing was not public, but the local newspaper had seen the docket. Photographers and press from three different counties had made the trip to cover the story. A murder, wounded police chief and kidnapped sheriff, had already made the newspaper and after the hearing, the prosecutor had promised a statement. Reporters were clamoring for a non-war related news story.

Bill Hill scanned the crowd from the steps of the Lincoln County Courthouse. He smiled, raised his hand to silence them and read from a prepared statement. "Gaston Leroy Carson was arraigned today on one count of aggravated assault resulting in a homicide, one count of attempted murder, two counts of assault on a law enforcement officer, two counts of kidnapping, and several minor infractions, including trespassing, and unlawful use of a firearm."

"Who was the victim?" a reporter shouted.

"The victim was a first generation Japanese American. His name is William Teramura. He was preceded in death by his wife, Keira. He has two children, both grown and living out of the area. He was the sole proprietor of the Asian Market on Yaquina River Road. Out of respect for the family, we are not divulging any further information about the family or the investigation."

"Can you tell us anything about Gaston Carson?"

"At this time, I can't comment on Mr. Carson. You'll have to ask his attorney."

"Who is his attorney?" another reporter called out.

"I don't have one on record. If he cannot afford one, we'll appoint one."

"He was indicted without an attorney?"

"It was a Grand Jury hearing to determine if he should be charged, not a trial. Thank you. That's all the questions for now."

Both Alice and Commander Goodman were in the crowd. "We need to get him some help," Goodman said to Alice. "I know you and Gaston were seeing each other. Are you certain you want to get involved in this?"

Alice had tears in her eyes. "I'm already involved. I love him."

"Then I'll give you this." He handed her a business card. "He's not cheap, but he's good."

"An attorney?"

"The best defense lawyer in the state. I got his card awhile back. I thought I'd never have to use it."

"If you know him, wouldn't it be better if you contacted him?"

"I already have, he's waiting for a call from you."

The name on the card was Barry Alexander, of the Portland law firm Alexander, Hearsh, and Lampman, the most prestigious law firm in the State of Oregon. Barry Alexander was known for defending some of the most notorious gangsters in the state, but since the repeal of prohibition, the number of his cases had decreased. He was glad to take on another high profile case. This one might even gain national attention. He flew to the Newport airfield and was taxied to the County courthouse.

Barry Alexander shaved his head daily. To protect his shiny dome from the elements he wore a stylish Fedora and went nowhere without it. He was unusually tall. Some said it appeared he had just grown out of his hair. Unlike many bald men of the day, he had no facial hair. Steel blue eyes peered through wire rimmed glasses. He wore an expensive gray wool suit with a vest. When he unbuttoned his coat and sat across from Gaston, a gold chain could be seen draped neatly from his watch pocket. He pulled out his gold watch and checked the time.

Gaston had been moved from the city jail to county after the Grand Jury indictment. Gaston wasn't surprised after hearing the charges. He'd had plenty of time to relive that night and was certain he was going to be framed for a murder the sheriff had committed or was covering up. He stared across the table at the man Alice had hired to represent him.

"You understand the charges, don't you?" Alexander asked.

Gaston nodded. "I've been set up," Gaston said. "Before you ask, I didn't kill anybody, my fingerprints are on the murder weapon, and I did shoot the Chief of Police, but there is an explanation for everything."

His attorney smiled. *An odd response*, Gaston thought.

"I'm ready to hear your side of the story. Mr. Carson, as your attorney our conversations are privileged. Think of me as a priest, if you will, I cannot reveal my conversations to anyone. If you lie to me, you are only hurting yourself. Your innocence or guilt is not important to me. I am only concerned with the best way of convincing the jurors you didn't do this."

"You don't care if I'm innocent? Let me tell you something," Gaston said. "If I know if I was defending an innocent man I would put a lot more effort into it than if I knew he was guilty."

"Good point, Mr. Carson. If you say you're innocent, then I'll do everything in my power to prove it. I'm ready to take notes. Are you ready to tell me your story?"

After Alexander finished with his notes and Gaston had assured himself he had told the complete story, he sat back. "Mr. Alexander, who is paying you?"

"I'm sorry; you didn't get to talk to Alice Fitzpatrick?"

"Alice? They won't let me talk to anybody. You're the first visitor I've had since I've been in here. They didn't even let me make a phone call."

"For the record, Alice Fitzpatrick gave me a $500 retainer. I'll make sure you have access to visitors. Give me a list of everyone you want to see." He slid his legal tablet across the table.

After Gaston listed all the people he could think might want to have visit, Alexander looked it over and smiled. "It's good you're keeping a sense of humor, Mr. Carson."

"I'm sorry?"

"Franklin Delano Roosevelt?" He laughed. "I think I'm going to enjoy defending you."

The next day Gaston was visited by Ensign Pastor. Danny handed him a paper bag with shaving supplies, underwear and clean socks. "You feel like telling me what happened?"

"I haven't got anything better to do."

After Pastor heard the long version of the story, he said, "Major would like to visit."

"Major, sure. He's on the list."

"Good. He has some secret crap he's not interested in sharing with me."

When Alice arrived at the county jail an hour later, she was told she couldn't visit because Gaston had exceeded his visitor limit for the day. Frustrated, she called Barry Alexander. "I haven't been able to see him. How's he supposed to mount an effective defense when he can only see one person a day?"

"I'm heading down your way tomorrow. I'll make sure you get to see him. I need to talk to you, anyway. Gaston's deposition states he was with you until shortly before the incident at the Asian Market. I may want to use you as a witness."

"So I can't see him until tomorrow?" Alice wasn't going to let this go easily.

"I'll call the prosecutor and get you in," Alexander promised.

An hour later, Alice received a call from the county jail. She would be allowed a one-hour visit.

*****

On Sunday, June 7 1942, Commander Yokota Minoru in Japanese submarine *I-26* lay submerged off the southern tip of Vancouver Island. Earlier that day the freighter *SS Coast Trader* departed Port Angeles, Washington, just across the Strait of Juan de Fuca from Victoria, Canada. The freighter was loaded with newsprint, bound for San Francisco. As the freighter left the strait and headed for open ocean, Commander Minoru brought his submarine to periscope depth. He had the *SS Coast Trader* in his sights. He shadowed the freighter at periscope depth at a distance of 200 meters. The day was clear and the water calm. It would be an easy kill.

The *SS Coast Trader* was a 324-foot freighter, first commissioned for the US Shipping Board in 1920. The 3286 ton freighter, originally named *SS Point Reyes*, was built by The Submarine Boat Company in Edison, New Jersey, was sold to Coastwise Line Steamship Company in 1936, and was put under charter to the US Army. Her home port was Portland, Oregon.

Commander Yokota Minoru had the ship in his sight. He trailed her as she turned south, steering a non-evasive course.

Onboard *SS Coast Trader*, Captain Lyle G. Havens had welcomed the nineteen US Army armed guards manning the deck guns. The submarine activity in the area had the crew on high alert, but they did not see the wash from the *I-26* periscope.

"Flood torpedo tube one," Minoru ordered, still peering through the periscope. "Fire one." Minoru checked his timepiece. It was 0710 Tokyo time, 1410 Pacific time. The fate of *SS Coast Trader* was sealed. Commander Minoru continued to watch. The ship exploded violently. Huge rolls of newsprint, each weighing 2000 pounds, flew a hundred feet into the air. As they came down, they toppled the radio antenna and the main mast of *SS Coast*

Trader. The freighter was dead in the water. "Down periscope," Minoru ordered. "We're going to surface."

Aboard *SS Coast Trader*, the captain immediately gave the order to abandon ship. Ammonia was leaking from the ship's refrigeration system and the men were being overcome by the gas. The starboard lifeboat was too badly damaged to lower, so the crew rushed to the port-side lifeboat, and successfully lowered it and two large cork life rafts. From the lifeboat, First Officer E.W. Nystrom watched the submarine rise and saw *I-26* on the conning tower. There was no doubt they were victims of an attack by a Japanese submarine. At 1450 hrs Captain Havens and his crew watched as their ship slowly disappeared under the water.

Commander Yokota Minoru recorded the kill in his log. He took the boat down to 150 feet. The floor was at 558 feet.

Captain Havens ordered a quick head count. All fifty-six were accounted for. He looked up as the first drops of rain fell. A storm was on the horizon. He ordered the life rafts be tied together and secured to the lifeboat. "Transfer all the injured to the lifeboat," he ordered. The water was icy cold and there was little chance for a wounded man to survive on a raft. As night approached, he prepared himself for the worst. He feared his distress signal had not gone out, due to the damage to the radio antenna. He addressed the men with him in the lifeboat. "Man the oars and start rowing toward shore. We're not going to be rescued tonight."

Captain Havens was jolted awake. The wind had picked up to gale force. The rafts had broken away from the lifeboat. The sea was rough with breaking waves. Without the life rafts, the lifeboat crew continued to row. It was 1600 the next day when they spotted a halibut schooner, the *Virginia I*, out of San Francisco. The crew was taken to the Naval Section Base at Neah Bay, Washington. Captain Havens and First Officer Nystrom gave the Naval authorities the approximate location of the rafts and several Coast Guard aircraft were dispatched to the site. Around 0600 the crew on the life rafts saw the Coast Guard fixed-wing aircraft circling in the distance and fired an orange signal flare. The pilot directed the Canadian corvette *HMCS Edmunston* to the rescue site. There was one fatality from exposure and hypothermia. Fifty-five of the original fifty-six onboard the *SS Coast Trader* survived.

After receiving news of the sinking of the *SS Coast Trader*, Commander Goodman was furious. It was three weeks after the incident, and he was only now finding out? "Ensign Pastor, my office now!"

Pastor could see the Commander was upset.

"I want you to go over to the jail and find out if Mr. Carson had any news of the sinking of the *SS Coast Trader*. Why was the news kept from me?" He handed Pastor a copy of the *Seattle Post-Intelligencer*. The headlines read *SUB SINKS SHIP OFF NEAH BAY; 55 SAVED*. Pastor looked at the date, June 10, 1942.

"What day is it today, Ensign?"

"Tuesday, June 30th, sir."

"I want to know how a sub sinks a ship off our shores and the newspapers find out about it before I do."

"You think Gaston can help you with that, sir?"

"Between you and me, I hope not. That boy is in enough trouble already."

When Pastor arrived at the jail, he had to wait in the lobby. Gaston was meeting with his attorney again.

After his attorney left, Gaston stayed in the visitor's room, handcuffed to a steel table. Pastor walked in and took a chair across from him. "The woman at the desk tells me you're more popular than Frank Sinatra at an all-girls school," Pastor said. "I had to wait an hour for your buddy to clear out." He could see Gaston was dejected.

"You know the difference between an attorney and a bucket full of snakes?" Gaston asked.

"I give."

"Nothing," Gaston said. "Absolutely nothing."

"The Commander wanted me to give you this."

Gaston took the newspaper and read the headline. "Holy smoke. When did this happen?"

"June 7th."

"Three weeks ago? Major and I were right there." He continued to read the article. "We were right there where they dispatched the rescue craft. They didn't say a word."

"The Commander has his shorts wedged between his ass cheeks over this. He wants to know if you knew about it and didn't tell him."

"I wish he would have come himself, so I could look him in the eye. This is the first I heard about it."

"That's good enough for me. Anything I can do for you?"

"Yeah, find out where Major has been. He hasn't come by to see me yet."

Pastor pulled at his lips with his thumb and forefinger. "Yeah, I forgot to get back to you. He's due to come here tomorrow. Something about evidence. You seem to be pissed at your attorney. May I ask why?"

"I gave him every bit of information I had and he hasn't interviewed anyone who can corroborate my story."

"If there's anything you need me to do, say the word."

"Thanks, Danny. I'll get back to you on that. Meanwhile, convince Goodman I didn't withhold information from him."

Chapter 22

It was 10:00 a.m. when Major arrived at the county jail. A yellow manila envelope caught the eye of the guard. He patted down Major and checked the envelope for contraband. In the visiting area, Major slid the envelope across the table. "I thought you might be interested in a conversation I overheard the other day."

Gaston glanced at the contents. It was a statement his attorney had asked for, trying to trace the activity of the sheriff the night of the murder. He was glad his attorney was finally starting to interview people for his defense. "Thanks, this may help, but I've got a bigger problem."

"Bigger than your freedom?"

"Maybe I can't seem to get the contents of my wallet. They're holding it for evidence."

"That doesn't seem right."

"A lot of things aren't right. The sheriff is the one who committed the murder, and I'm sitting in his jail. How likely is it I'll ever make it out of here?"

Major furrowed his brow. "From what I read in the paper, he has enough to hang you in a trial. Why would he want to harm you before then?"

"There are two reasons I can think of. Whoever came to the sheriff's rescue, not only knew he was in trouble, but they knew exactly where he was. They either helped the sheriff, making them eyewitnesses, or they were the ones who committed the murder and the sheriff was trying to cover it up."

Major took on a concerned look. "Maybe some of this is starting to make sense after all."

"Why do you say that?"

"There were two other people with the sheriff that night. All three were at the *Blue Whale*, sharing a pitcher of beer. The statement in the envelope only verifies where the sheriff was at

10:00 p.m. Your attorney didn't ask if there was anyone else who could verify my statement."

"At least my attorney is doing something. I thought he was sitting on his ass racking up hours and fees. I was starting to get nervous. Do you know the other two men?"

"Gene and Don, cousins of the sheriff. Come to think of it, the brothers were pretty nervous that night. They didn't finish their beers."

"Now that I know my attorney isn't just sitting on his butt, I need for you to contact him with this information. Those were probably the two who came to the sheriff's aid. Man, I'd like to get them in a room and pound the truth out of them."

"I'll see if he can get your billfold. What's in it that's so important?" A jailer came in the room and Major leaned forward.

"A phone number, but I'm not sure I should use it."

"The same number you called to get our equipment?" He raised his hands. "I know, I know, you can't tell me or you'll have to kill me. Sorry about the word choice."

"Forget it," Gaston said.

Gaston had been back in his cell less than thirty minutes when he was notified he had another visitor. He was very surprised to see FBI Agent Frank Billings. "Agent Billings. I didn't expect to see you here."

"I could say the same. Looks like you got yourself in a little trouble."

"I can tell you the whole story, if you have time."

"I'm afraid I can't help you with your dilemma, but I was hoping you could help me with mine. The men we arrested from the matching fingerprints, all have alibis. They say they were standing by your car when it was parked downtown and could have touched the trunk. We are about to let them go."

"I don't understand," Gaston said. "If you'd take a moment to hear why I'm in here, you'd find all of this is tied to the same group of men."

"Okay, but give me the short version. I was sent down here because the atmosphere around the cases has changed."

Gaston told him about the encounter and the events that led up to his incarceration. "We have another Asian American dead at the hands of a vigilante group. That should elevate my trial to Federal level."

"Well it would, but things have changed." He handed Gaston a bulletin.

Gaston read the large print: *INSTRUCTIONS TO ALL PERSONS OF JAPANESE ANCESTRY.*

Gaston had heard about the plan to intern Japanese Americans, but had dismissed it as something that just couldn't happen in the United States.

"You see the date, May 9?" Billings asked.

Gaston nodded, wondering where this was going.

"The defense of Allen Rich is going to be that he, as the head of the Civilian Defense, was trying to carry out President Roosevelt's Executive Order. Unless we can prove they were harassing Japanese Americans prior to Executive Order No. 9066, these guys are going to walk."

Gaston was aware that Japanese in the larger cities were already being rounded up and relocated to camps east of the Cascade Mountains. "There are a few isolated Japanese Americans. I've met with the family of Terry Nakamura. None of them want to harm America. Terry was second generation. He was born here. He had no connection with Japan."

"It's tough times. People are scared. It's all we can do to keep up with the hate crimes. The President has decided it's in the best interest of the country as well as the well-being of the Japanese descendants who live here, to move them to areas where they will be safe."

"Where does that leave me?"

"You are a fortunate man. Other than the assault on officers of the law, the other charges can be dropped."

Gaston let out a frustrated sigh. "You know there is no way for me to win a trial against Sheriff Johnson and Chief Myers. They're the law. Who's going to believe my story?"

"That's not my problem. Next time you see the sheriff doing something, I'd suggest you keep out of it."

Gaston shook his head in disbelief. "Then, you won't be needing more testimony from me."

"I doubt we'll be seeing each other again."

Alice visited Gaston July, 1. She looked tired.

"Have you been getting enough sleep?" Gaston asked, concerned. He looked at her and felt so helpless he could scream, but he knew that would only hurt her more. "Look at the bright side," Gaston said, trying to cheer her up. "They've dropped the murder charges."

"Have you got a trial date yet?"

Gaston pursed his lips and shook his head. "My attorney is going through a bunch of procedural things. He's got a hearing to drop all charges."

"I don't think Sam Johnson will go for that, let alone Police Chief Myers." Alice was despondent.

"I have some more good news," Gaston said.

Alice perked up. She wiped the tears from her eyes with a hanky and gave him a tight-lipped smile. "I'm ready. What has you so excited?"

"Major and his buddy, Talbot Miller, you remember me telling you about him? Anyway, they have become so frustrated with the war; they have decided to equip every civilian plane with Radio compasses, landing lights and all the latest gadgets for night flying. They are going to have a plane in the air every night and cover the entire Central and Southern Coast of Oregon looking for submarines."

"That's nice," Alice said. There was a complete lack of enthusiasm in her voice.

"I know you don't get as excited as I do regarding these things, but at least we'll be safer."

"Safer? What are they going to do if they spot one? Those boys are nothing more than defenseless targets for a submarine." She shook her head. "I will never understand war. Most of the people who get hurt are the innocent."

"You've got a point there. I'll take it up with Major."

"Gaston. Please get out of here."

"I'm doing my best."

Thursday, July 2, Alice brought Gaston a neatly pressed suit, dress shirt, socks, a tie, socks and shoes. He was to appear in court for a request to dismiss all charges. He felt it was the longest shot an attorney could make. It was a clear day and unusually hot without a breeze. He was brought into the courtroom, his handcuffs removed and he was seated next to his attorney. He leaned over to the tall man with the polished melon of a head. "I hope this isn't a wasted trip for you."

Alexander removed his glasses and whispered, "I don't make wasted trips."

Gaston turned and scanned the courtroom. There was no audience. *It must be a closed hearing*, he thought.

The prosecutor walked in wearing a baggy suit and loafers. It was the first time Gaston had seen him. He turned, smiled, and nodded at Gaston. *What was that?* The Judge entered and everybody stood.

"Be seated." The Judge, a man in his fifties, a full head of gray hair and bushy eyebrows picked up some papers on his desk. "I understand prosecution has received new information and wishes to petition the court."

"We have your honor. The prosecution wishes to drop all charges."

Gaston wasn't sure he heard right. He looked over at his attorney.

"The prosecution has dropped all charges against the defendant, Gaston Leroy Carson. Hearing no objection, Mr. Carson, you are free to go. Bailiff, make certain all the necessary discharge papers are filled out."

Gaston was speechless. He stood with his mouth open, afraid to make a move that might wake him up.

Alexander patted Gaston on the back. "How about I buy you lunch?"

"I can use some real food. You *are* going to tell me how you managed this, aren't you?"

"Actually, I'm going to tell you how *you* managed it. How do you like the *Bay View House*?"

"Never eaten there," Gaston said.

"Great place," Barry Alexander said. They were a little early for lunch and the restaurant had just opened. They sat by a window overlooking the bay. They could see the bridge spanning Yaquina Bay, the harbor with its many fishing and few pleasure boats, and the Coast Guard Station. The water glistened like a million diamonds in the bright sun.

"Do you men care for drinks?" a young woman asked. She wore a dark skirt and a white button-down blouse. Her hair was unusually short, but Gaston had noticed that short hair was becoming more popular with women since the war had started. Alice had said it was because long hair was not safe in the jobs women were taking to help the war effort.

"I'll have a double vodka martini with two olives. Shake it a few times, but don't let it get diluted."

It was the most specific drink order Gaston had ever heard.

"How about you, sir?"

"I think I'll have coffee, black, straight out of the pot. Bring it quickly so it doesn't cool." He tried to keep a straight face, but couldn't manage it. All three of them broke out laughing.

"I'm glad to see you haven't lost your sense of humor. You were in a tight spot," Alexander said.

"Honestly, I'm having a hard time believing I'm out." He slapped his hand to his forehead. "Damn, I've got to tell Alice."

"Hold off a few minutes. You need to know what happened."

Gaston held his breath and nodded. "Okay, you have ten minutes, but I warn you, I'm going to see my girl and celebrate."

Over drinks Alexander told Gaston the rapid turn of events that led up to the dismissal of all charges against him. He started out, "Have you ever heard of a wire recorder?"

"Sure, the same principle as a Dictaphone. I can't tell you how it works."

"That's okay. Your friend Major was able to borrow one from the library and place it under the pool table where the sheriff and his cousins play pool. After a week of trials, he was able to come up with the voice of Gene Johnson, bragging about shooting the owner of the Asian Market. The sheriff's voice is on the recording also talking about the attempt to remove the body. In short, your conspiracy was completely confessed and recorded."

"Is that legal?" Gaston asked, "listening in on someone's conversation without them knowing it."

Alexander smiled. He wiped a handkerchief over his shiny head. It was getting hot inside. "That was the argument I was expecting today, but when confronted, Gene Johnson broke down and confessed, claiming it was self-defense. The machete in the man's hand may help that stick. But you don't have to worry. The technology to record voices on a small device is so new, the courts didn't have a precedent. The prosecution offered a plea. Gene Johnson pleaded to involuntary manslaughter and six months. The prosecution was more than happy to drop the charges on you so as not to upset the community with a long trial that might bring down Sheriff Johnson and Chief Myers."

"Then I have Major to thank for my release."

Alexander wiped his head again. He pulled out his watch, "Look at the time, we need to get going."

"What about lunch?"

"I think we can get it at our next stop."

"Okay, I'm confused," Gaston said.

"We need to stop by the *Blue Whale*," Alexander said. "You can thank Major personally."

The second they entered the *Blue Whale*, Gaston knew there was something was up. The place was brighter than normal. A string of red, white, and blue lights hung above the bar.

Additional lights were strung around the perimeter of the room. A large banner shouting WELCOME BACK, GASTON! was hung on a wire across the center of the room.

People came out of the woodwork. The room erupted in cheers. Gaston stood there clamping his jaw, trying not to break down in tears. "I love you guys," he finally said.

Alice ran up and kissed him. "This is the happiest day of my life!"

"Mine, too," he said. "You put this all together?"

"What can I say? Major says he needs you back in the war."

"Do I see food over there?"

"Come on, everybody brought something. You'll have to try my potato salad."

"Why not, I survived your Irish stew."

"You crack me up, all your kidding around."

"Kidding? Me kidding? This is my innocent look."

Chapter 23

Commander Goodman was still steaming about the sinking of the *SS Coast Trader*. The local papers had picked up the story and he was getting calls of near panic from the citizens in the area. The official report from the Department of the Navy was that the *SS Coast Trader* suffered a boiler malfunction that caused an explosion. The Navy report gave no credibility to the crew sighting the Japanese submarine.

Local papers had also reported strange aircraft activity east of Brookings. In the newspaper account, a forest service lookout had heard a strange noise, sounding a lot like a Model-A Ford backfiring. This was highly unusual because he was in a fire-watch tower miles away from civilization and any roads. He searched the area and spotted a small plane circling the area. He called his partner to take a look. The early morning light was inching over the treetops making it difficult to distinguish, but they determined it was a single-engine pontoon plane. He called by radio to the ranger station in Gold Beach. It was 0624 hrs. The ranger station at Gold Beach forwarded the sighting to the Roseburg Filter Center, who attached no significance to the sighting. After all there were intermittent private flights along the coast quite often. At noon that day, after the fog had lifted from the forest valleys, smoke was detected. It was the start of a forest fire. There was no lightning, and no thunderstorm activity. The official report was the fire was a sleeper left over from a thunderstorm the previous day. Goodman shoved the report into a folder with a dozen other reports and called Gaston into his office. "Welcome back, Gaston. I'm glad to see they let you out. Frankly, I thought you were in a hole so deep, you'd never climb out. I saved some incidents for you to check out." He held the folder out for Gaston. "I don't know what to think of them."

Gaston took the folder. "Sir, I want to thank you for standing by me."

"I don't know what you are talking about."

"The attorney, sir. Alice told me you gave her his card."

"Glad I could help. Keep it quiet, will you?"

"No, problem."

Gaston had papers covering the table. He was using the kitchen in the Officer's Quarters as an office to review the folders. The aroma of fresh perked coffee hung in the air. He filled his cup and started reading. He went through the reports before he realized he hadn't touched his coffee. He was deep in thought when he was interrupted by Alice.

"Three people got citations last night for driving along the beach with their lights on. The local paper is warning fishermen the lighthouses will be under black-out rules at night. Do you think all this effort is doing any good?"

Gaston looked up from the papers and started gathering them up into a neat stack. "I guess there's no way to know for certain. The blackout is designed to prevent the enemy from knowing where the towns are. If we survive the war without being bombed, then maybe it worked."

"You know Civil Defense has been patrolling, making sure there are no lights that show, but the airport has new runway lights. How much sense does that make?"

Gaston gave her a look that said, "I don't really want to engage in this conversation right now."

"You didn't drink any of this, did you?" Alice took his coffee and poured it back into the pot and poured him a hot cup. Coffee was one of those items that were being rationed and it was becoming scarce, even on the base.

Gaston took a sip. "If you were the enemy and you were trying to draw our forces out of the Pacific and back to the United States, what would be your strategy?"

"Gaston, I'm not going to engage in a discussion about war strategy, just so you can make me look stupid."

"That wasn't my intent." He looked up to see Pastor walking in. "How about you, Danny? If you were the enemy and your mission was to get us to withdraw our troops from the Pacific to defend the homeland, what would you do?"

"I suppose I would launch an all-out attack against the mainland."

"Suppose you had very limited resources yourself, but still wanted to have the same effect?"

Pastor poured himself a mug of coffee. "I'm not sure what you are getting at."

"If I was Japan and I wanted to get the troops moved from the Pacific to guard the mainland, I would launch a propaganda campaign."

"You mean like drop leaflets, telling the people there will be a raid?"

"That might be part of it, but these submarine sightings have the population riled up. Fake periscope tubes are scattered along the coast, submarines are shelling lighthouses. It looks to me like nothing but general harassment, but I'd say they have been pretty effective in scaring the population."

"I'd say you're right there," Pastor said.

Gaston nodded and proceeded to set the stack of papers back into the folder. "We need to do something about those submarines." He finished his coffee and put the cup in the sink. "Alice, if the Commander comes looking for me, tell him I'm at the airfield."

The entire fleet of nine airplanes was lined up outside the hangar. Gaston looked at the measly bunch of planes; some were used for crop dusting, others for pleasure. *How are we going to win the war with nothing but a few civilian airplanes?*

Major spotted Gaston and reached out his hand. "Hey, Gaston, glad you stopped by, I want to show you the latest addition to our air defense system." They shook hands and Major escorted Gaston inside. The hangar was a cacophony of noise from all kinds of activity, including welding, hammering, grinding, and the up and down roar from revving airplane engines. Smoke hung like a cloud and the smell of burnt diesel was prolific.

"No, I can't believe you found one of those," Gaston said. Before them with three technicians hovering over and around her was an auto-gyro, similar to the one they had seen at the Coast Guard Air Station in Warrenton.

"What do you intend to do with that?" Gaston asked, looking over the rotor-wing craft.

"I haven't decided yet. I got it from the Forest Service. They thought it might be good for fighting forest fires, but it didn't have enough load-carrying capacity. I got it for a steal."

"And Sarah is fine with this?"

Major smiled and put his finger to his lips. "Don't mention it around her."

"Have you got a minute?" Gaston asked. "I want to run something by you."

"Sure, let's go back in the office where it's quiet."

They walked to the back of the hangar. The office door closed and the drone of an engine being tested muted to a low hum. A fan in a window was blowing in cool outside air.

"I was thinking about your many upgrades to the search planes. What is your plan if you spot another submarine?"

"I met with Goodman the other day. He's getting a new cutter equipped with depth charge racks and a 5-inch gun. He'll be patrolling the coastline. If we spot anything we will notify them of its position. They will respond and bomb the hell out of it."

"I hate to throw water on your parade. As soon as the submarine spots you, they'll be underwater in thirty seconds. By the time any vessel responds, the bastard will be gone, only to pop up someplace later. I've been thinking about it. We need to be able to respond immediately."

"I hear what you're saying. Just knowing we're out looking at them will deter them from sticking around very long." He looked at Gaston and grinned.

"Wait, you already have a plan."

"From the actual submarine sightings I could put together, I've determined there are only nine Japanese submarines stretched from Alaska to the tip of California. All of the damage they could actually do wouldn't amount to a tick on an elephant's ass, but their presence is causing near hysteria in the general population. The Navy has adopted a code of silence, if you will. They are doing their best to discredit any sightings and put pressure on the papers to keep it out of the news. You and I know the *Coast Trader* wasn't sunk by a boiler explosion. Turning the lights off in the lighthouses takes away the possibility the lighthouse will be shelled, but it also means our fishing fleets and commercial vessels along the coast don't have a clue where they are. As long as we are being harassed by a few submarines, the Japs are winning the propaganda war. Every action they've taken makes me believe they aren't here to mount a major attack. Their mission is to harass, hoping the public will panic and demand we put more forces along our coast."

Gaston was delighted, Major had come up with the same conclusion as he. "Well, you've certainly given this a lot of thought, but I haven't heard any solution."

"We need some military aircraft that we can call upon for a quick response."

"Yeah, if that was going to happen, it would have already been done. There isn't enough population along the coast to merit any military response, unless there is an all-out invasion."

"You're telling me it's hopeless?"

Gaston grimaced and fidgeted a moment before he responded. "We need to take out the subs, not by calling in a Coast Guard cutter that may take an hour to respond. We need to take it out when we see it."

"That's impossible. We don't have the capacity to carry bombs, or even launch them." Major shook his head. "Gaston, pardon the pun, but you bombed out this time."

"I thought you might say that. While I was sitting in the city jail, I was joined one night by a drunk logger. When he sobered up, I began to talk to him, more to get my mind off of my dilemma than anything else. He said his job in the woods was blowing stumps to clear land after it was logged. Have you ever handled dynamite?"

Major didn't answer and Gaston didn't rush him. He could almost see the wheels turning in Major's head. After a long silence and some hand gestures, Major stared in Gaston's eyes. "How would you like to take a ride in an auto-gyro?"

*****

Commander Goodman left a message with Alice for Gaston to contact him when he got in. It was after lunch and as soon as he got the message, Gaston rushed over to Goodman's office.

"How are things coming with the submarine spotters?" Goodman asked.

Gaston doubted the Commander would have left a message for such a report. "Fine, sir. They are ready to take flight tonight."

"When I first heard of the sinking of *SS Coast Trader,* I was upset that the Navy had kept me out of the loop until they came up with the cock-and-bull story about the boiler exploding. According to the Navy, there are no enemy submarines operating off our coast. Ships which are sunk are accidents at sea. Now that the Japanese descendents have been moved to internment camps, the public is beginning to believe us. But that could all change if we don't get a handle on this." He handed Gaston a single-page report.

Gaston read it. "Another airplane sighting and another forest fire, sir. The last one was dismissed as a delayed lightning strike."

"Is that what you think?"

"What I think is there is an unknown technology the Japs have. You remember the fisherman report off Winchester Bay? He saw an airplane being launched from a submarine. Mitchell Williams is a pretty good artist and he drew a sketch of an airplane that matches the description of the plane seen over the forest at Brookings. I don't believe in coincidence. I think the planes are one and the same, and, as unbelievable as it seems, the Japs must have developed a method of transporting and launching an airplane from a submarine."

"That's impossible," Goodman said. "It's been run by Washington and they say it's pure fiction. It can't be done."

"There aren't any subs off our coast either," Gaston said, sarcastically. "I'm interested in your explanation, sir."

"Think about it. An airplane is awkward. The shape doesn't lend itself to fit into a submarine. I don't see it. They must be launching from a ship or a secret land base."

"A ship?" Gaston shook his head. "You've got cruisers going up and down the coast. There are fishing boats out there every day. You can't just make a ship disappear during daylight hours...unless it goes under water."

"Then there must be a land base."

"I think that's even more improbable. The coast is pretty isolated. They would need a landing strip, fuel, and supplies. Someone would notice something. Why not accept what the facts have given us. If the submarine is not carrying torpedoes in its rear bay and the airplanes wings were detachable, I think it's feasible."

Goodman still wasn't convinced. "I can't think of a strategic reason why they would go to such lengths."

There was a knock on the Commander's door. "Come in," Goodman said.

Danny Pastor was at the door with a message. "Commander, I thought you would want to see this." He handed it to Goodman. Goodman glanced at it. "That will be all, Ensign Pastor." He finished reading the report. "They found incendiary bomb fragments with Japanese markings at the forest fire site, the one they dismissed as a lightning strike. Firefighters are hiking to the second fire. I guess that answers my question."

"Sir, if the Japs were successful in starting wildfires, it could be pretty devastating."

"Especially if the public knows the Japs are starting them. Funny how these things seem to come around full circle. That was why I called you in. Can you go back to Brookings and put a lid on any mention of these fires in the papers?"

"With all due respect, sir, how am I supposed to do that?"

"I don't need you to tell me how; it just needs to be done."

"Yes, sir. Is that all?"

"You've heard about the new cutter we're getting?"

"Yes, sir. It's front page news."

"I think it will do a lot to convince the Japs to stop messing around off our coast. We'll be escorting merchant vessels as they travel along the Southern Oregon Coast. Morale of the men is high right now; we are finally getting into the fight."

*****

"I'm going to fly back down to Brookings tomorrow morning," Gaston said to Alice over a glass of California wine. They were at the *Bay View House*. Gaston wanted to see if the food really was a good as Alexander had said.

While he was in jail, he silently resented the President for sending him out West, but looking across the table at Alice, he wasn't so sure. If he hadn't been sent out here, he never would have met her. Maybe there was such a thing as fate. He was beginning to cherish these moments. He longed for the war to be over so every day could be like this moment.

Alice had begun to accept the many trips Gaston was taking. He was such a mystery. She didn't know where he was getting his money. She had no idea if he was telling her the truth about knowing the President, it all seemed preposterous.

It wasn't that she didn't believe him, it was more of a lingering doubt that he wasn't telling her the whole truth. There were so many stories going around. From reading the papers, it seemed the Japanese controlled most of the western world and our Government was keeping secrets from the people. From casual conversations with people she trusted, it seemed at times the Government was outright lying to the people. She had a hard time believing Gaston was not a part of that lie also. Deep in her heart, she didn't want to be hurt again. Day-by-day it seemed she and Gaston were drifting apart. The meal tonight was no different than several they had had lately. Gaston seemed like he was in a distant place. All she wanted was for him to be close to her, look her in the eyes, kiss her passionately, and say everything will be okay. Instead everything was talk of the war. "Gaston, maybe it would be better if we stop seeing each other for a while." She was shocked the words had come out of her mouth.

Gaston set his wine glass down and looked straight into her eyes. It was happening all over again. Just as he was growing close to someone they would leave him. He felt hurt and then anger, but bit his tongue. He wasn't going to give up on this relationship as he had done on the others. "Alice, I know something is troubling you. What is it? You can talk to me."

"That's just it, I can't talk to you. You are in a different world most of the time. If you would at least be honest with me..."

"Honest with you!" He realized he raised his voice and lowered it immediately. "There is nothing I haven't been honest about. What are you talking about?"

"Never mind, you're clearly upset and I don't want to start an argument."

Gaston hailed the waitress and pulled out a ten dollar bill. He handed it to her. "Keep the change, we're leaving." He pushed away from the table. "We need to go somewhere where we can talk."

They ended up parked on the sand at Agate Beach. The stars were out and they had to make the trip down a rutted sandy road with the lights turned out. The stars were unusually bright. On the horizon the moon was just rising. "You want to walk?" Gaston asked.

"I'm in my high heels and nylons."

"So, take them off, I won't watch."

"And go barefoot?"

"I'm taking off my shoes and socks. It's a perfect night."

They walked along the beach. Moonlight glistened on the sand where the waves had broken and receded. "I've been as honest as I can be with you," Gaston said, taking her hand. "Everything I told you about my childhood is true. Is that what's bothering you?"

They walked along the breaking surf. The wet sand felt cool and soothing to Alice. "Gaston," she said, "I was hurt in a relationship."

"I know, you told me about your fiancé."

"Not him, there was another Margaret doesn't even know about. I moved out here to get away from him. It seems every time I get into a relationship, something goes wrong."

"Is something going wrong with ours? If there is, I don't know what it is."

"Jack was a salesman in the office where I worked in New York. He was a dashing young man with a smile that just wouldn't quit. I should have listened to my mother. I wish I was more like her. She could read a man like a book. She had my dad pegged from their first date. But I didn't listen to her. I was still in shock, recovering from the loss of my fiancé. I guess it was because I was vulnerable. Jack comforted me. We had an affair that ended abruptly when I found out he was married." She stopped and faced him, and started to bawl. "If you want to leave me, you can. I'm sorry I didn't tell you I'm a tainted woman."

Gaston pulled her close to him and hugged her. His eyes were filled with tears. He was struggling not to cry, himself. He fished a handkerchief from his pocket and wiped his eyes and handed it to Alice. He wanted to tell her it was all right. What was in the past didn't matter. She felt so close, like she was a part of him. As he started to speak his eyes drifted out to sea. In the shimmering moonlight a black object rose slowly from the water. It was a perfect silhouette of an I-Class Japanese submarine. "I'd better get you home, it's getting late."

*****

"I tell you it was right off the coast of Newport. If you hurry it's still out there," Gaston told the Commander over the phone.

"Thanks for letting me know. I'll put a couple of corsairs in the water in the morning."

"With all due respect, sir, that sub will be long gone in the morning."

"I don't have anything that could safely go after an *I*-Class sub at night. If I turn the lighthouse on, they will have a perfect bearing and could start shelling us. They would hear any boat I have a mile away. The best I could do is fire from the shore, and that would cause them to light up the town with artillery. I can't risk it."

Gaston was completely dejected. "Thank you, sir; I'll talk to you in the morning."

Gaston called the *Blue Whale*. Even though Major was planning on flying him to Brookings at dawn, he was certain Major would be polishing off his last few beers.

"What the bloody hell, mate," Major answered in his best rendition of a British sailors accent.

He's three sheets to the wind, Gaston thought. *Do I really want to do this?* "Major, I just got off the beach and there is an *I*-Class submarine surfaced in calm seas due west of Agate Beach. Can you send whoever you have spotting tonight over to verify?"

"Gaston, old pal, Punchy's going out tonight. Grayson will be spotting for him. Where did you say you saw this thing?"

Gaston gave him the coordinates as best he could. "We're still on for the morning?"

"Right When the sun winks over the mountains, I'll be there."

Chapter 24

Gaston packed his camera. The chance of him getting a picture of a Japanese submarine was slim, but he was hopeful. He thought about his latest call to the White House. It seemed like he had precious little to report. The President was interested in how the people were accepting the movement of the Japanese descendants to inland camps. Gaston had regretted to report, for the most part, the move had gone with very little incident. The highly Caucasian population saw nothing wrong with the uprooting of American citizens and treating them like prisoners of war. The President was also very interested in the submarine activity. Positive identification and location would help identify what happened to ships that simply went missing. It was a puzzle the War Department was finding increasingly harder to put together. Again, the President had thanked Gaston for his service and reminded him that serving his Country didn't mean he had to be shooting down Japanese Zero's, or shelling obscure islands in the Pacific. Gaston wasn't certain. At the airstrip, he parked outside the gate and showed his ID to the guard.

Major was in the hangar talking to three other men when Gaston walked up. He wondered if the man ever slept. The conversation seemed to be a somber one.

"Good morning, Major," Gaston said, in a cheerful voice.

Major pulled Gaston aside. "We nearly lost Grayson and Punchy last night. Punchy's plane is a complete loss."

"Oh, no! What happened?"

"I sent them out to look for the sub. Punchy's in pretty rough shape as you can imagine. He's in the hospital with several broken bones. Grayson is in the hospital with him. Neither was much on details. Both are pretty rummy. I hope to talk to them tomorrow."

"I can put off the trip to Brookings, if you like."

"No I want to go. It will take my mind off this fiasco."

"Fiasco?"

"My word for it. I'm not sure what went wrong. Get into your flight suit and we can get going. We have clear skies as far as we can see."

Gaston looked over the repairs to the biplane. The wings had new fabric and a new paint job. He smiled when he saw the name written in bold letters, *BINGO*. He climbed in and buckled his harness. He noticed changes in the cockpit as well. It had been modified since his last flight. There was a long, thin box nested between his seat and the fuselage. The RDF was displayed on the upper starboard side of the already crowded console. He rechecked his harness and gave *thumbs-up* to Major, who was checking the instruments in the cockpit behind him.

In ten minutes they were moving down the coastline at an incredible speed. He could see fishing boats looking like white dots off the rocky shores. He knew they were fishing for cod, sea bass, and red snapper. Halibut fishing boats were farther out. Crab boats were closer to shore, the floats neatly in a line marking the traps, some as close as a quarter-mile from land. Gaston leaned against the seat back enjoying the trip. The fresh air was sweeping his face and the smell of the ocean enveloped him. Farther out, nearly on the horizon, he saw a freighter with three escort ships heading north. He smiled. Everything about the day looked serene and peaceful. Then an unusual wake in the water caught his eye. His hand went to the radio mic. "Major, do you read me?"

"Roger. What's up?"

"See that freighter out there?"

"Got it."

"Does that look like a periscope wake to you?"

Major immediately took the plane down to about a hundred feet. He headed for the freighter and banked so he could read the name. He dialed the emergency frequency on the radio. Freighter *SS Isabella* and escorts, this is civilian spotter plane, *Bingo,* on your starboard side. You have a submarine at periscope depth trailing you. I say again a submarine at periscope depth is trailing you."

"Roger that, *Bingo.*"

One of the escort boats banked toward shore and circled around. As soon as the submarine saw what had happened, the periscope went down. He assumed the sub was in a deep dive. In a few more seconds, the boat was rolling depth charges off the transom. The sea erupted into a shower of explosions.

"I'd like to stick around and see what happens," Major said, "but I'm low on fuel."

"Roger," Gaston said. *For some reason the Japs have a lot of interest in the West Coast, especially the coast of Oregon,* he thought.

They touched down in Brookings and were met at the airstrip by Talbot Miller. He wasted no time. "Come with me," he said to Gaston. "I have the plane fueled and ready." Gaston loaded his gear into a brand new Piper J-5A, single-wing aircraft. "This is the perfect airplane for what you want, 75-horse Continental engine, cruising speed of 75 miles per hour. It's not going to break any speed records, but that's not what we're looking for."

"Sounds like you are trying to sell it to me," Gaston said.

"If you're in the market. It is a demonstrator, and I'm a licensed representative of Piper. Did I tell you it's a three-seater?"

"You're kidding," Gaston said, "there's hardly enough room for me and my gear. Where does the other person go?"

"I'm going to stay with *Bingo* and get her ready for our trip back," Major said. "How long will this take?"

"We'll be back in an hour," Talbot said.

Talbot had been right about it being the perfect plane. Unlike the bi-wing Boeing Stearman, this was a sleek aircraft. The wings and fuselage were aluminum. The wing was over the top of the cockpit, giving excellent downward visibility. The slow cruising speed was perfect for spotting and taking photographs. He fastened the harness and prepared his camera. He needed to take advantage of the midday sun when the trees and hillsides were not in the shadows.

In a few minutes they were over the site where the incendiary bomb had started the forest fire. The flames were out.

All that remained were a few wafts of smoke. Gaston could clearly see the firefighters below with their shovels and picks making sure the fire was out. "Can you take it a little lower? I need a few pictures."

Talbot dropped the plane until he was so close to the treetops Gaston could see the individual needles on the Douglas fir. A squirrel, startled by the plane invading his space, scampered down a tree and ran up another one. Gaston snapped picture after picture of the burned area. "Okay, that's all I need." Ten minutes later they set down on the airstrip.

When Gaston caught up with Major, he said, "You ought to look at one of these. The way the wings are set, you could drop a bomb from her if you wanted."

Major smiled. "Talbot and I have a little business to discuss over lunch; you're welcome to join us."

"Sure."

Before lunch, Major inspected the changes Talbot had made to one of his airplanes, a single-wing, two-engine Cessna T-50. It had a closed cockpit with side by side controls. The wings were under the cockpit. On each side of the cockpit an engine looked like it was built into the wing. "The biggest problem is the fuel consumption of this baby," Talbot said. "I can't get enough fuel rations to keep it in the air. I'm going to park it and use the Piper we were just in." He looked over at Gaston. "You sure you don't want to learn to fly?"

"Maybe some day," Gaston said.

Still looking at the Cessna, Talbot was showing Major a modification he was obviously proud of. "From the cockpit you can pull this lever, and you're going to love this." He pulled the lever and a metal tray on the bottom dropped down. "Bombs away!" Talbot yelled. "Ain't that a kick in the pants?"

"How big of a bomb could you hold?" Major asked.

"Two hundred pounds."

"Where are you going to get a 200-pound bomb?" Gaston asked. "I don't think the military is keen on letting civilians have live ammo."

"Party pooper," Major said, winking at Gaston. "I think we found a way around that."

"I'm not sure I want to know," Gaston said. "This isn't the kind of thing that will put me back in the brig, is it?"

Talbot wrapped his arm around Gaston's shoulder and pulled him close. "I hear you can get just about all the aviation fuel you want."

Gaston glared at Major, who shrugged and returned an innocent look. "Talbot, tell me about your mission."

After a sack lunch consisting of a peanut butter and jelly sandwich washed down with stale coffee, Gaston and Major got back in the biplane and headed north. Gaston was comfortable that Talbot would put the 500 gallons of high octane he had purchased to good use. He had also decided he would not tell the Commander about the plan Talbot and Major had concocted.

As they returned to the Newport airfield, Gaston and Major watched the last embers of the sun fizzle out in the Pacific. "You want to go over to the hospital with me and see how Grayson and Punchy are doing?" Major asked.

"Sure," Gaston checked his watch. He wanted to make sure he didn't miss another date with Alice. "Maybe they can tell us what happened."

They found Punchy and Grayson in the same room. Both men were awake and in good spirits. Gaston had never met either of them and was introduced. He stood back and let Major do most of the talking. He wanted to make mental notes, if anything they said was of importance to Washington.

"You weren't hot-dogging again were you?" Major asked Punchy.

Punchy hung his bandaged head. "Honestly, I don't know what happened. We were flying off Agate Beach, where we were told there was a sub sighting, but that's the last I remember."

Major turned to Tony Grayson. "Is that your story, too?"

"I remember a little more," Tony said. He had a concerned look on his face. "Honest, it was all a mistake."

"I thought so," Major said. "I should have dropped you two the first time you screwed up."

Gaston was shaking his head, trying to figure out what they were talking about.

"Tony, tell me the long version. Don't leave anything out." Major's tone was dead serious.

"Off the beach, we saw something, all right," Tony said. "We both thought it was the Jap sub. The moon was out, so visibility was good. It was clear. I don't know how we screwed up like we did."

"Get on with it," Major said.

"We were farther north than we thought. What I think we actually saw was the string of rocks off Beverly Beach. I swear to God, in the low tide and moonlight it looked just like a submarine. 'There she is!' I yelled to Punchy. We were going to buzz it, get down real low and check it out. Punchy was flying, so I can't speak for him, but when we hit, I guess we were both thrown from the plane."

"How about it, Punchy. What the hell happened?" Major was visibly angry.

"Pretty much like Tony said. I think my engine stalled when I started down. Maybe some bad fuel. All I know is, I started to drop down on the sub and—"

"Punchy said it was rocks," Major cut in. "Are you sticking to your story?"

"I don't know. I was busy fighting with the controls. The plane wasn't responding and ... I just don't know."

"It'll sort itself out," Major said. "If they find wreckage along Beverly Beach, I'll have to ground you."

Punchy was nearly in tears. "Not much chance of me flying again, anyways. My plane is a complete loss."

"What did you think of that?" Major asked Gaston as they left the hospital.

"Should be easy enough to sort out. A plane wreck that close to shore is certain to leave a lot of debris."

Gaston drove Major to the airfield. The night spotters were getting ready to make their next flight. "Gaston, you know there's a federal law forbidding civilian planes from being armed," Major said.

"Why are you telling me this?" Earlier Gaston had started to piece together what was going on, and he didn't want to know how many laws they were breaking. He thought of the long narrow container installed next to his seat in *Bingo*. Under his feet he had discovered a hatch, so neatly installed in the floor of the cockpit. He had missed it for most of his trip.

Major answered. "Because, I may need you to go my bail, and get Chrome-Dome to defend me if I get caught."

"Chrome-Dome? Really, didn't your mother teach you manners? His name is Barry Alexander. Have some respect. He saved my butt."

"I saved your ass," Major reminded him. "Chrome-Dome was the messenger."

"Okay, you're bringing this up now, because?"

"You owe me," Major said.

"You haven't got one of those recording contraptions set up around here, do you? I feel like this conversation could come back to haunt me."

"This is all your fault," Major reminded him. "I was content to call the Coast Guard if I saw a submarine."

"Okay, show me how this is all going to work."

They went over to the airplane, which was ready to depart. He introduced Gaston to the pilot, Travis Davis, and the spotter, Randy Paine. Randy was a high school senior who volunteered after school. "You ever hear of Lloyd Keeland?" Major asked.

"Can't say I have," Gaston said.

"He's a logger's boy from back in the woods. He spent a day with us teaching us what we need to know about dynamite and TNT. He and his dad make a living blowing stumps and boulders. He showed us a thing or two about these here sticks." He held one in his hand. "Looks a little like a flare, doesn't it?" He continued, "see this narrow box? It will hold eight sticks of TNT and two flares." He pulled out the first stick. "The thing to remember is the first two sticks are flares. That's very important. Without it you can't light up the target, and you can't light the dynamite."

"I'm starting to get the picture," Gaston said. "You don't expect to sink a sub with a few sticks of dynamite, do you?"

"Probably not, but we'll sure scare the hell out of them."

"I can't see this going very well. I've got to get back to the base," Gaston said. "Let me know how it goes."

"The reason I'm telling you this is you're going to be with me tomorrow night," Major said.

"I'm not sure I can do that."

"Why not?"

"I can think of a dozen reasons right off the top of my head."

"Don't be such a fuddy-duddy. This is what you've been asking us to do. Would you rather we fill the plane with TNT and crash into them?"

"Okay. If things go well tonight, I'll ride shotgun, tomorrow. Right now, I'm already late for a date."

Early the following morning Gaston was about to leave Officer's Quarters for another meeting with Major, when the phone at the front desk rang. Alice hadn't arrived yet, so Gaston picked up. "Officer's Quarters, Carson speaking."

"Mr. Carson, they have a boat ready to leave at the dock. If you want to be on it, you've got five minutes."

"Who am I speaking to?" Gaston asked.

"First Mate Nelson. Major is already aboard."

"Be right there." Gaston hung up and ran out the door. He didn't know what was up, but he knew if Major was a part of it, and it involved a boat, it couldn't be good. He spotted the 75 foot, *Six-Bitter*, as it was called, a wooden boat with twin gas powered Sterling engines and a crew of eight. A *Six-Bitter* was equipped with various armaments. This one had a 20 mm gun mounted on the foredeck.

"Permission to come aboard?" Gaston said to the Chief Boatswain's Mate. He knew him as Crabs, from bar room conversation. He wasn't about to ask how he got that nickname.

"Granted."

A seaman handed Gaston a Mae West as he gave him a hand getting aboard. Before Gaston had completely got his footing, the boat shoved off, headed for the bar. The fog was heavy, with visibility only a few hundred feet. Major was holding on to the netting around the rubber raft that served as a lifeboat. Gaston grabbed the netting and widened his stance. "You want to tell me what this is about?" Gaston asked Major.

"Travis and Randy didn't make it back last night. They got lost in the fog and never returned. This is the earliest we could mount a search.

"What about the Radio Direction Finder?" Gaston asked.

"I wish I knew more."

The boat paralleled the North Jetty and was hitting the first waves as they crossed the bar. The ocean was relatively calm with three-foot swells. The fog hugged the water making it difficult to get your bearings. In another minute they lost sight of land.

CG 299 had a top speed of twelve knots, and Gaston got another grip on things as the engines were revved to full power.

Major tried to light a cigarette and gave up. "This is going to be like taking a shot in the dark. The last I know, they were heading south and had made it to the mouth of Alsea Bay when we lost contact. If they lost their radio, they would have been flying blind. I'm told the weather is a little better down that way. We've also sent out a number of civilian craft."

Ten minutes out and Gaston could see the fog start to break up. In another minute he could make out sporadic houses nestled in the trees along the coast. As the fog lifted, the crew, along with Gaston and Major, took up posts along the railing. Another ten minutes and one of the seamen called out and pointed to some debris in the water. They maneuvered up to the floating debris, which looked like the rudder of a plane minus the tail fin. Not far off, what appeared to be a pontoon was floating.

"Major," Crabs asked, "were they flying a float plane?"

"That's not them. We're looking for a single-wing Piper Cub with fabric wings," Major said.

"Wait!" Gaston yelled, recognizing the debris. "We need to retrieve that debris." He slugged Major on the shoulder. "You remember that picture I showed you. If I'm not mistaken this could be the proof I've been waiting for."

"You may not have to wait much longer." Major pointed to a thirty-foot crab boat named the *Nelly Bee*. "That piece isn't from their plane either." There was noticeable excitement on the *Nelly Bee*. One of the deck hands was winching a large piece of airplane wing out of the water. *CG 299* pulled beside her and Crabs used a loud speaker to get their attention. "This is the US Coast Guard vessel *299* approaching. Fishing vessel *Nelly Bee,* prepare fenders and secure lines for a boarding party. Secure lines, starboard side."

They pulled up along side and secured the two crafts. Crabs told Major to check it out since the plane was one of his Civil Air Patrol fleet. Major prepared to board, to make identification. A rope was strung between the vessels and Major held on tight as he made his way from the taller railing of *299* to the deck of the *Nelly Bee*. Gaston held fast to the railing on the Coast Guard boat. "Just as you thought, it's a Jap plane," Major yelled up at Gaston.

They transferred the wing section to the *CG 299*. The fabric matched the rudder section they had already recovered. The weight of the engine would have dragged the rest of the plane under water. From what he could see of the wing section, the metal parts were burned and twisted, like they had been blown apart. Major climbed back aboard *CG 299* and the boats went their separate ways, continuing to search. A mile down the coast, near the mouth of the Alsea River they encountered another boat. This one had a line tied to a large piece of aircraft. As they approached, Major immediately recognized it from the plane Travis Porter had been flying. There was no evidence of the pilot or the copilot. The section of the plane was loaded onto the Coast Guard vessel and secured.

They continued searching another two hours, and around noon, Crabs called Major to the bridge. "The temperature of the water in this area and the currents make for a survival time of less than an hour. If they went in the water, they're most likely didn't survive. This is turning from a search and rescue mission to a search only. We're going to head back to port and let the civilian boats continue. I have to intercept a merchant vessel off Newport this afternoon and escort her to the mouth of the Columbia. Anything else we can do let me know. My report will say we found your craft and parts of an unknown second aircraft that appears to be Japanese in origin."

Major nodded. "Then get us back so I can put together a shore search."

As they returned to the dock, Major, who had been silent much of the return trip, grabbed Gaston by the sleeve of his jacket. "I'm not ready to give up on them. Can we use your vehicle to patrol the beach between here and Waldport?"

"I can do better than that," Gaston said. "I'll see if we can open the beach for a day and get everyone out searching for them."

When they returned to the base, Gaston called the Commander and was assured they would open the beach to search parties. He turned to Major. "How many people can you get out?"

"Plenty," Major said. "Let's stop by the *Blue Whale* and get the word out."

Gaston was able to borrow a new Jeep from the base motor pool. The *Blue Whale* had half-a-dozen regulars sitting at the bar and playing pool when Major and Gaston walked in. Major made his case and five people left the bar, promising to gather volunteers and mount search parties. The distance from Newport to Waldport was only ten miles. Gaston suggested, because of the limited access and rough shoreline, they break into five parties, each covering a one mile stretch on foot. The five parties would each search a mile of beach heading south from Newport to Seal Rocks. Gaston and Major would cover the five-mile stretch from Seal Rocks to Waldport in the Jeep.

Within an hour over fifty people had joined the shore search for the two missing men. Gaston and Major drove to Waldport and started up the beach heading north. They were looking for any sign of the wreckage or the men. They drove the Jeep along the base of the cliff, where driftwood and debris gathered at high tide. It was slow progress, slowing for piles of debris and obstacles such as rocks or washed ashore garbage from ships at sea. While examining a pile of driftwood, a piece of fabric caught Gaston's eye. "Over there, in that rubbish," he said to Major, who was riding shotgun. He turned the Jeep in that direction. Major bailed out and ran across the sand. He immediately waved for Gaston to join him.

On the sand was one of the men they were searching for. Major reached down and turned over the body. The body was pretty beat up and the skin a sickening color of blue. He choked up. "It's the kid, Randy Paine." Major broke down completely. "Oh, geez, he was just a kid."

Gaston put his hand on Major's shoulder. "I'll call it in on the two-way." He went back to the Jeep. He had a lump in his throat. The war was becoming personal for him. They waited until an ambulance arrived from Waldport.

"I'm going to have to contact his parents," Major said. "God, he was torn up awful."

They continued north on the beach, checking any and all debris. It was slow progress and another hour passed. Then, they spotted another body in plain sight, rolling in the surf. Gaston pulled the Jeep up to the edge of the water, got out, and ran through the surf. He was up to his knees in the cold water when he caught the man by the arm. He immediately let go. Major caught up with him. Gaston was standing in the breaking waves staring at the man.

Major was the first to speak. "I'll be a mother's uncle we got us a goddamned Jap."

Again Gaston radioed in the find and they waited for the ambulance that had picked up the boy to catch up with them. "What do you think happened?" Gaston asked. They had dragged the body to the sand. It was clearly a Japanese sailor. He was wearing oversized black trousers held up with a white cloth belt.

His shirt was metal gray. He looked to be very young. "What do you make of this?" Gaston asked again.

Major stated the obvious. "I'd say Travis and Randy encountered a submarine and something went terribly wrong." The anger caught up with him. "They will pay for this, if it's the last thing I do."

Gaston was filing all the information away. He wasn't about to make a quick judgment, but something inside him was about to snap. If he was asked to keep this quiet, he didn't know how that would be possible.

"Hurry up, you're burning up daylight," Gaston called to Major from the Jeep. Major hit the back doors of the ambulance twice and it took off south toward the nearest access road that connected to the Pacific Coast Highway. He ran up and jumped in the passenger side of the Jeep.

They still had three miles of beach to search, and one body was still missing. Gaston continued along the beach, maneuvering around the outcropping of rocks exposed by the low tide. In the distance he could see through a haze, the large rock outcropping that the Seal Rocks area was named for. He turned toward the embankment and started across soft sand. He was turning around. Their search had just about come to an end. He felt a tap on his shoulder.

Major said, "over there!" His voice had excitement in it. "Get over there, punch this thing." They pulled up to a clump of underbrush stretching out to the sand. "It's Davis," Major said, jumping out. He ran to the man's side and lifted him up to a sitting position. "He's alive!"

Gaston pulled a canteen of water from the Jeep and raised it to Travis's parched lips, but he was unconscious. His clothes were still wet. "Let's get him out of here." They laid him on the back seat of the Jeep. Major covered him with his coat.

Major patted Travis' cheek. "Travis, wake up. Can you hear me? How quick can we get to the hospital?" Major asked.

"We're about to find out. You recognize this stretch of beach?" Gaston asked, as he got out and locked the front hubs in 4-wheel drive. He started up an impossibly rutted road that angled up the bank.

"You're going to get us all killed," Major said. The Jeep crept up the embankment. One wheel lifted off the ground and the vehicle started to teeter. Gaston gunned it and the nose rose higher. He was certain they would tip over. He let off the gas, the nose dropped and he gunned it again. They climbed the rutted road like a bucking horse until they went over the top and slammed down hard. The path to the road was through a dense forest of wax leaf myrtle, coastal pine and Douglas fir. Fortunately, at one time, someone had cut a road and used it for beach access. The thick overgrowth made it nearly impossible to forge. They had to keep their heads down to avoid being swept off the rig by low hanging branches. They crawled at a snails pace making it seem longer, but the trip from the beach to the highway took less than five minutes. When they reached the highway, Gaston stopped and unlocked the hubs. In a few seconds he jammed the shift into high gear and they hit 60 mph along the straight stretches of the highway. They had no way of knowing if Travis would make it to the hospital while he was still breathing. As they pulled up to the hospital the ambulance with the two bodies was unloading the Japanese sailor. Gaston pulled up alongside. "We have a live one," he yelled. "Give us the gurney." He jumped out and grabbed the gurney from the two women who were operating the ambulance. "Help us," Gaston demanded. "Our man is alive!"

They lifted Travis Davis onto the gurney. "We need a doctor," Major called, as they rolled Travis into the hospital.

Chapter 25

"Gaston, I've got a meeting with the Navy Board of Inquiry tomorrow morning 0800. You're presence had been requested."

It was unusual for the Commander to walk over to the Officer's Quarters and deliver a message in person. That should have tipped Gaston off as to the seriousness of the situation, but he was unwinding from an exhausting, adrenalin packed day and it just came out. "Commander, I'm not in the Navy."

"I'm in no mood for humor, Gaston. You're going to attend this meeting if I have to lock you in the brig and have my MPs drag your sorry ass to my office."

"Oh eight hundred; got it, sir." Something had to be wrong. The Commander clearly was not in a joking mood.

Alice was already in her pajamas when he arrived at her apartment, and wasn't in a mood for his excuses. "I'll make it up, I promise," he said. She let him in and served him coffee at the table. "I am so sorry. I know you've heard it before. I promise it won't happen again. Please forgive me."

She stood up. "I don't know what to believe, Gaston. You've been so preoccupied with whatever you're doing. I'm not certain I can compete with that."

Gaston stood and reached out to her. "I don't want to lose you. Please understand, it won't always be this way." They hugged.

"I guess that is something to be seen," Alice said. "Please go. I need to get some sleep."

Members of the search party were invited to gather for a critique of their findings. The *Blue Whale* was packed. Everyone was talking about the Japanese sailor, who had washed up on the beach, and the youngest member of the CAP who had been killed. Rumors abounded of how the two were found, and what could have happened. The *Newport Times* was there in force. It seemed every reporter on the staff wanted a statement from the search party members. There were enough stories going around to fill a week of headlines.

"Major, tell them not to talk," Gaston said.

"Sorry, Gaston, that's beyond my control."

Gaston pulled Major aside. "Believe me, this isn't going to be good if these people talk to the reporters. If the news we found a Jap submariner on the beach gets in the paper, the entire coast will be demanding the authorities do something."

"Gaston, I'd like to help, but you've read the Constitution, does the First Amendment ring a bell?"

"I believe in the First Amendment as much as anybody, but we're at war and people could get hurt."

"Well, I'll give you this. You and I have most of the story firsthand. The rest have rumors and speculation. If we don't talk and Travis doesn't talk..."

"Oh shit! Travis," Gaston said. "We need to get to the hospital and make sure some reporter isn't pressuring him for a story."

"How do we get out of this?" Major asked. "I asked them all to show up here."

"I don't know. Buy them a beer and thank them for helping and send them home. I'll head to the hospital." Gaston left the *Blue Whale* in a rush.

All the way to the hospital Gaston thought of how he was going to get the staff to let him in to see Travis. As he pulled into the parking lot he'd devised a plan. He went to the front desk, leaned over, and read the name tag on the young girl. He held out his ID card, the one with the President's seal on it. "Amy, I need to see Travis Davis. It's a matter of National Security."

Amy looked at the card, the name, and the picture of Gaston. She stared at Gaston. "This way, Mr. Carson. We're a little short on doctors. I'll try and get permission from the one on duty."

"Ma'am, you did see the card?"

"Yes?" She looked confused.

"What part of 'National Security' don't you understand? We are at war; my presence here must be kept a secret."

She showed him to Travis' room. He put his finger over his lip. "Silence," he whispered to Amy.

Travis Davis was awake, sitting up in bed. He was receiving fluid through an IV. "Travis, I'm Gaston Carson, remember me?"

"Yeah. You were with Major."

"I need to debrief you. Do you think you can tell me what happened?" Gaston pulled his small notebook and a pencil from his pocket. He touched the tip of the pencil to his tongue and readied himself, but the room was silent.

"Travis?" He shook him awake. "You nodded off. You want to start again?"

"Give me a drink of water."

Gaston handed it to him. It was then he noticed how young Travis was. "How come you aren't in the service? You can fly a plane. You're in good shape."

"I tried the Army Air Corps. Maybe if they get desperate enough, they'll take me. My eyes aren't so good. I have to wear glasses. Now, the Army thought I'd be good, but it turns out I have flat feet. Maybe the Navy, God knows I can swim." He laughed. "Anyway, I'm here. I guess we got our own little war going on, don't we? You haven't heard what happened to Randy."

"He didn't make it," Gaston said.

"Oh, damn it! He was like a brother. His mom is going to kick my ass all the way to China." He put his hands to his head. "Jesus, he was younger than me."

"It wasn't your fault," Gaston said. "Why don't you tell me what happened? Start from the moment you left the airfield."

Travis gave him a tight-lipped nod. Tears were flowing. He wiped them away with the back of his hand. "It was just after dark, about 10:30 when we rolled down the runway. It was a perfect night. No moon, high clouds, very dark, but the air was still. We headed out over the ocean. With the blackout we were only able to spot an occasional car going down the highway. I remember thinking; *this is going to be a smooth trip.* I tested the RDF, it was good, so we turned on the spotlight and flew along the water, maybe a hundred feet up. We were about half-a-mile out. We were far enough south, I was afraid I'd hit Cape Perpetua, so I headed farther out to sea. I'm telling you, it was dark. There was nothing, land or sea that would give us a bearing, so I made sure we were well away from land. I circled and started back. We were just off the coast at Waldport when Randy tells me he sees something, could we take it down for a closer look." He took a drink of water. Gaston used the break to catch up on his notes.

He continued, "Randy, he saw something, all right. As sure as I'm sitting here, we came eye to eye with a Jap submariner. He was standing on the deck smoking a cigarette. We went around for a closer look. You won't believe this, but there was an airplane attached to that sub. The man dropped his cigarette, grabbed a wrench, and started shaking it at us. 'Let's try the dynamite,' Randy yelled. I brought her around one more time. When I got her into view again the man had retrieved a rifle and was shooting at us. I could see the muzzle flash. I dove down, heading right at him. Randy let the dynamite go. I felt the plane lurch and I lost control. That's the last I remember."

"We found you on shore, north of Waldport."

"Oh, yeah. I remember swimming. I have no idea which direction I was swimming. I just swam until I couldn't swim anymore. When I was ready to give up, my feet touched the bottom. I remember thinking, *I'm either drowning or I've reached shore.* A wave pushed me ashore and I crawled on the sand."

"You washed up near Seal Rocks. A little farther north and you would've been smashed to pieces."

"My mother always said there's an angel watching over me. Guess she was right."

"Travis, I've got to ask you to do something."

"What?"

"I need for you to forget everything you just told me. None of it happened."

"But it did. I just told you."

"Travis, I need for you to hear me." Gaston made eye contact with him. "If you tell your story to the newspapers, it will cause widespread panic along the coast. There is enough hysteria, without you telling what you saw. Do you understand what I'm saying?"

"I guess," Travis said, "but it's a hell of a story, don't you think?"

"It's a hell of a story for after the war, but for now, you didn't see a sub or an airplane on it, and you realize it's a Federal crime to arm a civilian airplane."

"Federal crime?" Travis looked worried.

"You didn't have any dynamite on that airplane did you, Travis?" Gaston was shaking his head slowly from side to side.

"Uhhh...no?"

"No, you didn't. You lost your engine and had to ditch. That's your story."

"You believe me, don't you?"

"I believe you, but that doesn't matter. I wasn't here either, understand?"

Travis curled his lips. His eyes filled with tears. "Poor Randy. He deserves better. He deserves to be treated as the hero he was."

Gaston put his hand on Travis' shoulder. "I'm sorry, man, I really am. We all have to make sacrifices." As he walked out of the room he considered going back to the *Blue Whale*, but thought better of it. Instead he headed back to Officer's Quarters. He wanted a drink, but he needed sleep more. His gut was churning. With all the lies, he hoped he wasn't digging a hole he couldn't climb out of.

Gaston dreaded the next call he was going to make to the White House. As bad as things were for him, it was worse for the President. Roosevelt had overcome adversity at every level and now he was fighting a war on two fronts. Gaston sure as hell didn't want to give him a third one, if he could help it. He hoped the story of Travis and Randy's encounter with a submarine carrying an airplane wouldn't do that.

Chapter 26

It was nearly 0800. Gaston walked across the base, still not sure why he was being included in a meeting with the Navy Board of Inquiry. He wasn't certain what the Board's purpose was, but he was about to find out.

He announced himself to the seaman at the desk. "Follow me, sir," the seaman said. He took Gaston down the hall to a small conference room. Standing with the Commander was a short stocky man in an officer's summer uniform.

"Mr. Carson," Commander Goodman said, as soon as Gaston entered the room. "This is Commodore Thackeray, from the NBI."

Gaston started to salute, caught himself, and extended his hand. The Commodore shook it. The man had a firm grip. His face was square, with a small mouth and tiny, piercing eyes.

"Shall we get started," Thackeray said, taking a chair at the head of the table.

Gaston and Goodman sat on either side. The table would seat up to ten. A pitcher of water and three glasses sat on a tray in the center.

Thackeray pulled out a thick folder from a worn leather briefcase. He opened it and spread newspaper clippings across the table. "These are a few of the articles that are fueling a wave of panic up and down the coast."

Gaston could see some of the articles were from the local *Newport Times.* "With all due respect, these are civilian businesses. Every time we mention the possibility of causing panic, the reporters throw the First Amendment at us. It doesn't have an exclusion for time of war."

"I'm not debating your efforts to keep these things from getting into the press. People are going to see things, and they are going to tell their stories. What I'm here to tell you is that there are always two sides of a story. The civilian side and, if I may, the official side. This year in Oregon alone, there have been seventeen instances where a story has been written that caused anxiety enough to prompt letters to State, as well as Federal, Congressmen. Most of those letters have demanded more protection be placed along the coastline." The Commodore got up and poured himself a glass of water. He returned to his seat, took a drink and continued. "The official position, and this is coming from the Department of the Navy, is that there is no Japanese presence along the West Coast. Commander, you have been in the middle of every one of these articles and have neglected to respond in an official capacity. Keeping silent is not a strategy that is helping calm the public. From this point on, the Navy is asking all Commanders to become proactive when an event occurs. Be the first to call the press and give an official account of what happened. We have adopted a plan referred to as the 3Ds. Rule one: Deny any Japanese involvement; Rule two: Deflect the conversation in another direction; and Rule three: Deflate the rhetoric. By doing this, the public will see there is a balance of information, no need to panic."

"Sir," Gaston said, "you're asking us to lie to the press and the American people.

"I'm not asking you to do anything. The Navy is ordering that these instances be treated differently than they have been in the past. Of course, Mr. Carson, you are not under our direct authority. I expect that you will bring this up with Washington, and do the right thing."

"I have my own 3D plan," Gaston said. "I like it better. Rule one: Develop a plan to defend the coastline; Rule 2: Destroy the threat; and Rule three: Deny there was a threat."

The Commodore chuckled. Commander Goodman clamped his jaw to keep from laughing.

"You're a civilian," Thackeray said. "Leave the fighting for those with the mettle to bear arms."

Gaston was insulted and wanted to lash back. Pound the little son-of-a-bitch into the ground, but he checked himself. "We've been using a similar strategy, but we haven't been putting out counterfeit stories, as you're suggesting. I can see where it may help. If that's what the Navy wants, I'll do my best to comply."

"That will be all, Mr. Carson," Thackeray said, standing and extending his hand. "The Navy appreciates your cooperation."

Commander Goodman stood.

As Gaston left the room, he heard Thackeray say to the Commander, "what the hell is he doing out here?" He didn't hear the Commander's response.

*****

The hangar at the Newport airstrip acted as the assembly place for the wreckage. The Japanese airplane was a Glen-model float plane. The report that was sent up the chain of command included a full accounting of the various sightings, and the suspicion it was being launched from a submarine. The report did not mention that it had been blown off the submarine by a makeshift dynamite bomb. The Commander never received a response. It was as if it had vanished and never been written.

Gaston had included the information in his report also. Washington was well aware of the technology to assemble and launch an airplane from a submarine, but not a single Defense Department Chief saw any advantage to the technology.

The *Newport Times* had numerous articles, none based in fact, saying there was an all-out attack by enemy submarines; their mission, the articles speculated was "to cause widespread terror by setting fires to our forests."

Gaston didn't disagree with the articles, but he did write a letter to the editor that disputed several wild claims. He noted there were only two positive submarine sightings off the Oregon Coast. Both of those had been disputed by the Navy. He made light of the fact the Japanese were trying to burn down our forests. "It rains so much out here, it would take a fleet of airplanes the size that invaded Pearl Harbor to start our forests on fire. The worst thing we can do is underestimate the intelligence of our enemy. They have the same weather reports as we have," he wrote, "and they know it's been the wettest year in recent history and our forests are nearly impossible to burn. Why would they waste the effort?"

The funeral for Randy Paine was an entire town event. Churches in the town tolled their bells at noon, and the entire town packed into the high school football stadium. The casket was covered with an American flag, and, because he was serving a mission for the CAD, the Coast Guard provided an Honor Guard of six to carry the casket.

Gaston was in the audience with Alice by his side. "This was a senseless death," he muttered to her. "We've got to drive those submarines from our coast."

Alice glanced at him and put her gloved finger to her lip. "Quiet, Major is getting ready to talk."

Major stepped up to the microphone. He tapped the mic. "When Randy Paine approached me because he wanted to help the war effort by flying in the Civil Air Patrol, I was excited to see one of our youth so enthusiastic to fight for our country. Randy was in his last year of high school. He told me he was headed to Oregon State College. He wanted a degree in Forestry, but he also wanted to fly. CAP gave him that opportunity. I remember when we first told him we were going to start night flying. He looked at me with those dark intelligent eyes and said, 'Major, it's about time we entered the Twentieth Century.' That's the kind of man he was. At 16, Randy was as much a man as any of our forces fighting the war. I'll miss you, Randy. We will all miss you."

Gaston and Alice both wiped tears from their eyes. "How many more young men will we bury before the war ends?" Alice asked.

*****

Ensign Pastor, dressed in his civvies, sat at the *Blue Whale* bar and downed what was, by his count, his sixth beer. "Okay, I'm ready to get the day started," he announced to Sarah who was on the other end of the bar wiping it down with a cloth.

"It's about time," Sarah said. "You got special plans?"

"I'm going to meet Gaston and Major at the hangar. They wanted my input on this new type of aircraft, they've been working on."

"Your input?" Sarah looked skeptical.

"It sounded kind of interesting...I might have invited myself."

"Your day off, huh?"

"Oh, hell, ever since Randy's death, Major is never around. I miss him."

"Yeah, you miss the free beers he gives you. It would do you good if you found something better to do with your time than suck down beers."

"If I wanted a lecture about my drinking, I would have married years ago," Danny countered.

"No decent girl would have you," Sarah said.

Danny took back the dollar tip he had left on the bar and walked out.

A fog hung over the area, but it was supposed to lift by noon. The sun was burning through the last of it when Pastor arrived at the airstrip. He showed his ID to the guard and walked to the hangar. As usual the hangar was a cacophony of sound. He put his hands over his ears as he approached Gaston and Major. They were leaning over the fuselage of the rotor-wing craft they had named *Beanie*. "What the hell is that?"

Major looked up at his friend. "Good, you're dressed for work. Hand me that pair of pliers."

Pastor picked up the pliers and put them in Major's hand. Major's head was still in the cockpit of the craft. "What the hell is this?" Pastor asked again. "It can't fly, can it?"

"We'll know in a few minutes," Major said. "You ready, Gaston?"

They pushed the craft outside. Major looked at the clear sky and smiled. He checked the sagging wind sock. "I think we're ready. Danny, you want to grab a jerry can and fill it up with high test? Gaston and I are going to take a ride."

"Who was your slave last week?" Danny asked.

Beanie was an unusual looking aircraft, but as Gaston and Major became more familiar with it they made it an integral part of their plan. Both had carefully outlined the details of their plan. If the Government wasn't going to fight the enemy on our coastline, they would. They had proven they could get close to the enemy and even drop dynamite on him, if they wanted. But to sink a sub, they needed to be more precise. Every time one of them mentioned, "sink a sub," they smiled. The code name for their mission was SAS. It was a covert operation the two had planned, and would soon carry out. Major had abandoned the plan to use dynamite with fixed-wing aircraft after the death of Randy Paine. Their new plan called for more precise delivery of the explosives.

Pastor lugged the can of gasoline over and set it beside *Beanie*.

Major had fetched some paint and some artist brushes. He handed them to Danny. "Since you're here, you can do this better than I. I want a red, white and blue beanie with a propeller on top, painted on the side. The letters *BEANIE* will be in white. I think that will look great, don't you?"

"No problem," Pastor said. "As soon as I get her gassed up."

"I didn't know you could paint," Gaston said.

"I've got all kinds of talent. You saw the sign in the *Blue Whale* when you got out of the brig," He pointed to himself, "I painted that."

Gaston stood back and watched Danny Pastor go to work. He was an artist all right. It took him only a few minutes to outline his design and start applying the bright colors.

"She's a beauty, isn't she?" Major said, admiring the awkward looking auto-rotor.

"I'm not sure *Beanie* is a she," Gaston said. "Sounds more like a guy."

"Sure, it's a girl," Major said. "In my mind, she's a girl. She's going to fly as graceful as a ballerina and sting like a bee."

"I hope you are right."

"You should give that a couple of hours to dry," Danny said, putting the lids back on the paint cans.

"No time for that, we've got to get a test flight in today. I'm the only one who's been up in this so far. I need to see how it handles with two onboard. Get your things on, Gaston." Major climbed into the pilot's seat. "Danny, you want to give that prop a spin?" The prop he was referring to was at the rear of the craft and was surrounded by a metal shroud.

Gaston buckled himself in. He felt like he was sitting on a canvas chair. In front of him was the normal array of instruments, but because of the side by side seating, there was no need for repetition. Below him, the bottom of the craft looked like the skin had been removed, but in fact, there had never been any skin there. Between his legs was a round, open bottom container that had been fabricated from an old milk bucket. He could see the ground directly beneath him. Overhead was a T-shaped bar that controlled the pitch of the overhead rotor, which was standing still at the moment.

The tiny engine started to whine in a high pitched tone. "Ready?" Major yelled to Gaston.

"Ready," Gaston called back. Even though they were sitting right next to each other, the whine of the engine drowned out their voices. He could feel the wind whistling past him even though they were standing still.

"Engaging," Major said. He flipped a lever in-between the seats and the large rotor overhead started to spin, first a thump, thump, thump, and then a steady staccato-like drone. It took only a moment and *Beanie* was off the ground, slowly moving foreword, then back, and then side to side.

"It's like floating in air," Gaston yelled. They were no more than a few feet off the ground.

"I'm taking it up," Major said. The words were hardly out of his mouth when they rose above the hangar, looking down at the airstrip, and the bewildered Danny Pastor. At a hundred feet off the ground, Major made a pass around the hangar and flew to the end of the landing strip and back. As they approached the hangar, a dozen people were standing pointing in awe. "Looks like we have attracted some attention."

"You want to fly it?" Major asked.

"Okay," Gaston said, not too sure he wouldn't kill them both.

"Grab the yoke."

Gaston reached overhead and grabbed the "T" handle. It had grips on it that reminded him of a motorcycle. "What now?"

"Pull back to go forward. Push forward to go back. The right grip is a throttle to slow down the engine. Don't worry, it won't let you stall. The grip beside your seat is to disengage the clutch, so you can free wheel. Better fuel efficiency that way."

Gaston played with the controls. He was amazed at the maneuverability of the tiny craft. He was able to bank right and left, and stop in midair. He had never experienced anything like it. "I could get used to this," Gaston said, taking it up, high above the growing crowd.

The Major reached on the dash, flipped a toggle switch, and the engine sputtered once and died. He saw a frightened look on Gaston's face. "Okay, Gaston, we've lost power. What are you going to do?" Major asked, calmly.

"I'm going to bail out!" Gaston said. "Wait, we don't have parachutes."

"Here's what you do if you lose power." He pulled the lever disengaging the overhead rotor and the craft floated down to the runway. It hit with a thud, but nothing was broken. The gasping crowd broke into a cheer. Major got out and bowed to the crowd and gestured for Gaston to do the same. Since the first time he had kissed a girl, his freshman year in high school, Gaston could not remember being more excited.

After the flight and the crowd had dispersed, Fairbanks approached Major. "I'd like to do a front page story on you and that contraption. When do you have time to sit down and give me all the details?"

"Not this week," Major said. "How about I call you."

"What was that about?" Gaston asked.

"I don't like that man," Major said. "I gave him a story on Randy and he didn't print it.

That night, as they sat in the *Blue Whale* celebrating the test flight, they heard the far-off sound of a thunder storm. Summer storms were not uncommon and nobody gave it a thought until Gaston walked out of the *Blue Whale* with Alice on his arm. "It's a beautiful night," Alice said. "I'm not ready to go home just yet."

Gaston was about to reply, when Major came racing out of the bar. "There's been a Mayday call from a freighter. You remember the thunder we heard. It was a torpedo. The Coast Guard is launching a search and rescue mission right now."

"You look like you're about to do something," Gaston said.

"I thought I'd go out and see if I can spot that SOB. You want to ride shotgun?"

"Are you taking *Beanie?*"

"*Beanie?* No. I don't think she's ready for action yet."

"I've got to do this," Gaston said. He kissed Alice. "I'll run you home."

"That's okay, you go with Major. I'll find a ride."

He kissed her again, this time on the lips. "You know I have to do this."

She nodded. It wasn't the perfect ending to the night she had hoped for.

Chapter 27

A corner of the hangar served double duty as an office and a radio shack for the CAP spotters. A woman, who, six months earlier, had been a stay-at-home mother of two, was now the radio operator for the spotters. As soon as Major arrived, she gave him a message. Major read it. "Damn the luck, Paul Frane in *Panther* spotted the Jap sub and couldn't seem to find the right frequency to warn the freighter. He called the Coast Guard, but they couldn't get out there in time. When will these people learn?"

By *these people*, Gaston figured, Major meant the merchant ship lines. "They should always ask for an escort, even if they think it's safe," Gaston said.

Panther was a single-engine, fabric covered, open cockpit Piper aircraft. It was an early, experimental, single-wing, single seater that hadn't been converted to accept a copilot. Paul Frane did double duty as as pilot and spotter. Even though the tiny plane had not been converted to launch dynamite bombs, it had the spotlights, landing lights and Radio Direction Finder required for night flying.

Panther landed as Major was topping off the fuel tank of his Stearman biplane. Major set the fuel can aside and ran over to the plane, as it taxied toward the hangar. Paul climbed out of the cockpit wondering why Major was standing there.

"What can you tell me about the sub?" Major asked.

"Long, black. The only reason I saw it was the freighters lights caught my attention. They should have been traveling with a single mast light. They looked like they were celebrating Christmas. It was like they were begging to be shot at."

"The Coast Guard is headed out. I thought Gaston and I would go out to keep a watch out for the sub."

"Well, it's out there and it knows we are, too. Be careful."

"I always am, "Major said.

Gaston finished topping off the fuel. "We're ready to go, Major."

"I'll get Paul to give the prop a twirl and we'll be off."

The runway was completely black as they waited for the engine to warm up. Major gave *thumbs up* and 2000 feet of lighted grass showed up in a narrow strip ahead of them. Major wasted no time getting his plane up to takeoff speed. Using less than half the runway the biplane lifted off. Almost immediately the runway lights went back out. The wind from the propeller was whipping Gaston in the face. It was exciting, as if all his senses were wide awake. The affect of the alcohol he had consumed earlier disappeared. They headed out to sea.

The Coast Guard vessels were equipped with a solid-white running light, and a red and green bow light. They also had searchlights. In addition, the newer ships had been equipped with forward looking radar to warn of other ships in the area or a land mass. When running along the coast, they used the many lighthouses and their flashing light patterns to keep track of where they were. The lighthouses were blacked out because of the war. A Coast Guard escort was almost always requested, but it was the merchant ship's responsibility to ask for it. There was no reason for a ship to be traveling with all its lights on.

Major and Gaston headed out to sea. It was uncommon for a submarine to wait around after a kill, so they weren't too concerned that they would become targets themselves.

The Coast Guard had deployed a new 327-foot "Secretary Class" cutter which had numerous depth charges aboard, just in case the sub decided to stay around. Additional armament included two 5-inch guns, one each on the bow and stern.

Gaston spotted the Coast Guard cutter right away. He could see the searchlights panning the water. He flipped a switch and the spotlight on *Bingo* was flittering across the water. It wasn't long before Gaston spotted debris. They circled and saw one crewmember desperately clinging to a wooden container. He radioed the Coast Guard. Major circled overhead until a rescue boat arrived. They continued to search until their fuel ran low.

"We need to head in," Major said.

"Roger. What is that!"

Major banked the plane and cut a tight circle. Gaston directed the spotlight and lit up the submarine. Immediately Gaston called the Coast Guard. Their location was over a mile south of where the crewmember had been rescued. Major continued to circle, worried that they were dangerously low on fuel. Gaston was having difficulty keeping his spotlight aimed at the sub. Each time they circled, he had to find it again. A black object against a black sea. They didn't seem too concerned they had been spotted. The third time they circled, Gaston saw a muzzle flash.

"It looks like the Coast Guard has a fix on us; let's get the hell out of here!" Major said banking away and heading back toward shore.

"Gaston, I'm not feeling so good. Could you get the landing lights?"

"Roger." He flipped the toggle on the dash.

Major called the radio operator and told her they were coming in. They needed a runway in one minute.

As the plane banked one more time, Gaston saw the field light up. In another minute the biplane set down softly.

"Another perfect landing," Gaston said, smiling as the plane came to a stop. He waited for the prop to stop spinning, unbuckled his harness, climbed out onto a wing, and jumped to the ground. He looked up at Major who was still in the cockpit. "Good job, Major. I'll bet you never made a smoother landing than that!" When Major didn't respond, Gaston climbed up on the wing and grabbed him and shook him. "Major, what's wrong!" His hand felt wet and sticky. He knew immediately it was blood. Gaston ran to the radio shack. "Get an ambulance. Major's been hit." He ran back to the plane and unbuckled the Major.

Gaston was a few pounds lighter and in much better shape physically than Major. He wrapped his arms around the man and physically lifted him out of the cockpit.

The radio operator came running out of the hangar. "The ambulance is on the way. How bad is it?"

"Bad," Gaston said. Major wasn't responding. He lowered him to the ground. "Go get a blanket. Let's make him comfortable." He laid Major on his back and unzipped his flight jacket. It was dark. All of the runway lights had been turned off. The hangar was under blackout rules. He saw a flashlight beam bobbing toward them. The radio operator shined the light on Major and immediately fainted, dropping the flashlight. Gaston grabbed the flashlight and shined it on Major. He turned away and vomited. The flight jacket was the only thing holding Major's organs together. All of Gaston's training at the Academy hadn't prepared him for this. Major was dead. When the ambulance arrived Gaston told the medics he was dead. As they carried Major away, Gaston dropped to his knees and cried. The radio operator, who had earlier fainted, recovered. She saw Gaston and hugged him. There were no words spoken.

Gaston stopped by Alice's apartment. He banged on her door.

She looked out the curtain and opened the door. "Gaston, be quiet, you'll wake the neighborhood." Immediately she could see something was very wrong. "What happened?" She took his arm and led him inside. In the room, under the light of an overhead bulb, she saw he was covered with blood. "Honey, speak to me. Is that your blood? Are you injured?" She grabbed a dishtowel and started wiping the blood from him. She got a pan of water and started washing him; still Gaston didn't utter a word. "Here, let's take your jacket off," she said softly. She unzipped his jacket and tugged on the sleeve. He pulled his arm out. She then removed the rest of his leather jacket.

"Major's dead," Gaston said.

"What? Gaston, I'm so sorry. What happened?"

Gaston let out a long breath. He shook his head still not believing. He stood. "Do you still have that bottle of bourbon in the cupboard?"

"Sure, I'll get you a drink."

"Get one for you, too."

She handed him a glass. "I'm sorry I don't have ice." She took her glass and sat at the table. Gaston had grown quiet again.

Gaston downed the glass of bourbon, reached for the bottle, and poured another drink. He began to tell her what happened.

It was daylight when Gaston woke up on Alice's bed. He had a dry mouth and a throbbing headache. His eyes were on fire and his tongue stuck to the roof of his mouth threatening to cut off his breathing. He shuffled to the sink, ran a full tumbler of water, and drank it down. He walked out on the back porch and used the toilet. On the way back into the house he realized he was in his skivvies. "Oh, shit," he said.

He looked over at the bed. Alice was sound asleep. He got another glass of water and downed it. Then the memory of last night hit him.

"It's Sunday, "Alice said, from across the room. "I'm going to mass. You want to join me?"

Gaston checked his watch, 0813. "Have I got time to go to the base and wash up? It's at 1000 hrs, right?"

Alice nodded.

Gaston dressed and crept toward the door. "You're not going to get into trouble, with me staying here, are you? I mean with me leaving this time of the morning."

"I don't know. We never discussed gentleman callers when I rented the place."

"I could use some time with God," Gaston said. "I'll pick you up at 0930."

"You better meet me there. That will give you a few more minutes."

"Okay, I'll meet you out front."

Gaston walked into Officer's Quarters and started up the stairs. "Hold on there, mate!" It was Danny Pastor.

"Danny, I really need to talk to you."

"I've got coffee on. No better time than now. Looks like you had a rough night. I want to hear all the dirty details. Who'd you spend the night with? It was Alice, wasn't it? I'm proud of you, boy. I didn't think you had it in you, but you've been proving me wrong about a lot of things."

"Major's dead."

Danny lost his silly grin and was suddenly speechless.

"Remember we left the party to help with the search. We found another goddamned Jap sub out there. It was the same bastard that sank the ship. The son-of-a-bitch had the balls to surface and watch the rescue." Gaston told him the rest of the story.

Danny didn't cry. He scrunched his mouth up, forcing his lips together. His eyes started to mist. "I need a drink," he said, and stormed out the door.

During mass, Gaston's mind wandered. He wasn't Catholic, so he didn't get what all the up and down fuss was about. He tried to follow the Latin in the missal, but he couldn't get his mind off the submarine that was terrorizing the coastline. He didn't know if it was one, two, or a dozen subs, but he knew the community couldn't stand many more attacks without breaking into all-out panic. His midnight call to the White House was tonight. He was going to tell the President everything. *There was no way the public would stand for submarines lobbing shells on shore, sinking ships right off their shores and launching airplane attacks against their forests. The public was not going to accept ships being sunk by torpedoes and being told it was a boiler explosion. How many boiler explosions could the public take before knowing the Government was lying to them? How many forest fires would they have to put out, before they realized the fires were not caused by lightning?*

Gaston felt a tug on his sleeve. Alice was kneeling again. He dropped to the hard board kneelers. If he ever became Catholic, he vowed to pay for padded kneelers, if the church allowed such things.

After the service, Margaret pulled her sister aside. She was smiling.

The Commander came up from behind Gaston. "Does she know?"

"I told her last night," Gaston said.

"How'd she take it?"

"We got drunk. Well, I got drunk. I don't remember the rest."

"I called Sarah. Have you spoken to her?"

"I'm planning on doing that right after breakfast."

"I'm sure Margaret is inviting Alice to breakfast at our house, I'll see you there, okay?" He patted Gaston on the back. "I'm sorry about Major. You two were spending a lot of time together." He went over and broke up the conversation between Margaret and Alice.

"I guess we're having breakfast at the Goodman's," Gaston said, joining Alice and her sister.

"I hope you don't mind," Margaret said.

"Can't wait," Gaston said.

As soon as he got Alice to his car, he said. "I'm starving. How do you do this fasting stuff on Sundays?"

"The sooner we get there the sooner we eat," Alice said.

"You want to take my car or yours?" Gaston asked.

"We can take yours, if you bring me back."

"No, I'm not going to bring you back. Your car will just sit here, and in a year it will be a pile of rust."

"Open the door for me, like a gentleman."

"I was going for it. You're really bossy today."

They got in the car and headed north. "Seriously, do you do this every Sunday?"

"You mean fast before mass?"

"Yeah."

"I'll tell you a secret. We have an eight o'clock service. That's the one I usually attend."

"I might be able to handle that," Gaston said. "Do you think your sister will have appetizers when we get there?"

"I'm sure you won't starve."

Gaston squirmed in the driver's seat, hoping Alice didn't mistake his growling stomach for passing gas. He swore he'd never drink that much again.

When they walked in the house the smell of fresh brewed coffee filled the air.

"Come in. Sit down, breakfast is on the table," Margaret greeted.

"That was quick," Gaston said.

"The kids like to go to early mass. I make them cook Sunday breakfast as punishment for not going to church as a family. I don't understand these youngsters. They seem to live in their own world."

"Where are they?"Alice asked.

"They're up in their rooms. They've already had breakfast. I rest my case."

"It's not that bad," Goodman said. "Let's say grace; I'm sure Gaston and Alice are not interested in the inner workings of our family. In the name of the Father, the Son, and the Holy Ghost..." Goodman said, bowing his head.

Again Gaston felt a pain in his stomach, it wasn't hunger this time. He wanted to have a life like this. A family where the people could sit down and discuss the events of the day, worship together, laugh together, and love together. He looked across the table at Alice. He wanted this with her.

The Commander handed Gaston a bowl of scrambled eggs. Then came ham steak, biscuits and country gravy.

"This is perhaps the best meal I have ever eaten," Gaston said to Margaret.

"I'll tell Sharon. She'll be tickled."

"What about Billy?" Alice asked.

"Sharon cooks. Billy does the dishes. Now if Gaston says these are the cleanest dishes he has ever eaten on, then I'll let Billy know."

There was laughter all around. Gaston felt the pain again. For moments like this, they were fighting the war.

After breakfast Gaston thanked Margaret and the Commander. "You understand why I have to eat and run?"

Goodman nodded. "Don't be too hard on yourself. Sarah knew the risk her husband was taking. Any day he went up in one of those things he was happy, even knowing it could be his last."

"You may be right, but I'm not sure she's thinking that way right now."

*****

"Major had his share of faults," Sarah said. "God knows he drank too much and smoked too much. But he was a generous man. I'm not expecting anyone to make him out a saint now he's gone, but I hope they will at least remember him for his generous spirit.

"The odd thing," Sarah continued, "Major had cut down his drinking considerably the past several weeks. It was like he had found a new interest. Something that promised to give him a purpose."

It was a short meeting. *Sarah was a tough woman*, he concluded. Not many women he had known in his life would have put up with Major's antics, yet Major and Sarah had been married twenty-two years. They had no living children, having suffered the loss of a child before he had reached his first birthday. Gaston had heard someone say that was when he started hitting the bottle.

Gaston had noticed a significant drop in Major's alcohol consumption also. He suspected it was *Beanie*. When he was around her he had seemed like a new person, one who believed he could make a difference in the war. Or maybe it was the loss of Randy and the near loss of two others. No matter, Major was different than the man he had first met. He considered Major a friend and would miss him dearly.

The *Blue Whale* was closed the day of the funeral for Major. Again, most of the town turned out and a good portion of the Coast Guard, as well. It was pouring down rain, and the event had to be moved indoors. There were over a hundred people standing outside. Sarah gave the keys to the *Blue Whale* to one of the bartenders and asked her to open up and invite the people to get in out of the rain.

Inside, Gaston was about to speak. He left his place next to Alice. Major's cremated remains were in a white ceramic urn atop a pedestal with a red velvet cloth. Flowers were in abundance; arrangements surrounding the pedestal and overflowing along the front of the stage.

Gaston approached the mic. "Many have spoken before me. My, but Major led a colorful life, didn't he?" The audience laughed. "I didn't know Major very long, in fact less than nine months. In that time I had my share of adventures, both good and bad. I learned I could trust Major in any situation. I guess if you fly you have to be a little nuts to start with, but you also have to be intelligent, quick-witted, able to make decisions on the spot, and courageous. Major was no saint but he had all the attributes of one. Like all of you, I will miss him, and like many of you, I am a better person for having known him. God bless you, Major. May you soar with the angels in Heaven as you have with the eagles on Earth.

At the reception in the *Blue Whale*, Sarah approached Gaston. "That was a beautiful eulogy you gave. I guess when you live with someone as long as we have, you tend to focus on the negative, not the things that brought you together in the first place. I wonder if you would do me a favor?"

"Anything," Gaston said.

"Would you spread Major's ashes over the ocean? We never talked about such things, but after hearing what you said, I think he would have wanted that."

When the reception wound down, Sarah kissed the urn and handed it to Gaston. "Goodbye, love," she said. "I'm giving you to Gaston, so you can fly with the angels."

Gaston walked out with the urn neatly tucked in one arm and Alice on the other.

"Gaston, wait up!" Danny Pastor caught up with them. "That was a nice thing you said about Major. He was a hell of a man."

"Yeah," Gaston said, wondering where this was going.

"I was wondering if I could go with you when you spread his ashes?"

"I suppose, I haven't thought about how I'm going to do it."

"Just let me know. He was my best friend. Hell, I'll admit it to the two of you, he was my only friend."

"I know he thought a lot of you, also," Alice said, touching his arm.

"You think so?"

"I heard him say it myself. He said you were like two peas in a pod."

"Aw, geez, you're just saying that to make me feel good."

"No," Alice said. "That's the God's honest truth."

Chapter 28

"I'm going on a night run to spread Major's ashes," Gaston told Danny Pastor over breakfast. "You up for it tonight?"

"Sure, who's flying?"

"I am." Gaston had a hard time to keep from breaking out laughing when he saw the look on Danny's face.

"You don't fly."

"Sure, remember the day we took *Beanie* up?"

"Yeah, I was there."

"I was flying her around until Major cut the engine. I brought her down. She's incredibly easy to fly. I've just been waiting for a calm night. You still want to do it?"

Pastor wrung his hands, thinking it over. "What the hell, I'll risk my life for Major. Why are we doing it at night?"

"It seemed appropriate, being it was a night flight that got him killed," Gaston said. "I'd give a hundred dollars to find that sub again and drop a Roman Candle on it."

"I know what you mean."

"You meet up with me at the hangar about 2200, okay?"

*****

Gaston's conversation with Danny had given him an idea. He went to the hangar and prepped *Beanie* for the flight. By the time Danny Pastor had caught up with him, he had topped off the fuel and pushed the tiny craft outside. It was dark. The stars shown so brightly, it felt like he could reach up and touch them. He stood for a moment and stared at the billions of worlds beyond his reach. "I know you're up there, Major."

"You sure this is safe to take out over the ocean?" Danny asked.

"Major just went through the engine. He said it was good as new. Get in, I'll tell Radio Ruth we're going to take off."

"Radio Ruth, I like that."

Ruth worked at her dad's radio repair shop during the day and volunteered two nights a week for CAP. Gaston opened the door. "We're going to be taking off. No need for lights on takeoff, but I'll need them to land. I'll call you. We're going out about five miles, drop his ashes, and return. It shouldn't be more than twenty minutes."

"And your call sign is *Beanie*? I saw the mascot painted on that thing."

"What can I say? Major had a sense of humor."

Gaston was in the left seat, Danny was in the right. One of the men in the hangar prop started Beanie, and Gaston sat on the ground making certain he remembered what each control did.

"What are we waiting for?" Danny asked.

"I'm just trying to remember what to do next."

"This is where I get out," Danny said. "Where the hell is Major?"

"See that bucket between your legs. He's in there."

"Holy shit, that looks like dynamite! Tell me I'm not sitting on top of a dozen sticks of dynamite!"

"Okay, you're not sitting on a dozen sticks of dynamite." Gaston engaged the overhead rotor and revved the engine to a scream. He tilted the rotor forward and the craft rolled about ten feet before it hopped into the air.

"So what is in the can?" Danny asked.

"A flare, thirteen sticks of dynamite, and Major."

"Shit," Danny said. "You've gone off your rocker."

"See that lever on the right side of your seat? Don't touch it until I tell you to."

Gaston flipped a toggle switch attached to the overhead handle bars. The ocean below lit up in a fifty-foot circle. They were no more than a hundred feet above the gentle swells.

"I think this is far enough," Danny said, nervously.

"Just a little farther. I'm taking him back to the place he was shot."

"What was that?" Danny asked excitedly.

"Looked like a muzzle flash," Gaston said, flipping off the spotlight. He steered the tiny craft in the direction of the flash. His heart was beating rapidly.

Just then a spotlight started darting across the sky. It was just what Gaston was hoping for. He took *Beanie* down to fifty feet off the water and turned on his spotlight again. They were gliding above the swells headed straight for the sub. The spotlight from the sub went out again, but Gaston had a bead on them. Another shot. This time he heard it whistle past his ear.

"Grab the flare and light it," Gaston said.

"Flare! How do I know which one is the flare?" Danny was in near panic.

"It's the one without the fuse. It's in the center of the pack."

Danny reached down and pulled out the flare. He struck it and the entire craft was lit up by the bright red light. He held it outside the craft as far away from him as possible.

"Quit shaking that flare. You're going to drop it."

"Drop it?"

"No, don't drop it until I tell you!"

Another muzzle flash and one of the tiny tires on the craft blew, causing Gaston to rock the craft from reflex. He caught himself and aimed for the submarine again. They were very low and very close. Gaston could see the panic in the sailor's eyes. He dropped the rifle and ran for the open hatch on the deck. Now the entire rear deck of the craft was lit up by the flare and the Spotlight.

"Light the dynamite," Gaston yelled.

"I don't want to do this, Gaston."

"Light the damn dynamite and then drop the flare."

Danny touched the flare to the fuse and threw the flare out. They were hovering only ten feet above the deck. The sailor on the sub seemed petrified. He was frozen between the open hatch and his rifle. He glanced toward the rifle and back at the hatch, like he couldn't make up his mind.

"D-D-Dynamite!" Danny yelled.

Gaston dropped down and hovered over the hatch cutting the sailor off. The sailor jumped overboard. "Pull the lever now!" Gaston yelled.

Danny didn't have to be told twice. He pulled the lever and thirteen sticks of lit dynamite along with Major's ashes dropped straight down into the open hatch of the submarine. Gaston wasted no time getting *Beanie* as far away and as high as he could. He took the craft up to five hundred feet and turned in a broad circle toward land. When he thought he was far enough away, he turned toward the open ocean and hovered. It seemed like an eternity. He shook his head, *what went wrong?* "It should have blown by now," Gaston said.

The sky lit up in a flash and a moment later the shockwave hit them. Then there was another flash, followed by a muffled explosion.

"Take that you bastards!" Danny yelled.

This time the shock wave caused them to rock sideways. Gaston struggled to regain control.

"Yeah!" Danny yelled. Gaston glanced over at him. He was pumping his fist on one hand and giving the sub a single finger salute with the other.

"Ditto," Gaston said. He had to keep both hands on the rotor yoke handle to keep the craft under control. Then another flash came and a shock wave that nearly knocked them out of the sky. It seemed the entire sub lifted out of the water, split in two, and disappeared in seconds.

Gaston struggled to control the craft and remembered he had engaged the rotor clutch to make the craft hover. He had forgotten to disengage it. He flipped the lever and disengaged the clutch. *Beanie* took off toward shore at better than a hundred miles per hour. Gaston called Radio Ruth and told her they were close. He really had no idea they were already over the airstrip. The lights came on below them. Gaston made a sharp turn and cut power. The craft was only ten feet off the runway. It auto-rotated to the ground. As soon as *Beanie* bumped the ground, the runway lights went out.

Danny wasted no time getting out of his harness and running away from *Beanie*. Ten feet from the craft he stopped, bent over, put both hands on his knees and lost his dinner.

Gaston had been too busy to process all that had happened. He stayed with *Beanie* until two men emerged from the hangar and offered to push her inside. Gaston got out. "Take good care of her," he said. "Oh, you may want to change that tire."

Gaston was shedding his flight gear, when Danny caught up to him. Danny was wiping his mouth with the back of his hand.

"Damn you, Gaston, you nearly scared the shit out of me."

"What do you think? A pretty good send off for Major, huh?"

"He would have liked it. I can hear him telling the story at the bar."

Gaston grabbed Danny by the shoulders. "You know you can't mention this to anyone?"

"No! Do you realize how many beers this would get me, just telling the story?"

Gaston shook his head. "I need your word. You won't mention this, even to your sweetheart in the heat of passion."

"Come on, Gaston, I can't promise that."

Gaston held him at arms length. "You mention this to anyone, and I'll make a liar out of you. You need to be silent."

"How the hell will you keep it silent? You saw that explosion. It doesn't take Albert Einstein to know a sub was sunk out there. You don't think the explosion wasn't seen from land? Hell, the Coast Guard is probably on the way to investigate already."

"It was just another boiler explosion, or a live torpedo, or what ever accident can happen to a submarine at sea. We were nowhere near that explosion, understand?"

Danny put his hands to his head, hardly able to contain himself. "Geez, Gaston. You are one serious son-of-a bitch. You're swearing me to a code of silence?"

"I like that," Gaston said. "Now let's go back to the base and get some sleep."

EPILOGUE

SIX MONTHS LATER
There were no more submarine incidents along the Oregon Coast for the duration of the war. Official word from Washington was the "Code of Silence" imposed by the Department of the Navy was one of the most successful campaigns of the war. By denying the attacks, Japan was robbed of the propaganda they were seeking for their efforts. After shelling, sinking ships, and starting forest fires, the people along the West Coast didn't panic. Japan considered their operation a failure and ordered their submarines back to fight in the Pacific.

In the *Blue Whale*, there was the occasional mention of the huge explosion out to sea, but there was no mention from Danny Pastor or Gaston Carson regarding the incredible events of that night. The closest anyone came to putting it all together was Major's wife, Sarah. After Gaston had told her he had spread Major's ashes out to sea that night, she said, "I saw the explosion. That's just like Major; he went out with a bang."

Gaston smiled. Danny asked for another beer.

Alice was sipping on a stubby bottle of Olympia. "Did you hear, the Coast Guard shot down some balloons with Japanese writing on them?"

"No shit, I heard they had bombs attached to them," Danny Pastor said.

"I heard they were weather balloons, way off course," Gaston said. "Maybe I should go investigate."

Made in the USA
Columbia, SC
05 October 2022